D0253997

*"I'm a big girl," ~~Billie said~~. Her voice came out low and sultry. "Didn't you know?"*

"Aye," Iain answered. He stood so close, she could smell the subtle, musky scent of his aftershave. "There's very little about you I haven't noticed. Including the fact that you don't look after your own welfare."

Billie was afraid he was right. If she really looked after herself, she would make a point of avoiding Iain as stringently as he had avoided her. Sadly, she realized, that wasn't going to happen. Since she had last seen him, she had nearly convinced herself that the attraction between them was all in her overheated imagination. Now Iain was back in her life, even if only temporarily, and she felt as if someone had hot-wired her nervous system and jump-started her heart.

And judging from the flicker in his eyes, Iain was tuned and ready for takeoff, too....

Dear Reader,

Welcome to another month of fabulous reading here at Silhouette Intimate Moments. As always, we've put together six terrific books for your reading pleasure, starting with *Another Man's Wife* by Dallas Schulze. This is another of our Heartbreakers titles, as well as the latest in her miniseries entitled A Family Circle. As usual with one of this author's titles, you won't want to miss it.

Next up is *Iain Ross's Woman* by Emilie Richards. This, too, is part of a miniseries, The Men of Midnight. This is a suspenseful and deeply emotional book that I predict will end up on your "keeper" shelf.

The rest of the month is filled out with new titles by Nikki Benjamin, *The Wedding Venture;* Susan Mallery, *The Only Way Out;* Suzanne Brockmann, *Not Without Risk;* and Nancy Gideon, *For Mercy's Sake.* Every one of them provides exactly the sort of romantic excitement you've come to expect from Intimate Moments.

In months to come, look for more reading from some of the best authors in the business. We've got books coming up from Linda Turner, Judith Duncan, Naomi Horton and Paula Detmer Riggs, to name only a few. So come back next month—and every month—to Silhouette Intimate Moments, where romance is the name of the game.

Yours,
Leslie Wainger
Senior Editor and Editorial Coordinator

Please address questions and book requests to:
Silhouette Reader Service
U.S.: 3010 Walden Ave., P.O. Box 1325, Buffalo, NY 14269
Canadian: P.O. Box 609, Fort Erie, Ont. L2A 5X3

# Emilie Richards

## Iain Ross's Woman

### THE MEN OF MIDNIGHT

Silhouette®
INTIMATE™ MOMENTS®

Published by Silhouette Books

**America's Publisher of Contemporary Romance**

If you purchased this book without a cover you should be aware
that this book is stolen property. It was reported as "unsold and
destroyed" to the publisher, and neither the author nor the
publisher has received any payment for this "stripped book."

 SILHOUETTE BOOKS

ISBN 0-373-07644-4

IAIN ROSS'S WOMAN

Copyright © 1995 by Emilie Richards McGee

All rights reserved. Except for use in any review, the reproduction
or utilization of this work in whole or in part in any form by any
electronic, mechanical or other means, now known or hereafter
invented, including xerography, photocopying and recording, or in
any information storage or retrieval system, is forbidden without
the written permission of the editorial office, Silhouette Books,
300 East 42nd Street, New York, NY 10017 U.S.A.

All characters in this book have no existence outside the imagination of
the author and have no relation whatsoever to anyone bearing the same
name or names. They are not even distantly inspired by any individual
known or unknown to the author, and all incidents are pure invention.

This edition published by arrangement with Harlequin Enterprises B.V.

® and TM are trademarks of Harlequin Enterprises B.V., used under
license. Trademarks indicated with ® are registered in the United States
Patent and Trademark Office, the Canadian Trade Marks Office and in
other countries.

**Printed in U.S.A.**

## EMILIE RICHARDS

Award-winning author Emilie Richards believes that opposites attract, and her marriage is vivid proof. "When we met," the author says, "the only thing my husband and I could agree on was that we were very much in love. Fortunately, we haven't changed our minds about that in all the years we've been together." The couple has lived in eight states—as well as a brief, beloved sojourn in Australia—and now resides in Ohio.

Though her first book was written in snatches with an infant on her lap, Emilie now writes full-time—unless the infant, now twelve, reminds her that it's her turn to do car pool. She loves writing about complex characters who make significant, positive changes in their lives. And she's a sucker for happy endings.

For George Ross, the fifth laird of Balblair,
and all his descendants

# Prologue

Even though it was blasphemy, Margaret Henley wished that she had not lived long enough to see the terrible black cloud creeping toward Druidheachd. She would not be alive when it settled over the tiny village in the Scottish Highlands, and although she didn't know the exact hour of her own death, she knew it would be well before Druidheachd faced its greatest test.

How she wished that the second sight that had so often warned her of tragedies in the lives of village folk had dimmed with age, as her eyesight had.

A voice called her back to the present. "Mum, ye've no' eaten for a day, and ye've no' been out of yer bed! Now, I will no' have such a thing in my house. Either ye let me help ye to a chair by the window, or I'll be calling Dr. Sutherland to come and take ye to the wee cottage hospital. And that's a fact."

Margaret opened her eyes and decided that her eyesight had not dimmed enough, either. Unfortunately, she still could see Flora, her terrible scold of a daughter, glaring down at her. "I've no wish to get up."

"And I've no wish to bury ye in yer bedclothes! If ye're that determined to die, at least get out of bed and put on yer best dress."

Something bubbled deep inside Margaret, something she had believed impossible. She could feel the corners of her mouth lifting and laughter struggling to free itself. "Flora, ye're a trial, and I rue the day I conceived ye."

"Shall I call the good doctor?"

With great ceremony Margaret sat up. Her joints creaked audibly. Hadn't she eaten enough good mutton fat in her ninety-odd years to keep them well greased? "I'll never ken why I see the things I do."

"Because the good Lord intended it that way, and because ye're a crotchety old woman who's too strong to stay abed over a vision now and then." Flora wasn't young herself. When she bent to help her mother swing her legs over the side of the bed, her own joints creaked in protest.

"I'd sooner have died!"

Flora held out a hairbrush to Margaret. "Shall I brush it for ye?"

"What bits there are, I'll brush myself." Margaret took the brush and began making short strokes that chiefly polished her scalp.

"There's gossip from the village." Flora set her hands on her narrow hips and pursed her lips. "But I think I will no' tell ye 'til ye've eaten."

"I've no wish to hear yer gossip." Margaret paused, her arm uplifted. "Unless it concerns the laird."

"Aye, it does."

"Then I'll have my breakfast at the window."

Margaret waited until Flora left the room before she got out of bed, dressed and crossed to the little wooden table at the wide window that looked out over the mountains. She was quite spry enough to eat with Flora and her husband, and did so on occasion, but most of the time she pleaded fatigue or the ache of old bones so that she could enjoy her solitude. Flora did prattle so about nowt.

Flora returned with a tray. "A lovely, fresh bap and porridge with cream. Ye're as thin as a stick. And when I'm an old woman, I hope my own daughter is as good to me."

"Ye *are* an old woman, and ye have only sons."

Flora folded her arms. "I'll no' tell ye a wee morsel of news 'til ye've eaten it all."

Margaret was famished, but she grumbled anyway, since it was expected. Then she poured an extra dollop of cream from the pitcher Flora had thoughtfully provided—she really was an excellent daughter—and ate all but a token spoonful. Finally she buttered the bap and savored every last yeasty morsel. "There, will ye be satisfied now?"

"Enough." Flora took the chair across from her mother. "And I've been the soul of self-discipline to wait so long to tell ye."

"It's certain I am there'll be a reward waiting in heaven," Margaret said dryly.

"Lady Mary Ross had her child last night."

"Hallowe'en night?"

"Aye. Here, in Druidheachd. At the cottage hospital with Dr. Sutherland doing the delivering."

"A child at last."

"But that's no' all." Flora sat back, obviously savoring the rest of what she had to pass on.

"Let's have it all. I could die before ye finish."

"Melissa Sinclair had her bairn at the same time! The very same time."

"Surely ye dinna mean the same moment?"

"But I do, and that's no' all." Now Flora leaned forward eagerly. "Jane MacDougall had her child at the same time, as well. All three weans were born at the same moment. It's no' even known which was born first, Mum. Think of it!"

"And who did the delivering, if Angus Sutherland was catching Lady Ross's bairn?"

"Jeanne Maxwell was on duty, and she caught the Sinclair child. And Jane MacDougall caught her own!"

"No!"

"Aye. Dr. Sutherland tossed the laird's son into his arms like a poke of potatoes and ran to deliver Jane's child, but she'd no' waited. She'd done it herself."

"Son? The laird has a son?"

"As do they all! All boys. Born," Flora was practically foaming at the mouth from excitement, "at midnight! Exactly at midnight as the clock struck the hour!"

"No." Margaret realized her mouth was wide open. She snapped it shut, afraid her teeth might slip out. "I can scarce believe it!"

"Have ye heard the like? Have ye *ever* heard the like?"

But Margaret was staring out the window and hardly heard Flora's question. Three laddies born at midnight. Three!

And now she understood so much more than she had before. As clearly as she had the first time, she saw a portion of the vision that had kept her in her bed for a day. And when her sight cleared, and the autumn rusts and bronzes outside her window came back into view, she saw something new.

Three lads. One with hair as black and curly as the laird's own, one with the penetrating gray eyes of his innkeeper father, and one with the red hair of the ne'er-do-well fisherman who had fathered him. Three lads, laughing and tumbling on green grass below her window. Three lads running through the bens and braes of the Highlands, growing together, facing life together.

Three lads and a dark cloud that was no longer quite so dark.

"'Tis a sign. They can no' be separated," she said. She turned back to the table and saw that Flora was still sitting across from her, although Margaret didn't know how much time had passed. "The three laddies of midnight. They've started this life together, and they can no' be separated."

"But the laird will no' agree to that, even if the others will."

"Aye, he'll agree. And it will be the end of the curse that has haunted his line for eight hundred years."

"Ye're daft, Mum."

"And will continue to be 'til the day I'm laid in the kirk-yard."

"Shall I tell anyone what ye've said?"

"Aye. Tell all who will listen." She paused. "And, of course, they all will." Margaret turned back to the window. She heard the clatter of cutlery, then the retreat of Flora's footsteps.

Three wee laddies of midnight. Margaret ached to hold the infants, but she knew that she would soon enough. For she would not be disobeyed. Even the laird had respect for the visions that were Margaret Henley's alone. One by one the bairns would be brought to her, and she would be certain that their paths intertwined forever.

Someday they would be the men of midnight.

Even though it was blasphemy, she wished she could live long enough to see that day.

# Chapter 1

A monster was said to live in Loch Ceo, a fearsome creature with the scales and fins of a fish and the head and mane of a horse. A creature fifty feet long who either roared like a lion or wailed like a lovesick coloratura—depending, of course, on who was telling the story.

To Iain Ross's knowledge, no one had ever spotted the monster floundering in the Loch Ceo shallows dressed in blue denim and russet wool, but that was what Iain saw now. If he wasn't mistaken, someone—a lad by the looks of it—was drowning in the loch.

Whistling for his dog, Iain started down the tower stairs of Ceo Castle. He almost never climbed as high as the walkway; he almost never even set foot among the ruins. But the sunshine had been such a prize after an early autumn snow that he had found himself strolling toward it, dog at his heels, before he'd even had time to reject the idea.

Now he was sorry he'd been so hasty.

"Hollyhock, you bloody hound! Where the hell are you?"

There was no answering whine. Hollyhock—definitely not Iain's choice of name or pet—had vanished again, which was Hollyhock's only talent. In the months since Holly-hock had been forced upon Iain, the puppy had been res-cued off the ledge of a cliff, dug from a bog on nearby Cumhann Moor and pulled out of the path of a speeding Austin-Healey. Apparently Hollyhock had as many lives as a cat, with none of a feline's intelligence or reserve.

The winding tower steps were treacherous, solid stone made slick by centuries of trudging military feet. He took them as fast as he dared, but there were precious few hand-holds, and one misstep could spell disaster. It seemed as if minutes passed in which he was making no headway, but fi-nally he emerged on the bottom level and began his sprint toward the loch.

Iain couldn't imagine how the boy could have fallen into the water, but there was no other explanation. No one swam in Loch Ceo, not even on the hottest day of the hottest summer. The water was suitable for penguins, never peo-ple. The occasional tourist tried a quick dip and usually—but not always—lived to regret it. Now that autumn had arrived, the water temperature had dropped still farther.

And there was always the monster.

The distance from the castle to the loch was short, but trees bordered the loch now—as they never had during the centuries when Ceo Castle had been occupied—and Iain was forced to slow his pace as he avoided branches and tree trunks. He could glimpse the blue sparkle of water through rust-colored leaves, but he knew he wasn't moving fast enough. In water this cold, a boy as slight as the one he'd glimpsed could drown in moments.

He finally reached the loch's edge. There was a drop-off of ten feet into water that was well above his head. Farther down there was a sandy beach where he could wade into the deeper water, but there was no time for wading. With a hand shading his eyes, he scanned the loch, but nothing broke the surface, not even a ripple. And then a head emerged, a head with short dark hair slicked back from a face as white as anything Iain had ever seen. He glimpsed huge, frightened eyes and a mouth working soundlessly, and with a flying leap, he was in the water, too.

*  *  *

Billie Harper didn't know where the dog had disappeared to, but she was rapidly ceasing to care. Because if she didn't get out of the loch herself in approximately two seconds or less, she was going to die.

Which would do the dog no good at all.

Billie had thought she knew everything about cold water. There was an ice-cold sinkhole just half a mile from the mobile home in rural Florida where she'd grown up. She could still remember the sting of that water on a sun-heated body and the way it robbed a child of breath. But she also remembered that, eventually, she *had* been able to breathe. Now she wasn't sure her lungs would ever inflate again.

She had been fighting her way toward the shore for what seemed like hours. She wasn't sure how she had gotten this far out. She had seen a dog struggling in the loch and had gone in after it—which was an all-too-typical Billie Harper kind of thing to do. She had ended up in water above her head before she'd had time to do more than attempt a gasp, and now, no matter how hard she tried, she couldn't seem to get back to her starting point.

The part of her mind that was still working clearly was amazed at the part that had now ceased to function. Time seemed to have stopped, and even panic, which had hit her with the force of a cannonball, was beginning to recede. She was still fighting, but she was no longer as determined to win. There were worse fates, she supposed, for a no-account junkman's daughter, than to end up in a loch in the Scottish Highlands, just a stone's throw from the ruins of a medieval castle. In all her childhood dreams, she had never fantasized a better ending than this one.

She hoped it would be mentioned in her obituary.

That thought wasn't her last. As her mind slowed, she thought she heard a splash. It might have been her own arms flailing helplessly. She really didn't know. Everything was grinding to a halt. Her mind, her will, even the beating of her heart. The water closed around her, almost like a friend. She realized that she could have given up easily if she weren't such a fighter. She'd always enjoyed the fight. Until the past year, there had been little about life that she hadn't enjoyed.

She flailed once more, and this time she contacted something solid. There was a moment of wild hope. Perhaps she'd almost reached the shore and had hit the stump of a tree or a boulder at the water's edge. But a last glance told her that she was still too far from shore for that.

She wondered if, instead, she might have found the monster. If so, that would make even a better obituary. She flailed again, weakly, then, with a sigh, she gave herself up to the water.

A woman.

There had been a moment as he locked his arm around the victim's chest when Iain had been warned. But there hadn't been time to contemplate. He had known that he had only minutes, at best, to complete a rescue. He had to get in, grab the boy and get him out, but at first the shock of the water temperature had been so great that he had wasted precious moments unable to move.

Still he *had* moved. After the worst of the shock, he had put everything else out of his mind and made his way toward the place where the boy had been. There were ripples and occasionally hands splashing, even dark hair floating on the water. He had reached the place as the boy went under again and grabbed him just in time.

Except that the boy wasn't a boy at all.

Iain had never been so cold. He peered down at the body lying on the beach yards from where he had jumped into the water and realized that he had rescued a full-fledged woman. She was thin, and her hair was shorter than his, but she was unmistakably female. Her breasts, braless and clearly outlined by wet, clinging wool, had been soft against his arm, and she had the longest eyelashes he had ever seen.

Also the palest skin.

He was afraid he was going to have to breathe life back into her, although he was fighting for every breath himself. He knelt on the ground and turned her to her side. With the heel of his hand he thumped her back twice, then again. She gave a weak cough and a reassuring gasp, but her chest still refused to rise and fall as it should.

He only debated for a moment. He turned her once more and cradled her neck in his hand so that her head fell back. Then with his other hand he pinched her nose, took a deep breath and sealed his mouth to hers.

Even though he was chilled clear to the bone himself, she felt like ice against his lips. As he puffed air into her lungs he had an impression of skin and lips that were as smooth as Highland butter. He lifted his head and watched her chest. He could see her nipples outlined through the thin wool and contracted from the cold, but there was no movement. When she didn't breathe on her own he tried again, stroking her neck to find her pulse as he did.

The pulse was there, weak and thready, but at least her heart was still beating. He puffed once more, and this time, as he watched her chest, he saw a gentle rise and fall. He counted slowly, to still his own fears. Seconds passed, and her chest rose again, this time on its own. She coughed twice and sucked in another, larger breath.

Gratified, he watched her struggle to clear her lungs. But he didn't rest on his laurels. She no longer was in as much danger from the water she'd inhaled, but hypothermia was just around the corner.

Iain couldn't think of anything to do but carry her along the back path to Fearnshader, his home. There was no one else about, no one to rush her into the cottage hospital that served the village of Druidheachd. If he took the loch road home, he might be fortunate, someone might pass them on the road, but he didn't have much hope of that. Fortune had overlooked him any number of times.

He shivered and supposed it was a good sign. *His* body, at least, was fighting for survival. Hers was a different story. Although she was breathing regularly now, she lay as still as a finely wrought piece of driftwood.

He shivered again and again before he could lift her in his arms. By the time he had his arms under her back and legs, he was trembling so hard he wasn't sure he could get back on his feet. But stand he did. She was all bones and tightly drawn skin, with no excess padding to protect her from the cold, but she was a full-grown woman and not a feather in his arms. He could hardly remember feeling so weak, and an old fear that he had learned to keep at arm's length crept subtly closer.

A dog barked just beyond the trees and out of sight. Iain whistled, but it was a poor attempt, and the dog continued to bark.

"Hollyhock!"

In seconds a shaggy-furred, skelly-eyed mongrel came bounding through the trees. Just feet from Iain, Hollyhock stopped and shook, spraying Iain and his charge with tiny droplets of water.

Immediately Iain realized why the woman must have gone swimming. "You're a wee scunner and a death threat to boot! Get on home with you, Hollyhock!"

Not at all chagrined, Hollyhock took off down the path that would take them the back and shorter way home, and Iain staggered after him.

For a large estate, Fearnshader had relatively few employees. Now Iain wished that he'd desired seclusion less and assistance more. There were moments in the fifteen minutes that it took to stumble to his house when he wasn't certain he was going to make it.

But he did make it at last. He hadn't stopped at any point to do more than observe the woman in his arms to be certain she was still breathing. She hadn't shifted once or even moaned. When he shoved open the door into one of Fearnshader's cavernous hallways, she was as still as she had been on Loch Ceo's shore.

"Is anyone about?" He shouted his question.

He hadn't really expected an answer. The staff normally took Wednesday afternoons off, and even his housekeeper, who sniffed at such blatant sloth and disloyalty, was in Glasgow nursing her sister. When no one replied, he spared time for a curse before he started through the house.

He had to get the woman warm. There was no time for a telephone call to the doctor. He had to get her back into water. Warm water, this time, water lapping over every part of her to raise her temperature and restore a normal blood flow.

The nearest bath wasn't far from the head of the stairs. He spared the steps one glance. He had made it this far with difficulty, and he still shuddered from the cold. Even carrying a sizable burden for such a great distance hadn't warmed him. The stairs wound and twisted, and for a moment he wondered if he would make the top. But there was little choice.

At the top he teetered. In that split second he knew he was exhausted nearly beyond endurance. With disaster just inches away, he remembered a scene from an old American movie a former lover had forced him to see. Penelope had fancied herself another Scarlett O'Hara, but now Iain had proof he was no Rhett Butler. Butler had carried his lady up the steps for a night of passionate lovemaking. Iain swayed back and forth, struggling to maintain his balance, and could think only of a bath.

With a last surge of strength he stumbled forward.

In the bathroom he set his burden down in the tub. From experience he knew that the water would take minutes to heat, and he damned British plumbing as he fired up the water heater. There was a small electric furnace in the corner for the use of foreign houseguests—few Scots would expect or use such a thing. Now he turned it to its highest setting and shut the door to retain the heat.

The woman's lips were blue, her skin nearly the same. The room might heat quickly, but her clothes held the frosty waters of Loch Ceo against her skin.

He didn't think twice about his next decision. He crossed the room and put his arm behind her to urge her forward. When she slumped against his opposing arm he lifted her sweater and inched it up her back and over her head. Then he shifted her weight and did the same with the sweater's front. In a moment she was naked from the waist up and pounds of icy, sodden wool were on the floor by the tub. Her jeans were more difficult to remove. He managed the zipper, despite fingers that were nearly numb, but the heavy denim clung to her slender hips and buttocks.

He struggled on and hoped she didn't regain consciousness as he stripped her. He imagined her panic and supposed there was little he could say in his own defense before she assumed the worst. He cursed softly and urged the denim lower. Until he'd thought about her reaction, he hadn't given much thought to exactly what he was revealing. Now, despite his own fears, he was aware of small but perfectly-formed breasts and a waist as narrow as a reed.

He loosed the laces of her boots and slipped them off, tossing them to the floor behind him. Thick woolen socks came next and, finally, the jeans. Her legs were as shapely as the rest of her.

The tub was old-fashioned and narrow, a point in its favor, since she was as limp as a rag doll and still unconscious. He was able to prop her into a sitting position while he turned on the water, but the stream that issued from the spout was nearly as cold as the loch.

He was fast reaching human limitations. She was freezing and so was he, and the bloody room was still chilled. His gaze fastened on the shower, a modern one with its own instant heating unit. He couldn't blast her with warmth from above, not as she lay unsuspecting and inert beneath it.

But he could get in, hold her upright and let the water warm them both.

He kicked off his shoes and stepped into the tub. With his last ounce of strength he lifted her under the arms until she slumped against him. Then he turned on the water.

Billie was on fire. At least, she thought she was. She wasn't quite convinced, because she didn't remember ever being so cold. While fire swept across every inch of her body, she shivered helplessly.

Something rose in her throat, an unfamiliar and humiliating sound. She moaned and was immediately ashamed.

"Look, it's all right," a voice said. "You're safe now." A pause. "Even though it may not quite seem that way."

She didn't know what to make of the voice. Sometimes as a child she had fallen into such a deep sleep that, when she'd finally awakened, it had taken her long seconds to remember who and where she was. Now the answers to those questions were elusive again.

But she was sure she wasn't a child.

One step at a time she came back to life. She had heard the voice, although she didn't understand what it was saying. She had felt fire singeing every nerve. Now she recognized the sound of running water and felt it pelting her body. And she felt something else.

A man's arms around her.

It took precious moments to remember how to open her eyes and additional precious moments to act on the memory. Once she had, the first thing she saw was white. She studied it carefully, struggling to glean clues.

The voice spoke again. "You went swimming in the loch. I dragged you out and brought you here. Your temperature had dropped dangerously. I'm sorry, but this was the only way I knew to warm you quickly."

The voice rumbled against her cheek, a voice with a lilting accent. And then she knew what she was looking at. A man's sweater stretched across a male chest. She lifted her head and saw a shoulder. It was as difficult as anything she had ever done. Dizziness swept her, and she would have fallen, except that the man's arms were firmly around her. She could manage only one word, and hardly that. "What?"

"You were drowning. I saved you, and now I'm warming you."

"Oh." Bits of memory returned. Walking down a road. She was in Scotland. That slammed from one part of her brain into another and woke her a little further. She had been out exploring, and she'd seen something . . . "A dog."

"Mine, I'm afraid. He's fine. He got out on his own."

She was glad, although now that she thought about it, the animal had been six miles beyond ugly. She remembered going in after him. Stupid. Very, very stupid.

"I carried you home. You're at my home. The only way I knew to get you warm was to stand you up in here and let the water run over you, and you couldn't stand alone."

It all seemed quite sensible. The Brits were sensible people, after all, and the Scots as sensible as any of them. Not at all like their American cousins, who jumped into freezing water to rescue dogs.

"Look, don't be upset, but I had to remove your clothes to get you warm."

She heard the man's voice more clearly this time, but it was still taking her too long to make sense of it. She computed his words one by one. And then she understood. She was in a foreign shower held against the broad chest of a stranger with a deep voice and an educated Scottish accent.

And she was buck naked.

She lifted her head farther and found that the worst of the dizziness had passed. She stared into eyes as blue as any she'd ever seen, at a face that would have made her draw her breath—if every breath didn't singe her lungs. "Naked?"

His expression expressed regret. His eyes couldn't quite manage it. "Well, you're still wearing your knickers. And I'm completely clothed, which seems as good a proof as any that I don't intend to harm you."

Billie couldn't drum up an iota of outrage. Instead, she began to laugh. Softly at first, then louder. It bubbled up inside her, despite everything that told her to compose herself.

"Shh..." Iain tried to calm her. Hysteria was an expected response. He stroked his hands along her back in reassurance until he realized what he was doing and how his own body was responding.

His hands stilled immediately. "You're going to be fine. The moment the tub fills a little farther I'm going to get out of here and turn my back so you can slide down into the water and cover up completely. Then, when you've warmed enough, I'll find you something to wear, and we'll get you in to the hospital."

"What's the point of turning your back?" She gasped the words between painful bursts of laughter. "You've seen everything there is to see already, haven't you? Not that there's...so much!"

"I'm afraid that's not going to make things any better."

"Maybe not. But at least there's no...question I'm still alive!"

"None." Iain could feel her shaking against him. The sensation was all too much like a woman in the throes of ecstasy, and his own body didn't seem to know the difference. He held her away from him a little. The water was creeping up his leg. It was nearly deep enough now to cover her. "Look, I think we can sit you down now. I'll help. You're still weak."

Billie sobered a little. She *was* weak. In fact, she felt like the proverbial dishrag. "Good Lord, I almost died."

"Aye. You did."

"And you rescued me."

"Little enough, considering you tried to save my dog. Although next time, I'd appreciate it if you'd just let him go under for the third time."

"You must be freezing, too." She managed to move away a little to get a better view. "You're still dressed."

All he had to do was glance down to view again all the delights he had uncovered, but he didn't. "Safer that way, don't you think?"

"Why? Do Popsicle women appeal to you?"

Something continued to stir inside him. He kept his gaze firmly planted on her face, but he remembered far too well what the rest of her had looked like. "Let's get you under the water."

She smiled. "I think I can...manage that much alone. You take care of yourself."

He was dazzled. Even allowing for her wretched physical condition, her face was almost ordinary. But when she smiled...

When he didn't respond, she continued. "Look, I'll be all right, eventually." She muttered the rest. "Though this will flat out ruin one hell of an obituary."

He realized she was an American, and judging from her accent, from the southern states. He'd been paying too much attention to other things to notice. He slowly unwrapped his arms, his eyes still fixed on her face, and monitored her progress as she was forced to stand on her own.

When she didn't collapse he covered his exit from the tub with polite conversation and turned off the shower. "I'm sorry this happened. We're famous for our hospitality in the Highlands. We usually treat our guests with more consideration."

Billie lowered herself to the tub floor, or rather, her legs gave way. The water lapped around her, and she slid down to let it cover her. She tugged the curtain closed, although, considering everything, it was only a formality. Through a crack she could see that her rescuer was flooding the bathroom floor with water from his clothing. She watched him reach for a towel. His back was politely turned. Quite obviously she had been rescued by a rare breed. A gentleman.

"I suppose I'm a guest," she said. "Although my mother's family...came from Druidheachd nearly a century ago."

"Is that so?"

She leaned her head back and closed her eyes. She couldn't remember ever feeling so tired. Her speech slowed. "She was a MacFarlane...of the Druidheachd Mac-Farlanes. One of the last, I guess. From what I've been able to tell...there are none left here. You don't know any MacFarlanes, do you?"

There was a long pause. For a moment Billie thought she might have fallen asleep and missed his answer. Then he spoke from the other side of the curtain.

"Not a one. Nor have I ever cared to. In the Middle Ages your family put a curse on mine. And we've lived eight hundred years to regret it."

## Chapter 2

There wasn't much Billie could tell from a bathroom. From the state of the plumbing, she had suspected her rescuer's house was old. But after all, what qualified as new in Druidheachd? In her explorations of the village she'd heard a house with a hundred years of moss and ivy adorning its stone walls called "that new cottage at the end of the High Street."

It took a shaky trip into the hallway before she began to understand that she hadn't landed just anywhere. Wrapped in the folds of a terry cloth robe—as luxurious as any she'd seen—she stood just outside the bathroom door and gazed around her.

She had landed in Dracula's castle, the Addams' Family mansion, or a Scottish combination thereof.

"Look, I thought I told you to stay put."

She glanced to the right to see her rescuer striding toward her, a pile of clothing across one arm. For a moment she just stared. This was the man who had held her naked against his sweatered chest. This was the man who had risked his safety for her, this Heathcliff come to life. Only *this* man made her childhood fantasies of *Wuthering Heights* romance seem lacking in creativity and drama.

She recovered enough to murmur, "Where the heck am I? Did I float all the way to Buckingham Palace?"

"Hardly." Iain stopped just in front of her. "You're still much too pale."

"And shivering," she acknowledged. "But standing on my own two legs and covered from head to toe, which is the way I like it."

Something gleamed in his brilliant blue eyes. She couldn't help herself. She grinned. He didn't smile back. "You've had a nasty shock, Miss..."

"Harper. Billie Harper." She extended her hand.

His hesitation was so fleeting she wasn't sure if she'd imagined it. He took her hand for the briefest moment. She had an impression of both strength and caution. "And I'm Iain Ross."

"Iain Ross, I'm more than pleased to meet you. You might say I was dying to meet you, but that would be a little too close to the truth, wouldn't it?" She repeated her warmest smile. "And this is your..." *House* seemed a little inappropriate under the circumstances. "Home?"

"It's called Fearnshader."

She leaned against the wall. Her legs were behaving strangely. In fact, all of her was behaving strangely. She was resilience personified, but even she couldn't ignore the effects of a close brush with death. "You know, I think I'd better sit down," she said.

"There's a bedroom right across the hall where you can change and rest. I've called the hospital. Dr. Sutherland will come by in a bit to check on you. He thought it best not to move you yet."

"I'm sorry. Haven't I been enough trouble?"

His eyes gleamed brighter. "From what I've heard, the MacFarlanes have always been trouble."

"You can say that again. My mother claims there was never a more troublesome bunch of people anywhere. Except possibly the Harpers." She pushed herself away from the wall and teetered dangerously. Instantly he slipped his arm around her waist to hold her steady. "I think I can make it alone," she said.

"And I think you can't."

"And you're not a man to be defied?" She risked another smile.

He seemed immune. He just lifted a brow. "Only rarely does anyone take the notion to try."

"Better watch out. I take all dares." Despite her words she leaned against him gratefully. She was used to a body that did her bidding. Today, both legs seemed to have minds of their own.

He was warm against her, dry and one hundred percent male. She was medium height—there had never been anything extraordinary about her—and he loomed above her, six feet and counting. With his black Byronesque curls pushed back from a broad forehead and his sharp, aristocratic features, he was a man to swoon over. But then, in *her* weakened state she could have swooned over anyone. Weakness seemed to be the specialty of the day.

"How big is this place? What did you call it?" she asked.

"Fearnshader. And it's large."

"Fearnshader." She struggled to pronounce it as he had. His accent was light, almost more English than Scottish, but the burr and the lilt were still there. "I like that. Do you know what it means?"

"Place of alders. There's a grove of them to the west."

"I love the way you name your houses here. My father had a name for our place, too. Tin Can Estate."

"I suppose that's a joke."

"Absolutely. It sure as heck wasn't an estate." She let him help her across the threshold into the bedroom he'd indicated. Her breath caught. It was a large room with windows of multiple diamond-shaped panes looking over a formal garden that still, despite neglect, was a thing of beauty. "Oh, how lovely. How perfectly lovely."

"Let's get you to bed."

"Men have been saying that to me for years."

She heard a strangled sound coming from his throat. She looked up at him and saw that he was trying not to laugh.

She smiled brilliantly—if tiredly—at him. "Life's way too short to take it seriously," she said.

"Did you discover that today?"

Her smile disappeared as he led her to the bedside. "No, I almost *proved* it today."

"So you did."

"Have I said thank you?"

"In any number of different ways."

"I can't say it enough. If you hadn't jumped in to rescue me, I would have gone out with a splash, but this is definitely better." She lowered herself to the bed. "I owe you big time."

He stepped back. "Is there anything you need? I put the kettle on, and I'll be back up with some tea in a bit."

"The magical cure-all. You'd like my mother. She gave us tea for every ache and pain." She watched him move away. When he was nearly to the door, she spoke. "I know what I can do for you, Iain."

He faced her. "Oh?"

"Sure. If the MacFarlanes cursed your family, then a MacFarlane—or a reasonable facsimile—ought to be able to lift the curse. Just tell me what to say, and I'll say it."

He didn't smile. "I'm afraid it would take considerably more than a word or two. All the king's horses and all the king's men . . ." He shook his head.

"Oh, I'm sorry." She was stricken by the bleak expression in his eyes. She had been teasing, hoping for another smile. Instead, for a moment he had looked completely desolate. "I really am sorry. I didn't realize . . ."

The expression disappeared as quickly as it had crossed his face. "What didn't you realize?"

What could she say? That she hadn't thought an adult man might really believe in something as absurd as a curse? "I didn't realize how long I'd kept you here when you must be exhausted, too," she said lamely. "Don't worry about the tea. I'll just lie down for a while and wait for the doctor. You take care of yourself."

"I'm a master at doing just that."

She made a face. "Until today, I thought I was pretty good at it, too."

Exactly what had he done? Iain slouched on a kitchen chair, his arms folded across his chest, and waited for the tea to steep. The house had never seemed so silent, but after Billie Harper's musical chatter, Piccadilly Circus would seem like a tomb.

He had leapt into Loch Ceo to save a drowning lad, and instead he had ended up with a full-fledged woman. A Druidheachd MacFarlane, at that. He couldn't imagine why he'd thought she was male. Her hair was short, but now that it was almost dry, it brushed her neck and forehead in soft, feminine wisps. Her eyes were the same chocolate brown as her hair, huge and rimmed by thick black eyelashes, and her generous, impertinent mouth was punctuated by deep dimples that flashed a continuous message of humor and goodwill.

She wasn't pretty, not according to the standards set by the women who had paraded through his nights, but despite a brush with death, she was so filled with life that energy exploded in every word she said, every movement she made.

She was so filled with life, and he was so drained of it.

He got up from his chair, despite legs that still didn't want to hold him, and walked to the window. The view was of the alder grove. The trees had been there forever, long before the house, perhaps as long as Ceo Castle. An old tree died, a sapling sprang up to take its place. The Rosses had always protected the grove. As a child Iain had been told that protecting the trees was his responsibility, along with a thousand other duties that went along with being the laird of Druidheachd. At his father's side he had walked the lands belonging to his family and learned what was expected. He had felt such pride that someday all this was to be entrusted to him.

Now he would gladly give up all of it, every structure, every stone, every tree. All of it in return for the things he'd never had.

He didn't know how long he stared at the alder grove. He was so lost in thought that he didn't hear footsteps.

"I really couldn't sleep."

He turned to find Billie standing behind him. She was dressed in his university rugby shirt and knit trousers rolled and rolled and rolled.... "You really don't take orders well, do you?" he asked.

"Not well at all. I really am sorry." She didn't smile. "But there was something about being alone again, right after everything." She shrugged. "You know."

"Do I?"

"It's silly. But when I shut my eyes, I feel the water closing over me."

Sympathy penetrated his own black thoughts. She looked in need of holding, but he knew he wasn't the man to do it. "I've made tea. Sit over there and I'll pour some."

"That would be nice." She took the closest chair and looked properly grateful to sit again. "This is some place, Iain." She hesitated. "Is it all right to call you Iain? I know I'm awfully informal sometimes."

He couldn't imagine her being awfully anything. In clothes that were large enough for two of her and with worry wrinkling her brow, she was completely adorable. He had the ridiculous urge to touch the silky wisps of hair feathering along her cheek, to tug the neckline of the jersey just a bit lower.

But he didn't need to be reminded why he'd always stayed miles away from adorable, cuddly women. "You're welcome to call me whatever you please," he said.

She looked up at him through eyelashes as long as a sleepless night. "If I get to know you better, I probably will," she said, with flash of her dimples. "And I'm Billie."

He turned away, far too enchanted for a man who prided himself on maintaining emotional distance. "All right."

He set cups on the counter and poured the tea. There was no reassuring steam. Frowning, he felt the pot. It was cool to the touch.

*How long had he stood at the window and stared at the alder grove?*

For a moment he couldn't think what to say. Then the impeccable manners drilled into him throughout a seemingly endless childhood took over. "I'm sorry, but I'll have to make another pot. This one seems to have gotten cold already." He moved to the stove. As he filled the kettle, he tried to ignore hands that were less than steady.

"Oh, listen, that always happens to me. I make tea, get involved in something, and the next thing I know the tea's cool enough for ice and lemon."

"You're very kind, but I'm afraid I'm just absent-minded."

"It's no wonder, is it, when you risked life and limb today for me?"

For just the briefest moment he let himself imagine what it might have been like if he hadn't completed the rescue. He would have drowned along with her, because, despite his flaws, he wasn't a man who would have given up searching in order to save himself. The water would have closed over him, and he would have died, the last of his line.

And with him would have died the hopes and fears of centuries.

"This really is some place," she said.

He tried to shake off his thoughts. "I can't figure out if that's a compliment or a critique."

"Well, neither, as a matter of fact. It's a statement. I think I'm in a fairy tale. Gargoyles looming from ledges, life-size portraits of dour old men, stone walls as thick as a prison, wind rattling glass older than my great-grandparents. I've been listening for the spooky organ music, but so far I've been disappointed." She smiled to let him know she was joking. "Really, it's breathtaking. It's just so wonderfully old. And large. There must be fifty rooms. I peeked at a fair number on the way down."

"What fairy tale?"

She considered, one long finger resting against her cheek. "Well, *Sleeping Beauty,* I think. Everything is so quiet here, like time's been suspended. Which reminds me. Are we really alone?"

"Quite."

"Your...wife isn't home? Your children? Your servants?"

"No wife or children to *be* at home, and the staff is off for the day. Which is why I took on the task of warming you myself."

"I see. Ordinarily you pay someone to strip and heat all the ninnies you rescue from the lake."

"Ordinarily."

"Which reminds me, where's the beast I tried to save? I want to give him a piece of my mind."

"Hollyhock? I don't know. Probably throwing himself in front of cars out on the loch road."

"Hollyhock?" She gave a laugh that bubbled from the very tips of her toes. "Hollyhock! Iain, that's the ugliest dog I've ever had the displeasure to see! You should have named him Stinkweed. Or Skunk Cabbage."

Despite himself, he smiled, too. "I didn't name him. A small friend of mine did. She gave him to me, too, which is why he's still alive."

"I want to see him dry. Is he really as bad as I think?"

"Worse, I'm sure."

She got up from the table and went to the door. It was one of nearly a dozen on the ground floor that opened to the outdoors. She gave a piercing whistle that nearly shattered his eardrums. He hadn't even known that female physiology was capable of producing such a sound.

He was about to warn her that Hollyhock came for no man—or woman—when a rat-brown, moth-eaten ball of fur streaked into the kitchen, nearly knocking her off her feet. Before he could intervene, Hollyhock had leapt up to greet her, puppy paws planted somewhere—Iain refused to notice exactly where—above her waist.

"Now, this just won't do," Billie said. She shoved the dog to the ground and firmly held him down before Iain could move. "Hollyhock, sit!" She continued to keep her hands just below his neck. "Now listen, mutt, this is just not the sort of place for that behavior. This place has class, and you're going to be way too big to get away with these shenanigans. You have to learn some self control."

Iain could swear that Hollyhock was nodding.

Billie lifted her hands and backed away. The moment Hollyhock stood again, she shoved him back down to the floor. "Sit!"

Hollyhock cocked his head. His long dark ears flopped against his neck as he assessed her.

"That's right. I mean it. You'd just better toe the line. Or else." She moved away again, turned her back and went to the table. Hollyhock remained motionless. When Billie was settled back in her chair she snapped her fingers. Then, and only then, did the dog bound over to her.

She ruffled his ears and kissed his nose. Riveted by the impossible, Iain watched in silence. "You know, you're not really so bad," she murmured to the dog. "You're going to be a knockout when you're grown. Now listen, honey. I know it's hard to do what you're told, but you have to, because if you don't, this man here's going to make mincemeat out of you. *¿Comprende?* Now, sit." She gave him a playful shove, and he lowered himself to the floor obediently.

"Where did you learn to do that?"

"What? Teach him manners? Oh, we always had dogs when I was growing up. I was kind of in charge of them, and there were way too many to let them run wild. So, I learned how to keep them in line."

"I've never seen anything like it. I had a trainer work with Hollyhock. Private lessons, at that. And he couldn't do a thing."

"Then he doesn't know dogs."

"How many dogs did you have?"

"Probably a hundred or so. Over the years, of course." She looked up from scratching Hollyhock's ears. "My father runs a junkyard. And people are always dropping off dogs there and at the county dump down the road. My father has a heart the size of Florida. He just can't watch an animal suffer. So, when I was a little girl, if there was any hope for the dog at all, he'd bring it home, and we'd take it in until he could find it a new home. Of course, half the time or more the dogs stayed on. But we're way out in the country, so nobody ever complained.''

''A junkyard?''

''Sure. A salvage yard. I like to think Daddy was into recycling before anybody else thought of it. He found and sold all kinds of things. They say one man's trash is another man's treasure, and my father built his life and business around that.''

Iain tried to imagine.

She leaned back in her chair. ''It was a great life for a kid. My brothers and I had every toy, every piece of play equipment a kid could want. You just wouldn't believe what people throw out.''

''I suppose I wouldn't.''

''We were never bored. But speaking of boring, I'll bet I'm boring you.''

''Boring me?'' He gave a wry smile. ''Never that.''

''So, tell me about yourself. Or is that too personal? I'm still feeling my way. Things that are perfectly appropriate at home may be considered the height of rudeness here.''

''And it's perfectly all right to ask for a life story back...home?''

''Probably not. But that's never stopped me. There's always so much I want to know.''

''What do you want to know right now?''

''Well, who is Iain Ross? How did you come to live in this...this house? What do you do for a living? Why did my family put a curse on yours? That sort of thing.''

Who is Iain Ross? It was a question without an answer, because for years now he'd striven not to be anyone in particular. He gave as noncommittal an answer as he could. ''I was born here. And I don't do anything for a living except manage what I was born to. As far as the curse goes, it's ancient history and completely forgotten, except that everyone knows one existed. No details available.''

Billie whistled softly. Hollyhock jumped to his feet. After a few friendly but firm commands he sat once more.

"Now, how many people can condense their lives that easily? There's absolutely nothing to you, Iain Ross."

He couldn't help himself. He met her eyes and wished he hadn't. Hers shone with warmth tangible enough to caress him. "I'm certain you wouldn't be the first to think so."

"You know what? I think that's just a prologue. The real story must be much more complex and interesting."

"I wouldn't count on it." The kettle had heated, and gratefully he poured boiling water into the newly readied teapot. While he waited for this pot to steep, he leaned against the stove. "What are you doing in Scotland, Miss...Billie?"

"My dissertation."

He lifted a brow in question.

"Yes, believe it or not, this ditzy woman sitting at your table asking insensitive questions, this idiot who jumps into polar water just for the fun of it, is working on her doctorate."

"In what, if I might ask?"

"Folklore. You know, there's such a crying need for folklorists. I've always been such a practical person. And when I get out of school and need a job, I can always train dogs."

"How did your studies bring you here?"

He watched a cloud pass over her face. He hadn't been sure such a thing was possible. "It was sort of spur of the moment. I changed subjects at the very end. I'd planned to do something closer to home, but things didn't...work out."

She looked up, and he watched her will away her sadness. "Instead, I came here. I've always been fascinated by the way ancient folktales and legends weave their way into modern lives, so I'm going to study the most prominent stories in this area and see how—or if—they affect day-to-day living."

"I'm not sure I understand."

"Would you like an example?"

"Go ahead."

"Well, there's a story where I come from in Florida about a woman named Betty Gray, way back in the early 1800s, who had never been able to have children. One day she was walking in the woods near her home when she met up with a tiny man sitting on a tree stump. The man pointed deep into the grove, and she heard a baby crying. Betty started toward the sound, but when she'd gone a few yards, she turned around, and the little man had disappeared. Fifty yards into the grove she found a baby lying under a tree. She brought the baby home, and she and her husband raised it as their own. But almost more interesting..." She paused. "Is this incredibly dull?"

Her eyes were glowing with enthusiasm. He tried to remember the last time he had felt anything like it. "Not even a wee bit dull."

"Well, for nearly a century after that, whenever a woman couldn't conceive, she was told to walk in the woods every day. It was called following Betty Gray. People in the area still talk about 'following Betty Gray' whenever something unexpected and wonderful comes into their life."

"And this is the sort of thing you'll be studying?"

"It's second nature to me. I just naturally grew up with an appreciation of old things. Anyway, that's why I came to Druidheachd. I thought I'd kill two birds with one stone. Research my own history and work on my dissertation. Life's way too short to do just one thing at a time."

He didn't say anything for the moments that it took to pour their tea. He spoke when he set the cups on the table. "I don't know what you'll find here. As I understand it, the MacFarlanes have been gone from Druidheachd for a good long while."

"You'd be so surprised." She leaned forward. He couldn't avoid the warmth or sparkle in her eyes. "Iain, you wouldn't believe what people remember. It's all there. All the stories of generations. All I have to do is find people who listened carefully as children and are willing to talk to me."

"Then you'll be around for some time?"

"Yes. I've taken a room in a wonderful little house just past the village. An old woman named Flora Daniels lives there. I can't wait to see it in the spring and summer when everything's in bloom."

"You'll be here through summer? You don't have to go back?"

"No. I've got a small grant to help with my expenses." She cocked her head. "And I bet you're wondering if you'll have to rescue me on a regular basis. Well, I'm impulsive, but not stupid. I promise I won't intrude on your privacy again."

"Won't you?"

She bent to fondle Hollyhock's ears, and her expression was hidden from him. As he watched, she easily persuaded his dog, *his* ignoramus of a pet, to lie down at her feet. "Unless you count jogging your memory a little from time to time," she said.

"My memory?"

She sat up and faced him again. "Well, sure. You see, I think you know more about what passed between our families than you're letting on."

"And why do you think that?"

Chimes rang through the house before she could answer. Iain knew it would be Dr. Sutherland at the door, but he didn't stand. He waited. "Why?" he repeated, when the house was quiet again.

"Let's just say that in the last year or so I've learned to tell—and it was about time—" she grimaced "—when someone is coming clean with me or not."

The chimes sounded again, but Iain didn't move. "Coming clean?"

"Being one hundred percent honest. And don't be offended, Iain, that's very different from telling a lie. I'm certainly not saying that you're lying."

"Then what are you saying?"

"Well, just that you haven't decided to tell me every little thing you know. That's the reaction I'm getting from most people in the village, as a matter of fact. As soon as I tell them I'm a MacFarlane, they don't look at me as an American tourist anymore. Suddenly, I'm something else. And I'd like to know exactly what."

"There are some things it's better to leave alone."

She spread her hands helplessly. "I'm incapable."

The chimes sounded their third—and final, Iain imagined—appeal. He stood. "Here's a friendly warning, Billie. Explore our folktales and our legends to your heart's content. But stay away from your own family history. You might find some things you'd rather not know."

She looked genuinely sorry, but she shook her head again. "I just can't do that. You see, I believe that the old stories our ancestors told still affect us. And I have a feeling, Iain, that we've both been affected by this one. I don't know why, and I don't know how. But I saw the look on your face when you heard who I was. I'm a scholar and more than a bit of a sleuth. And there's nothing I like better than tracking down answers."

# Chapter 3

The man standing at Fearnshader's entrance was a stranger to Iain. "May I help you?" Iain asked.

"Actually, I believe I'm here to help you." The man extended his hand. "I'm Alasdair Melville, Dr. Sutherland's new associate."

Iain took his hand for a perfunctory shake. "I'm sorry. I was expecting Dr. Sutherland himself. I'm Iain Ross."

"Yes, I know."

Iain stepped aside. He had already cataloged his impressions of the new doctor. Several years younger than he was, tall and slight, sandy brown hair, a friendly, respectful smile. There was nothing about Alasdair Melville that wouldn't blend perfectly into a crowd. There was nothing about the man, but something about the name.

"You dinna remember me, do you?" Alasdair asked.

"I'm sorry, no. Obviously I should?"

"Oh no. It's been a long time. You would no' be expected to remember. But I remember you."

Iain wondered if the man was just being polite, or if this was another teapot filled with cold water. "A long time? Were we at school together, then?"

"No. I'm John Melville's son. He was your father's gamekeeper."

John Melville. A glowering, towering man who was quiet to the point of near silence. Strict, uncompromising, a shadow who stalked the Ross lands with a smaller, slighter shadow edging along beside him. Iain smiled in recognition. "John's son. Of course. It *has* been a long time. And now you're back in the village."

"Aye. Who'd have thought it, after all these years?"

"And your father, how is he?"

"Dead these ten years."

"I'm sorry for your loss."

"Thanks, but I was lucky I had him as long as I did." Alasdair smiled.

There might not be anything particularly striking about Alasdair Melville, but he had a smile that probably put his patients at ease immediately. Iain sensed competence as well as a determination to succeed.

"And now, where's our swimmer?" Alasdair asked.

"She's in the kitchen, chattering away. I doubt you'll find anything seriously wrong with her."

"I'll need to look at you, too."

"That won't be—"

Alasdair held up his hand. "It will be if I want to go back and face Dr. Sutherland. I'll end up like his last associate if I dinna check *you* over, too."

"And how did his last associate end up?"

Alasdair drew a finger across his throat.

Iain laughed and started down the hallway. "How did you find your way back here after all these years, Melville? I'd have thought you'd consider yourself fortunate to be almost anywhere else and working for anyone other than the man who brought you into the world."

"You'd think so, would you no'? But this suited me. Childhood memories and all that. And I wanted an old-fashioned practice, with people I could get to know well and a variety of ailments to keep me on my medical toes."

"Well, I'm sure you'll get that." Iain made all the correct turns and stopped outside the kitchen door. "But you

won't see anything of real interest today. Both Billie and I
are as well as can be expected."

"Billie, is it?"

Iain pushed open the door. "Billie, the doctor's here."
There was no young woman sitting patiently at the table
where he'd left her. For a moment Iain was concerned, then
he saw her standing beside the stove rearranging the copper
pots and saucepans that hung from a cast iron grid. "Just
what are you doing?"

"These are all wrong, Iain. A good cook puts her most
important tools in easy reach."

"You're supposed to be half dead, woman. You're not
supposed to be training my dog or rearranging my kitchen."

"I've never been good at sitting still, even when I'm at
death's door." She grinned ruefully, then she crossed to
greet Alasdair, her hand extended. "I've got a feeling I'm
not in the presence of old Dr. Sutherland."

Alasdair introduced himself. Iain thought the young
doctor held Billie's hand a fraction longer than politeness
required.

"I'm really just fine," Billie said. "Better than that. Just
the tiniest bit wobbly, but even that's going away."

"So much the better," Iain said dryly. "I've a mop and
bucket in the corner. You can start on the floors immediately. Then by all means proceed to the rest of the house and
do whatever seems fitting."

"You scowl so wonderfully, Iain. I'm frightened half out
of my mind. Does everyone always do exactly what you
say?"

Alasdair laughed. "Has he been browbeating you,
Miss . . . ?"

"Harper," she supplied. "And no, he's much too upper-
class for that. He just lifts a brow and makes me feel small
and insignificant."

Iain knew his scowl had been replaced by a smile, even
though he also knew what a bad idea that was. Billie Harper
was unexpected sunshine in a cloudy life. "Insignificant will
be the least of it unless you sit down over there and let this
man examine you right now."

Her eyes sparkled. She looked up at him through her ridiculously wonderful lashes, and something deep inside him responded with a silent hallelujah. "I live to obey you, my lord," she said.

And for a moment Iain found himself wishing it were true.

"You really were quite fortunate Iain saw you, you know," Alasdair said.

Billie had been thinking just exactly the same thing. She'd left Flora's cottage that morning to explore the Scottish countryside. And in the few hours that had elapsed she had nearly died—and nearly fallen in love.

She turned to watch Alasdair, who had volunteered to drive her home. She had to remind herself which way to turn. She still felt disoriented in a car with the steering wheel on the right. "I'm fortunate he's a stronger swimmer than I am."

"Iain was always the best at everything. As a lad I nearly worshipped him. I wanted nowt more than to be him." Alasdair chuckled.

The town's new doctor was easy to talk to and pleasant to look at, with a nice laugh as well as a warm smile. Billie imagined that he would find his way into the villagers' hearts and homes with little difficulty. "Then you knew him as a boy?"

"Aye. My father was Lord Ross's gamekeeper."

"Wait a minute. If his father was Lord Ross, does that make Iain..."

"Lord Ross? Oh, probably, although I'm no' sure the title is more than a mark of respect. But he is the local laird. He owns a fair share of this part of the Highlands. I could no' even guess how wealthy he is. His family's been here for centuries."

"That part I know." Billie leaned against the headrest and closed her eyes. "And yours, Alasdair? Has your family been here forever?"

"No. And I did no' finish my growing up here, either. We left Druidheachd just before Lord Ross's death and settled to the east. But when I learned there was a chance to come back, I jumped at it. I've never forgotten this place.''

''I can understand that. It's like another world . . . or another century.''

''Will you be here long?''

''I plan to be.'' She was too tired to elaborate. The events of the day had caught up with her. ''You'll have an advantage, won't you, since you lived here as a boy? I don't think this is the sort of place that accepts strangers immediately.''

''No? Have you had trouble?''

''Oh, no. It's just that people are naturally wary. It takes time to gain their confidence. You shouldn't have that problem.''

''We'll see. I've been here only a few days. Iain did no' even know I was back.''

''Do other people remember you?''

''A few, certainly. The other two lads of midnight remembered me . . . with a little help.''

''Lads of midnight? Is that a club of some sort?''

''You have no' heard of our famous wee laddies of midnight?''

She scented a tale and opened her eyes. Her fingers itched to pick up a pen. ''Tell me.''

''Well, Iain's one of them, you know. Three babies born in the village hospital exactly at midnight on Hallowe'en. No one knows which one came first. There was an old woman in the village, a seer, who claimed that the births were a sign and that the three laddies had to be raised together. And so they were.''

''Together? In the same house?''

''At times, surely. They were passed around like good whiskey. It's a strange thing, really, that their parents agreed, but after a while they became such strong friends that no one could separate them anyway. No' even when Duncan was taken off to America. When he came back that next summer it was as if they had never been apart.''

Billie was fascinated. She forgot she was tired. ''What were the births a sign of?''

"I'd say a need for better prenatal care." Alasdair flashed her a smile. "Dr. Sutherland would have known the three weans were due at the same time if their mums had just come in to see him more often. But Lady Ross planned to travel to Glasgow to have her baby, and Andrew's mum planned to have him at home."

"No, seriously, why were the three boys supposed to be raised together?"

"I'm no' certain I ever heard. But now they're the men of midnight. All still living here. It's an odd story, but a charming one, is it no'?"

Billie closed her eyes again. It *was* an odd story, exactly the kind she liked most. "I came to the right village."

"Pardon?"

She smiled sleepily. "Sometimes I have the damnedest luck."

Three babies born at the same hospital on the same night at exactly the same time. A folktale in the making. A legend evolving in front of her eyes. Billie sat on a stone bench under a rose arbor twining with leafless, thorny branches and watched Flora Daniels planting tulips. It was nearly dark, and Flora had been working since early afternoon.

"Are you sure you don't want some help?" she asked.

"And let's say ye were feeling strong enough, would ye know what to do?"

"Believe it or not, I would. I have a middling green thumb."

Flora pushed back her wide-brimmed hat to peer at Billie. Every time Flora went outside she covered every inch of her body, but it was much too late to protect her complexion from the sun. She was in her eighties—or possibly older—and there wasn't a place on her face to fit another wrinkle.

"Be that as it may," Flora said, "if ye planted my bulbs, then they would no' be my bulbs anymore, now would they?"

Billie grinned. "I'll be quiet and watch."

"Ye dinna know how to be quiet."

"Do I annoy you too badly?"

"Ye dinna annoy me at all." Flora went back to her digging.

"Flora, why haven't you ever mentioned the men of midnight to me?"

"Have ye asked about them?"

"How could I ask if I didn't know?"

"And what have ye heard?"

Billie repeated Alasdair's story. She had already told Flora all about her near disaster, about meeting Iain and her drive home with Alasdair. Flora had promptly gotten up from the garden, gone inside, mixed a special blend of herbal tea from her own garden and forced Billie to drink the entire pot. Billie intended to mosey on down to the hotel pub in a little while to see if she could rid herself of the taste.

"That's the story," Flora said. "Ye've heard it all."

"Do you know why they were supposed to be raised together?"

"No."

"Doesn't it seem odd to you that their parents agreed to it? I mean, Iain's father was a lord, for heaven's sake. Were the others nobility, or at least prominent citizens?"

"No' a bit of it. Duncan's father was the innkeeper, and Andrew's father a bit of a scoundrel, as it were. But remember yer Scottish history, lass. Fostering was an important tradition here. In the olden times a highborn lad was often sent to live with a humbler family to learn the things he might no' learn at home and to forge new alliances."

"Interesting. So a tradition from the past continues. But there's been no hint of why it was necessary?"

Flora was silent. Billie sat back and waited. She had sensed when she first met Flora that the old woman probably knew everything that Billie needed to learn about Druidheachd, but that she would only dole out the information bit by bit, as it suited her.

"There was a black cloud," Flora said at last. "Hanging over the village, it was. And until the lads were born..."

"Until they were born..." Billie prompted, when it seemed clear that Flora had finished.

Flora shrugged.

"And it's gone now?" Billie tried again. "The black cloud's vanished?"

"No. I dinna think it has."

Billie knew a scholar's frustration. "Fat lot of good they did then, huh? Well, at least Iain had friends, or has them, I guess. I sensed loneliness there, Flora. He seems to have everything, but..." Now her own words trailed off. She and Flora were a team. Neither of them seemed to be able to finish a thought out loud.

"Our Iain's had his share of misfortune."

"Has he?" Billie paused for one heartbeat, another... "Do you know about the curse my family put on his?"

Flora's hand paused in midair. The tulip bulb she was holding seemed doomed to flower in space. "Ye know about the curse?"

"Nope. Wish I did. Iain mentioned it in passing. You know, 'Here's a towel, here's a bathrobe. By the way, your family put a curse on mine about a million years ago.'"

"Then ye told him ye were a MacFarlane?"

"I might as well have told him I was a Martian. I gather being a MacFarlane is nothing to brag about here. And really, we're not that bad, Flora. A little pigheaded, a little unconventional, maybe. My mother married the local junkman, after all, her with a master's degree in linguistics. In the mornings she finishes odd pieces of furniture that Daddy finds and in the afternoons she works on the definitive book about the subtle connections between Hungarian and ancient Finnish. And she speaks Gaelic whenever she's lecturing us, which, frankly, is more often than not. We're a pretty obnoxious brood."

"Are there lots of MacFarlanes, then, in America? MacFarlanes from here?"

"Not anymore. Mom was an only child of an only child, and a passel of relatives were killed in both world wars, not to mention all the ones who passed on before them at the end of a hangman's rope. I don't think there are many of us left. Maybe some very distant cousins somewhere who'd rather forget their roots than be reminded."

Flora laughed. "Ye do go on!"

"Awful, isn't it? Can you tell me more about that curse?"

"Do ye think I dinna know what ye're doing? Ye go on like that, and then ye slip in a question. I've faith ye'll find what ye need . . . when ye need to find it."

"Now, what on earth does that mean?"

"Ye're a smart lassie. Ye'll figure it out."

"Lord, I think I've met my match."

"I think ye may very well have," Flora said. "But no' the way you mean." She lowered the formerly doomed bulb to the hole she'd dug for it and began to cover it with soil. "Aye, I think ye've met yer match, Billie MacFarlane Harper. And it's glad I am that I'm still alive to witness it."


"No, it's not short for anything." Billie smiled at the man seated at the table beside her. The Sinclair Hotel pub was crowded, and it hadn't seemed odd to her that a stranger had asked to join her. "Billie for Billie. My mother was sure I was going to be a boy, like all her other kids. She said it took a couple of weeks to notice I wasn't. By then the name had stuck."

Andrew MacDougall grinned back at her. He was a large man, with shoulders wide enough to thrill a football coach and hands powerful enough to crush a brick. He had hair the dark russet of autumn maples and a smile that could turn a woman inside out. Sitting beside him, Billie thought she could still hear the thundering echo of all the women who had fallen at his feet.

"And are you liking Scotland, Billie?"

"Oh, I'm liking it a lot. It's the strangest thing, but I feel at home here, as different as it is from what I'm used to."

"Aye, I suspect it's quite different."

"But people are people for all that, aren't they? Same hopes, same fears." Same stories, she hoped. She was in the pub tonight to see if she could hear any. She sipped the bitter brew that Brian, the barman, had recommended to her, and watched Andrew over the rim of her glass.

"We share common traits, that's for certain."

"Have you always lived here?"

"Aye, I was born here. I work on the oil rigs, but I make my home here when I'm no' on duty."

Billie knew what a common name Andrew was, but she wondered if she was talking to one of the infamous men of midnight. He seemed to be around the same age as Iain, late twenties, perhaps a year or two older. Flora had said there was a Duncan and an Andrew. She wished she had tried to worm last names out of her—not that she would have been successful.

"I heard the strangest story today." She glanced down at her drink. "Do you know about the men of midnight?" She looked up again quickly.

"Aye."

"Are *you* the Andrew I heard about?"

"And what would make you think so?"

"Oh, you're about the same age as Iain, and you're from Druidheachd."

"Then you've met our Iain?"

"Your Iain?"

"How did you meet him?"

"Andrew, why doesn't anybody in this part of Scotland answer a question directly?"

"Do we no'?"

"Andrew, I'm feeling inordinately frustrated."

He sprawled back in his chair, but he never took his eyes off her. "How *did* you meet Iain?"

"I'm sure you've heard already. Haven't you?"

He grinned. "So, you're the fish who thought to feed herself to my creature."

"Your creature?"

"Aye, she's my very own darling. She's belonged to my family for centuries."

"You keep your own private monster in the loch?"

"Tell me, Billie, did you really jump in to save Iain's dog?"

"I'm sure Iain's already told you. You are the right Andrew, aren't you?"

He laughed. "Iain has no' told me a thing, but the story's all over the village how the American lass jumped into water cold enough to freeze a witch's...nose and nearly drowned.''

"Terrific. I'm sure everyone will take me seriously from now on.''

"And should we? Are you a serious person?''

"Only about things that matter. Like finding out if you're the Andrew who was born at the same moment as Iain and someone named Duncan.''

Andrew rose. "I'll be back.''

"Primed and willing to talk, I hope." Billie watched Andrew stride away. He didn't get far before someone stopped him to chat. Someone else joined them. She realized it would be a while before he made his way to her table again, because quite obviously, with his easy charm and warm hazel eyes, everyone liked to talk to Andrew.

Billie sipped her ale and continued the survey of the pub that had begun before Andrew had asked if he could join her. The gray stone hotel was centuries old, comfortably shabby and sturdy enough to withstand an earthquake of monumental proportions. This room was everything a British pub should be, dark, crowded and buzzing with hearty conversation. It was also smoke-filled, which was less appealing, and vaguely dungeony. She had always been the slightest bit claustrophobic, and now, after a morning of practicing drowning, she found herself looking for windows and exits.

"Do you mind if I join you?''

Billie halted her survey to gaze up at the man standing over her. He was older than Andrew by at least a dozen years, and from the frown on his face she suspected he would be less appealing company. "Well, I'm waiting for someone to come back.''

"No problem. I'll leave when he does.''

She nodded, because she was in no position to make enemies.

"I'm Jeremy Fletcher.''

Billie held out her hand and gave her name, and Jeremy took the seat across from her. "You're an American?''

"Born and bred. But a Scot by descent, as well as about fifty other things on my father's side."

"I thought maybe you were. You have the look."

"Do I?" She wasn't at all sure he'd meant it as a compliment. He was a handsome man, but one who seemed never to have learned to smile. He had thick silvering hair and darkly tanned skin, and he wore his expensive sport coat like a man used to fine things.

"It's rare that we have visitors this time of the year." Jeremy signaled the barman for a drink, then turned back to Billie. "Who comes to Scotland just before winter when there's the south of France or Spain?"

"I've always prided myself on doing things backward."

"Are you enjoying yourself?"

"Sure. It's a tourist's delight. Today I swam for a while, then I toured one of your wonderful manor homes." She favored him with a brilliant smile to see if she could evoke a glimmer in return. "I'd say Scotland in the autumn is highly underrated. There are hundreds of things to do."

"I've never thought so. I try to stay away as much as possible."

"Why come back at all, then?"

"I suppose I need a place to gather myself for the next foray out."

"Then you work out of the country?"

"He works anywhere there's someone weaker than him to take advantage of," Andrew said.

Billie looked up to see Andrew standing beside the table. She glanced back at Jeremy to see how Andrew's words had affected him. "MacDougall," Jeremy acknowledged. "You've changed not at all."

"Nor have I any intention of changing," Andrew said. "Now if you dinna mind, the lady and I were having a conversation."

"So she told me." Jeremy rose. He was just a fraction of an inch shorter than Andrew. "Are you staking a claim, MacDougall? Does Miss Harper know she's chosen a man who'll live and die here without anything to show for it?"

Billie hit the table with the palm of her hand. "Listen, I'm sitting at a pub just trying to have a drink and a friendly conversation. I'm not looking for a proposal of marriage. So thanks for your concern, Mr. Fletcher, but since the conversation's not friendly anymore, I'd appreciate it if you'd leave."

Neither man moved. For a moment Billie expected one to take a swing at the other. Then Jeremy twitched his shoulders to straighten his coat and moved around Andrew. Billie watched him settle at the far end of the bar.

"I don't know what that was all about, but I could have done without it," she told Andrew.

Andrew lounged across from her again. "I'm sorry, but he'd be a good chap to stay away from."

She narrowed her eyes. "Oh really? I suppose I've just got to quit sending out all these signals that I'm on the prowl. Maybe it's the way I dress." She looked down at her faded jeans and bulky red sweater, then up at him again. "Or maybe in Druidheachd a woman can't sit in a pub without giving every man in it the wrong idea?"

Andrew leaned forward. He wrinkled his brow, but his eyes danced. "Billie, does this mean you will no' be coming home with me tonight?"

She couldn't help herself. She burst into laughter.

"I almost hate to break in."

Billie looked up to find a new man standing over her. She didn't know whether to smile at him—under normal circumstances, he would have been a man to smile at immediately—or throw her arms over her head for protection.

"I'm Duncan Sinclair." He held out his hand.

She extended hers warily. Duncan's steel gray eyes were doing a quick but thorough investigation of her. "An American?" she asked, judging from his accent.

"Right. And a Scot. This is my hotel."

She remembered Flora's words. *Duncan's father was the innkeeper.* She looked straight at Andrew. "Is this the Duncan of men of midnight fame? Is that why you left? To bring him over here? And *are* you the Andrew? You can't weasel out of it this time. You owe me a straight answer for almost embroiling me in your little feud with Jeremy Fletcher."

Duncan made a place for himself at the table. "So, we were born at the same time. It means nothing."

"Duncan thinks that the villagers make much of it because they've nowt better to think about," Andrew said.

"And what do you think?" she asked.

"I think Iain just walked in."

Duncan muttered something under his breath as Billie turned. Iain stood framed in the doorway. Her heart did a Charlie Chaplin skip. She watched him scan the room until his eyes settled on her. She didn't smile, and she didn't breathe.

"Damn, he's coming over here," Duncan said.

Billie didn't take her eyes off Iain. "I thought the three of you were friends? Don't tell me you're having a fight and I'm caught in the middle of this one, too."

"No."

"Dunc's never understood his place in the scheme of things here," Andrew said.

"What place, and what scheme of things?" she asked.

"They're doing it," Duncan said.

"Doing what?" Billie reluctantly tore her gaze from Iain and looked around. The only thing that seemed out of the ordinary was that the crowd around them had thinned, probably just to let Iain through. "Who's doing what?"

"Billie, what are you doing here?" Iain asked.

She gazed up at him and couldn't think of a word in her own defense.

He frowned at her. "You're supposed to be resting."

"I am, unless you count nearly provoking a fistfight."

"Pull up a chair, Lord Ross," Duncan said. "I'll stand for a drink."

Iain pulled up a chair beside Billie. She noted that he had his pick of chairs. Everyone in the vicinity seemed to have moved away. "Where's everybody gone?" she asked. "Is it time for their favorite TV program or something?"

Duncan muttered under his breath and signaled for a drink for Iain.

Iain folded his arms and leaned back in his chair. "We're a superstitious lot," he said.

"And?"

"And sometimes it gets the better of us."

She watched the way his gaze roamed over her. She wished that she had done something short of plastic surgery to make herself more attractive tonight. "Would someone please tell me what's going on?"

"There are those who believe that together the three of us have power," Andrew said. "And they'd prefer no' to be near in case we decide to use it."

She contemplated that. "Power? Supernatural power?"

"It's not that well-defined," Iain said. "Let's just say that the unknown has its own kind of power."

"Medieval curses and magical births and black clouds." She whistled softly. "Mysterious creatures in the loch. And yesterday someone told me that there's a local ghost who warns people of danger. My Lady Somebody-or-Other."

"Don't believe any of it," Duncan said.

"Duncan's the resident skeptic," Andrew said. "And sensitive about ghosts, considering that his lady love…" He laughed at the way Duncan narrowed his eyes. "I'll say no more."

Billie filed that exchange away to investigate at another time. "What an odd and wonderful place this is."

"Then you don't find us ridiculous?" Iain asked.

She sensed much behind the question. "That would be the last word I would use."

He shifted his weight, and suddenly they were nearly nose-to-nose. "Maybe you should run away, too, Billie. Perhaps the others have the right idea. You're sitting here with the mysterious men of midnight, and you have no idea where it might lead. If you stay in Druidheachd, you might find out."

"I'm beginning to think you'd like me to leave. Is it because I told you that if I stay, there'll be no secrets that are safe, not yours, and not anyone's?"

"And yours, Billie? We all have secrets. You'll be no different."

The other two men were silent. Billie knew they were watching, but she couldn't tear her gaze away from Iain's. "Not me. I'm an open book."

He reached for her hand. She hadn't even realized hers was cold until he'd enclosed it in his. "Are you? Or do you reveal so much about yourself because you don't want anyone to look beneath the surface?"

She couldn't answer. For once in her life, she really couldn't answer.

Andrew answered for her. "This one's different, Iain," he said. There was no laughter in his voice. "And she deserves better than you're going to give her."

"Are you by chance warning me?" Iain asked without taking his eyes off Billie. "Or are you declaring your own intentions?"

"Wait a minute." Billie pulled her hand from Iain's. "I must really have more to recover from than I thought. I'm kind of slow on the uptake tonight, but I'm catching on. Are you two arguing over me? Because you're way out of your league. I've chewed up and spat out better men than both of you."

When neither one answered, she stood. "I think I'll call it a night before anything else goes wrong." She rounded the table and started toward the door, but halfway across the room she felt a hand on her shoulder. Without looking, she knew it was Iain's.

"It's late, and it's dark. Let me take you home."

"I'm walking, thanks. You stay and fight with Andrew."

"We weren't fighting." His lips were very close to her ear. In the midst of the noisy pub his words were for her alone. "He was warning you, Billie. He doesn't like my record with women."

She faced him. "Your record has nothing to do with me. You pulled me out of a lake. You didn't offer for my hand in marriage or proposition me—although, come to think of it, you did strip me naked. But you don't owe me anything more, Iain. You can wave at me when you see me crossing the street, and that can be that."

His face was inscrutable, his words even more so. "I'm beginning to understand the past."

"What are you talking about?"

"A man and a woman and eight hundred years of hell."

"If I could get one straight answer tonight, just one, I'd be a happy woman."

He dropped his hand.

She waited for him to say something more, but clearly he thought he had already said too much. "Good night, Iain." When she looked back from the doorway he was sitting with his friends again. Not one of them was smiling.

# Chapter 4

"She's way out of her league." Andrew downed a dram before he turned to stare at Iain. "She has no idea, does she, Iain, how irresistible you can be?"

Iain didn't want to respond, but something goaded him. "I don't believe I asked for your assessment of my effect on women."

"No' on women. On one woman. I like Billie. She's fresh and original, and she has no guile. I can no' see what you find so engaging, since she's everything you've always stayed far away from."

"Are you trying to annoy me?"

"No. I can annoy you without trying."

Duncan brought his fist down on the table just hard enough to get their attention. Iain turned to look at him. "Are you going to add your piece, Dunc?"

"We've managed all these years not to fight over women. Why start now?"

"Aye. Why?" Iain asked. "I can see just as clearly as you, Andrew. And I've no wish to ruin Billie's life." Andrew didn't answer. Iain leaned toward him. "Shall I stay away from her, then?"

"No' on my account." Andrew shook his head. "But for God's sake, Iain, tread carefully."

Iain felt a surprising trickle of relief. He had more than his share of reasons for not pursuing Billie Harper, but he was glad that Andrew didn't plan to, either. And he was afraid to examine that more closely.

"Fletcher's leaving," Duncan said. "And I hope he doesn't find his way here again for a while. Brian tells me he had to step between him and another man last night. I remember he was always trouble when we were kids."

"Fletcher?" Iain turned toward the door. "Jeremy Fletcher?"

"Yeah. The one and only."

"So he's back." It took Iain a moment to spot him. Fletcher had stopped on his way out the door to talk to another patron. One glance at the back of his head and Iain felt a familiar knot tightening in his gut.

"Whenever Fletcher's back in the village I yearn for the old days," Andrew said. "There was a time when a man could be driven away for good and forced to find a new home."

"Aye, the good old days." Iain forced himself to look away from Fletcher. "When a man's tongue could be cut out or his eyes gouged. When we weighted women with stones and threw them in Loch Ceo to determine if they were witches."

"Dinna get on your high horse. I'm no' a vigilante. I'll take our present day system of justice, too, but Fletcher brings out something primitive in me."

"You'd have been a sight in belted plaid with your claymore and dirk," Duncan said. "I shudder."

"He has his eye on Billie," Andrew said.

"What did you say?" Iain snapped to attention.

"I was sitting here with her, and I got up to get Duncan. When I came back he'd taken my place, and I did no' like the way he was looking at her."

Iain told himself that Billie was safe. It was a pleasant stroll to Flora Daniels' cottage, less than a quarter of a mile. The way was not well lighted, but neither was it deserted.

Dark had settled in hours ago, but it was early enough that people would still be up, eating late suppers or watching their favorite programs. All Billie had to do was shout....

She had nearly drowned without so much as a call for help.

He cursed under his breath and stood.

"So, you're going after her," Andrew said.

"You knew I would. You can't have it both ways, Andrew. Which shall it be? Am I to be Billie's savior or her destruction?"

Andrew shrugged. "You'd be the one to know that, Iain. I've no way of telling, do I? I'd say you've both inside you. Now we have only to wait and watch to find out which emerges victorious."


She would never learn to pace herself. Billie had hardly gone a block before she realized how badly she had overdone it today. The next time she nearly drowned, she would consider it a good morning's work and take the rest of the day off.

Wind was howling like the drone of a bagpipe, gusting between houses and bending leafless saplings nearly to the ground. She pulled her jacket tighter and tried to concentrate on the exotic flavor of the experience. She was in Scotland, in the tiny village of her ancestors, and she was experiencing what they must have experienced a thousand times.

She was beginning to understand why there were no more MacFarlanes in Druidheachd.

"May I walk with you?"

Her heart beat faster at the unexpected male voice from the shadows behind her. She faced what she thought was the right direction and found Jeremy Fletcher. "Lord, you really startled me!"

"Thinking about something important, were you?"

"I was thinking how cold it is. I've got a new understanding of windchill tonight." She started back down the walkway, and he joined her.

"You're making an early evening of it," he said.

"Funny. I was just thinking it was a late evening. It feels like midnight."

"Do you walk alone often? I should think that's not suitable in most American cities."

"I've never been hurt or threatened. I use discretion." She wondered if she should have used some tonight. After his encounter with Andrew at the pub, she wasn't sure she liked Jeremy Fletcher, and she wished he hadn't followed her.

"I'm surprised that Iain or Andrew didn't offer to bring you home."

"Iain did, but this seemed perfectly safe. I hope I wasn't wrong," she added pointedly.

"Oh, I don't know. I'm not certain that a woman alone is safe anywhere in the world. Even in a place as remote as Druidheachd."

"Then it's good I know how to take care of myself, isn't it?"

"Do you? Have you studied self-defense?"

"Never needed to."

"Curious. I'm surprised, really. You Americans always seem to be preparing for the worst."

"I didn't say I was unprepared." Billie knew they had reached the most deserted stretch between the hotel and Flora's house. The last house she'd passed was already a good ways behind her, and ahead was a small footbridge that crossed the picturesque burn that meandered through the village. From here the route climbed steadily, bordered by woods for a hundred yards or so before more houses appeared.

Billie stopped and faced Jeremy. "Shall we part ways now? I'm sure you didn't mean to go this far, and I'm afraid I'm too tired to be much company."

Jeremy put his hand on her arm. "Your company is desirable, conversation or no conversation."

Billie took a step backward, but she didn't take her eyes off him. "Let's cut to the chase, Jeremy. I'd like to be alone now. I just want to go home and go to sleep. We can take a walk some other time."

"I'll assume that if I was Iain Ross, you might feel differently?"

"You can assume anything you want as long as we say goodnight here." She was aware that his hand still lingered on her sleeve. She waited for him to remove it.

His fingers played over her arm. "What is it about Iain, do you suppose, that attracts so many women? Because there have been many, mind you. More than you could possibly count."

"I'm not sure why we're talking about Iain." She took another step backward, even though she didn't want him to think she was retreating. "I don't know him much better than I know you. And what he does and who he does it with are no concerns of mine."

"Do you know how wealthy he is?"

"Sure. I asked him for a detailed accounting in our first five minutes together. Would you please take your hand off my arm?"

He smiled and wrapped his fingers around her wrist. "You Americans are always in such a hurry. There's no reason to rush off."

"Sure there is." She relaxed her arm and moved closer to him. As his grip relaxed, she twisted her wrist sharply and freed herself. "Good night, Mr. Fletcher."

"You've a way to go as a goodwill ambassador."

"And you've a way to go as a gracious host. Now that we've set diplomacy back a century or two, let's call it a night." She didn't want to turn her back on him, and she didn't want to back away. She remained where she was, tensed and ready for anything, and hoped that he would give up and leave.

He clamped a hand on her shoulder, and his fingernails dug into her flesh. "Not without a kiss."

"Try it and I'll bite your nose off."

He actually looked taken aback. For a moment she thought she'd made her point, then his eyes narrowed and his fingers dug in harder. "Where do you think you are, girlie? There's no one around to hear you shout, and no one to believe you later when you complain. You're a stranger here without a friend. And I can do whatever I please.''

"You can *try* to do whatever you please."

"And you think a wee slip of a lass could stop me?"

"I think this wee slip could make a good stab at it." She didn't take her eyes from his. "But if you just drop your hand and go away, this wee slip will forget anything ever happened here."

"Not without a kiss."

She knew he wanted nothing less than humiliation, and she was determined not to give it to him. She had made a vow, a recent one, that no man would ever humiliate her again. "Drop your hand or I'll scream. There were lights on at the last house."

He jerked her toward him, and, expecting exactly that, she swung her elbow up as he did, ramming it into his chest. He gave a surprised grunt, but he didn't release her. His eyes narrowed, and he barred his teeth like a mad dog. "Now you're in for it," he gasped.

She stomped the heel of her shoe down on his instep, then did it once more for good measure. He grunted again, and his grip on her loosened just long enough for her to break free. She knew better than to run toward Flora's. She needed civilization around her and quickly. She started back the way she'd come.

She had always been fast, but Jeremy was faster. His arm closed over her throat and jerked her off her feet. She couldn't breathe, but she knew how futile it was to struggle in that position. She managed to turn in his arms, and air rushed back into her lungs. With a great deal of satisfaction she kneed him sharply in the groin.

This time he howled in pain and dropped his arms. She spun and started to run again. She expected to make it this time, but Jeremy was tougher than she'd thought. She could hear him gaining on her as she veered left and covered the distance to the last house, which was now completely dark. She was just opening her mouth to scream when she saw the lights of a car approaching.

Hope filled her and doubled her speed. The lights drew closer. She was almost in their range.

The name he hurled after her could have come straight from a Hollywood action flick. She needed only seconds before she would be clearly visible, but Jeremy's newest injury hadn't slowed him enough to give them to her. He tackled her and threw her to the ground. There was a hedge running beside the road, and she knew they were no longer visible. With her face buried in the soft ground, she couldn't scream. She kicked with all her strength to break Jeremy's hold, but, facedown, she had no sure target.

Brakes squealed, and a car door slammed. "Get your hands off her, you bastard!"

Billie recognized Iain's voice. She twisted and squirmed, and suddenly she was freed. She rose to her hands and knees and turned to see Iain and Jeremy struggling on the ground behind her. Impressions collided one with another. Jeremy was the larger, but Iain was angrier. He had his hands around Jeremy's throat and was trying to choke the life out of him. Then Jeremy was on top, although Iain still had him by the throat. Jeremy raised his hand. Something glinted in the moonlight, silver flecks against a smooth, solid surface.

"No!" Billie threw herself forward and knocked him off balance. The rock in Jeremy's hand glanced off the side of Iain's head. Jeremy cursed and grabbed for her.

She saw two openings and one chance. She slammed the side of her head against his vulnerable throat and grabbed for something far more vulnerable between his legs. He howled in outraged agony and rolled off Iain.

Iain jerked upright. In a moment he had Jeremy pinned to the ground. "You've gone too far this time, Fletcher."

Jeremy groaned in response. Iain lifted Jeremy's shoulders and thumped his head against the ground. "Did you hear what I said?"

"You do anything...anything! You tell anybody...I'll tell what I know!" Jeremy gasped. "I'll tell her first!"

Iain slammed him against the ground again. "I don't care what you bloody well tell anybody, you bastard!"

"Iain, let him go." Billie grabbed Iain's arm.

Iain didn't move. "Did you hear me?"

Jeremy lay still. "You'd better bloody well...care, Ross."

"There are things I can tell, too."

"Iain!" Billie tightened her grip on him. "Get off him now. Let him go. We can go to the police and tell them, and they can find him."

"Go to the police...and you'll wish you'd never been born," Jeremy said.

Iain slammed him against the ground one more time.

"Iain!" Billie tugged at him.

"Move away, Billie."

She knew better than to argue. She stepped back warily. Indecision was apparent in every line of Iain's body, but finally he dropped his hands and stumbled away from Jeremy. "Get up and get going," he said.

Jeremy rolled to his side and rose. He limped away without looking back at either of them. They stood in silence and listened to his footsteps dying away.

Billie didn't know what to say. Everything she tried in her head sounded absurd.

"Where the hell did you learn to fight like that?" Iain asked.

"Excuse me?"

"You fight like a bloody sailor! My God, I'm glad it wasn't my...private parts you were after!"

"I was a cook on a tramp steamer. I was!" she added, at his disbelieving grunt. "For a year and a half between college and graduate school. I went all over the world, and a couple of old men on board made sure I could handle myself when I had to."

"You are certifiably mad."

"I'm a terrific cook, too."

He grunted again.

Billie put her hand on his arm. "Iain, what did he mean? What did he mean about telling what he knows?"

"It's the kind of thing a man says in a fight."

"Bull...loney," she finished lamely. "He was talking about something between the two of you."

"Which is where I plan for it to remain."

"Look, I got just a little bit involved myself, don't you think?"

He faced her. "What happened before I got here?"

"More dirty fighting. I was doing pretty well until he tackled me."

"How did it start?"

"I was walking home, and he followed me. When I asked him to leave me alone, he wouldn't. You were mentioned, a kiss was mentioned, next thing I know, I've got my knee in his groin. But obviously not hard enough. I haven't had enough practice lately."

"What did he say about me?"

"That you're incredibly wealthy and you have the sex life of a rabbit." She shrugged. "I guess that about sums it up."

He coughed. "Bloody hell, woman."

"Should I tell the police?" She paused. "Are there police to tell?"

"Of a sort. One bobby for the surrounding area. He's out of town at the moment."

"What do you think I should do?"

"I can't tell you that."

She tried to imagine reporting this to the police. She knew what the ensuing ruckus would do for her reputation in a village like Druidheachd. Any hopes she had of getting people to trust her with their stories would be dashed. "Do you think he'll come after me again?"

"I've never heard of him manhandling a woman before, but he's unpredictable."

"He must have been carried away by my beauty and charm."

"I haven't even asked if you're all right." He wiped her cheek with his fingertips. "You're covered with dirt."

His touch was so gentle that she wanted to close her eyes and savor it. "Rolling around on the ground does that to a person."

He dropped his hand. "Are you hurt anywhere? Scraped? Bruised?"

"All the above, but nothing serious. How's your head?"

"Still on my shoulders, thanks to you."

"To me?"

"Aye. He'd have knocked me unconscious with that rock if you hadn't grabbed his . . . hadn't intervened."

"Just returning the favor of the morning."

"Let's get you home."

"No." She put her hand on his arm. "I don't want to scare Flora to death. I'm going to have to go somewhere and clean up first."

He studied her. "Maybe that's a good idea. I'll take you back to the hotel."

"I'm really not in the mood for another beer and verbal joust."

"Upstairs to Duncan's suite. Maybe Mara will still be there. You couldn't be in better hands."

"Mara?"

"Duncan's lady."

"Well, I'm sure she'll just be pleased as punch to meet me."

"She will be."

She smiled at what she thought was a compliment. "I haven't said thank you, have I?"

"Don't."

"Why were you driving this way?"

"I was looking for you."

Something warm and liquid spiraled through her. "Were you?"

"I saw Fletcher leave just after you did. I just wanted to be sure you were all right."

"Then you do think he's dangerous."

He didn't answer for a moment. "Jeremy Fletcher would like nothing better than to take everything that belongs to me," he said at last.

"I don't belong to you, Iain."

"Be glad you don't, Billie." His eyes were bleak. "Be tremendously glad that you don't."

## Chapter 5

Mara was a woman to hate on sight. She had hair like moonbeams and eyes the pale green of new spring leaves. Her features were delicate, and she moved with ethereal, feminine grace. Billie really did want to hate her.

But it was impossible.

"I dinna think you should go after the dirt so hard," Mara said, squinting into the mirror from behind Billie. "You've scraped your cheek, as well, and from the looks of it, it'll be bruised. Would you like me to do that for you?"

Billie turned obediently and handed the facecloth to Mara.

"Sit there in the light," Mara said. "I'll be gentle."

Duncan's apartment was spacious and comfortable, and nothing at all like the rest of the hotel in decor. There were no Victorian furbelows here, just straight, clean lines and the occasional piece of modern art, its subject matter more appropriate to California than Scotland.

A child's toys dotted the floor. A stuffed seal lay against the leg of the sofa, and open books with colorful illustrations nestled in stacks under the television table.

Duncan had a daughter. Billie had learned that much already. Her name was April; she was seven, and not Mara's child by birth, but obviously loved as much by Mara as if she were. She was asleep in the farthest bedroom, so Billie hadn't had a chance to meet her yet. But she had met Primrose, a brother, it seemed, of Hollyhock's and almost as ungainly.

Billie took the offered spot and closed her eyes. Her fingers dangled by her side, and a long, wet tongue slurped at them. She looked down to see Primrose alongside her. "What do you suppose Duncan and Iain are doing?"

"They said they were going for more ice. I'm thinking they stopped in the pub for a wee dram to take away Iain's headache."

"*I'm* Iain's headache. Make me disappear, and he'll be as good as new."

"There are certainly some in the village who believe I could do it."

"What? Make me disappear?"

"I've a reputation of sorts."

"What sorts?"

"A bit of this and that." Mara smiled. "Are you ready?"

Billie knew it was not her day to have questions answered. She closed her eyes and waited for Mara to begin. When nothing happened, she opened them again. Mara was frowning.

"Is something wrong?"

"No. Nowt."

Billie could smell a lie a mile away. "You look pale. Are you all right?"

Mara took a deep breath. "A bit unsteady. That's all."

"Maybe you should sit down."

"No. I'll take care of you, no' you of me." Mara began to gently wipe Billie's forehead.

"The last time somebody did that I was five or younger."

"Did you never get into scrapes after that?"

"I was in them all the time. My mother gave up and taught me what to do for myself so I wouldn't even have to trudge back home in between."

Mara laughed. "So, you were an adventurous bairn."

"That's what my mother called it, too. The spin doctor of northern Florida. Nearly everyone else said I was a trouble-maker, but I was too busy having adventures to know it."

"But you were the least troublesome, Billie. Next to your brothers, you were an easy child."

Billie opened her eyes. "How did you know I had brothers?"

Mara paused, her hand in midair. "I thought you said so. Did you no'?"

"No."

"I must have misunderstood."

"I did—*do* have them. Three. Older than me, and a hundred times more trouble. So, you were right."

"A lucky guess, then."

"Tell me about yourself, Mara."

Mara's hand paused again. She had progressed to Billie's cheek. "What would you like to know?"

"Well, what brought you here? Iain said you're not from Druidheachd originally."

"I've land up on Bein Domhain that I bought from Iain. It's a wee croft, with sheep and a garden. I built the cottage by myself. It's exactly as it might have been if my ancestors had built it on that spot."

"It sounds wonderful. I hope you'll let me see it one day."

"Aye. You've a standing invitation."

"Why did you choose Druidheachd? Is your family from here originally?"

"No' too far. I feel at home here."

"I do, too. As a matter of fact, Iain claims that hundreds of years ago my family put a curse on his."

Mara stepped back. Her hand dropped to her side. She seemed to grow paler. Billie took her arm. "Mara, are you all right? Please. I insist you sit down for a minute."

Mara sank into the chair beside Billie's and handed her the facecloth. "I'm sorry."

The door opened, and Iain and Duncan walked in. Iain was holding an ice pack to the side of his head where Jeremy's rock had grazed it.

"Mara's not feeling well," Billie said.

Duncan crossed the room and knelt in front of her. Mara leaned forward and whispered something in his ear. Billie got up to give them more privacy and joined Iain.

"Your face is still dirty," he said.

"I guess I'll have to give up hope of impressing you with my ravishing beauty."

He set down the ice pack and took the cloth from her hand. "Hold still. I'll be impressed by ravishing cleanliness, instead."

Billie told herself there was nothing sensuous about having her face washed. She was exhausted and shaken from the encounter with Jeremy and worried about Mara. But as Iain swirled the cloth over her face, she was suffused with warmth. She watched his expression. It didn't change, but some new emotion was reflected in his eyes.

When he had finished, he lightly traced her cheek with his fingertip. "You may have a bruise."

He was standing so close that she could feel the warmth of his body mingling with her own. His fingertip was rough against her cheek, and the intensity of his gaze made it impossible to look away. "It won't be the first." Her voice emerged low and husky, and she didn't smile.

"You have the most wonderful eyes."

She had just been thinking the same about his. They were so profound a blue that there was nothing to compare them to. "I should go home now, and you should vow never to be caught within miles of me again. I've brought you nothing but trouble."

He smoothed a wisp of hair over her ear. "This had very little to do with you, Billie. If Fletcher hadn't seen you with me, he wouldn't have gone after you."

His fingers lingered against her earlobe. The warmth inside her was pooling in very specific and intimate places. "You're not going to tell me why he hates you, are you?"

"There are many things I'm not going to tell you." His fingers trailed slowly down her neck to the collar of her sweater.

"Like what?"

"Good try."

"Iain."

Iain turned at Duncan's summons, but he didn't move his hand. "Is there anything we can do, Dunc?"

"That's up to you."

Billie's curiosity was piqued. "Would you like me to leave?"

"No," Mara said. "Unless you choose to."

Billie frowned and looked up at Iain. "Iain?"

"I don't know," he said in answer.

"I think you have a pretty good idea, Iain," Duncan said. "Although it's never been directed at you before."

"At me?"

"Yes. And Billie, too, apparently."

"I'm in the dark here," Billie said. "Which is beginning to feel as familiar as my favorite sneakers, by the way."

Iain didn't look at her. "Mara has some unusual... talents. I think this concerns one of them."

"Mara has second sight," Duncan said bluntly. "She often sees the future, less often the past. I was skeptical once myself, but I'd be an idiot to be skeptical now."

"That's how you knew I had brothers," Billie told Mara. "It never occurred to me."

"Then you believe in the sight?"

Billie hesitated. Did she believe? She wasn't sure, but unlike many of her academic colleagues, she was reluctant to throw out any source of information just because it couldn't be proved in a laboratory. "Well, I've seen it demonstrated before."

"Then you've an open mind?"

"Some people would say my mind's so open it doesn't contain a thing."

"They'd be fools," Iain said.

She looked at him, surprised. His gaze was warm and something else. Protective? Alarm threaded through her. Iain was taking Mara's claims absolutely seriously. And he didn't expect to find out anything good.

Mara closed her eyes and leaned back in her chair.

Iain moved away from Billie, as if to attempt to distance himself from his feelings. She watched him and swore he was torn between staying to see what Mara would say and leaving. She went to Mara and knelt beside her. "Is there something you want to tell me?"

"Your future is dark to me. I can no' see a bit of it."

"What then? My past?"

"No. No' yours. The past of your family."

Billie heard Iain draw a breath. Mara opened her eyes and pointed at him. "And yours, Iain, though I've no' seen a thing about you or your family before now."

"You don't look well, Mara. Are you certain you want to go on with this?" Iain asked.

"I've wee choice." She motioned for him to join them.

Billie watched indecision continue to play across Iain's features. Finally he stepped forward. Mara held out a hand. He hesitated, then took it.

Mara closed her eyes again and held out her other hand to Billie.

Billie was torn, too. A part of her rejected the drama of a joust with the supernatural after a day filled with more than enough excitement. She had come to Scotland to lick wounds, not to have more inflicted.

"Billie?"

Billie had been drawn to Mara at first sight. Now she couldn't make herself refuse the woman who already seemed like a friend. After mere days in the home of her ancestors, Billie was already up to her ears in intrigue.

She grasped Mara's hand, but she didn't know what to expect. She had a cousin with the odd ability to find lost items and sometimes even people. Billie had seen his ability demonstrated more than once, but those experiences had been nothing like this.

Mara was silent for so long that Billie began to wonder if whatever she had experienced had already faded away. As Mara continued to sit silently with her eyes closed, Billie glanced up at Iain. He was frowning, but as if he felt her gaze on his face, he turned. The moment his eyes met hers, Mara began to speak.

"You had ancestors...many hundreds of years ago. Billie..." Mara was silent. "I've no name for her. Your ancestor." She looked increasingly troubled. Her lovely face was suddenly twisted by sorrow. "She was a bonny lassie, brave and intelligent. Spirited, like you, Billie. The pride of her father's heart. The joy of her mother's days. She was protected by...brothers."

She was silent again for nearly a minute, struggling with sadness. A tear ran down her cheek when she finally continued. "She was to marry her cousin, who she did no' love, but that was no' so important in those times. She looked forward to raising strong, courageous sons and having a good and useful life."

"Mara," Iain said, turning his gaze from Billie, "don't go on if this troubles you so."

"And your forefather, Iain. He was good and brave, the best at all he ever tried. He was to lead his clan when his father died. They were never supposed to meet, those two. Their families were in conflict. They were...enemies."

Mara rested her head against the back of her chair. For a moment she seemed too upset to go on. Billie waited. Beside her, Iain was obviously uneasy.

"She walked one day, beside the loch," Mara said. "She was with her maids, and there were men to guard them." She opened her eyes. "I dinna know what to call them. I know nowt about this time. I have no' the right words."

"That's all right," Billie said. "It doesn't matter."

Mara stared at her, and Billie had the strangest feeling that she was seeing someone else. "Her women were attacked by men from Iain's family. The guards were overcome. The maids were...thrown to the ground and..." Her face expressed her horror.

"Don't go on with this, Mara," Iain said sharply. He tried to withdraw his hand, but Mara held it tightly in hers.

"She jumped in the water to drown herself. It was better...."

Billie shuddered. Suddenly it was as if she were there. She could imagine the horror of that moment, of a medieval woman with so few choices that drowning herself was the best of them. She could hear the screams of the women on shore, feel the cold water closing over her head, just as it had this morning. For a moment she couldn't breathe again. Then she felt a hand on her shoulder and looked up to see Iain staring at her. She gulped for air. She didn't know how much time had passed, but concern shone in his eyes.

"She was rescued," Mara said. "As she was drowning, for she could no' swim, she was rescued by your ancestor, Iain. He came upon the scene and stopped the violation of the women. And when he saw the lady in the loch, he dove in to rescue her."

Billie wasn't a seer, but she could read Iain's thoughts. A part of that history had repeated itself today.

"His men were gone when he came out of the water carrying her. They knew he would be furious, for in spite of the feud between the clans, he was no' a man for violence. He revived her. When she opened her eyes and saw him, she knew he would no' hurt her. They looked at each other and knew they were destined to love each other always."

Iain shook his head, as if such romantic nonsense was incomprehensible to him. But his eyes were still wary.

"And it was then, as they stared at each other and saw how their fates were intertwined, that her cousin, her betrothed and his men, came upon them. They would have put your ancestor to death, Iain, but the lady begged them to spare him. She told the story of how he had saved her, and as a gift, her cousin set your ancestor free. But he was told that he must never show his face to her again or he would die a terrible death."

Billie was entranced—and skeptical. She was also aware that Iain hadn't removed his hand from her shoulder.

"Is there more?" he asked, after Mara had been silent for a long time.

"Aye, there's more, and none of it is clear to me." Tears filled her eyes. "But there is such pain there, such sadness."

"Damn it, I don't understand why you have to go through this!" Duncan crossed the room, knelt and took Mara in his arms. "I don't understand why it has to be you!"

"Because it does," Mara said simply.

"Mara." Billie put her hand on Mara's knee. "I know what you've just experienced is very real to you, but could it just be a twist on what's happened to Iain and me today? A story suggested by everything that's gone on since we met? The rescue from the loch, the fight with Jeremy, and my saving Iain from having his head bashed in. Can you always tell the difference between what's real and what your imagination suggests?"

Mara smiled sadly. "Always."

Billie looked to Iain for confirmation that she was on the right track. He shook his head, as if to warn her not to say more.

"This isn't to be discussed outside this room," Duncan said. "Mara's earned the respect of people in the village, but the less said about her second sight, the better. I don't want her to become the village fortune-teller and sideshow freak."

"Then you think this really happened?" Billie looked from man to man. Iain didn't even acknowledge her question. Duncan shrugged noncommittally.

Mara slipped her hand from Iain's and used it to cover Billie's. "You know it happened, Billie dear. For a moment, you saw it, too. The story's buried deep inside you. In the same way birds fly a thousand miles to nest where their ancestors have nested before, you've come back to find answers here in Druidheachd. Each of us has the secrets of generations inside us. And it's time for your secrets to be revealed."

Mara looked up and focused on Iain. "And yours, Iain. The time's arrived to put the agony of centuries behind you, too. The time has finally arrived."

Iain drove a vintage Jaguar, a car designed decades before for comfort and durability. The leather interior had spiderweb cracks that added to the ambience of money so old it had faded and decayed from the touch of a thousand hands. Billie snuggled against the seat and watched him drive. He had magnificent hands, long-fingered and broad. She was fascinated by the only ring he wore, a worn circle of plaited yellow and white gold, a wedding ring, from the looks of it, but worn on the right hand instead of the left.

"I've had the strangest day," she said at last.

He laughed. There was no humor in it. "Are you going to report Fletcher?"

"Probably not formally, since it will just be his word against mine. But it might be good to let your bobby know what happened, in case he threatens me again."

"I'm going to be sure he doesn't."

"Don't, Iain. I don't want you involved anymore. Apparently you two have enough going on between you without me to add fuel to the flames."

"What do you think about Mara's story?"

"How much of it have you heard before?"

He glanced at her. "What do you mean?"

"I mean you didn't seem overwhelmed with surprise. You've heard at least some of it before. Maybe Mara has, too, and just doesn't remember. Maybe she's just repeating something that's already circulated."

"Then you think she's telling lies?"

She was outraged. For a moment she couldn't speak; then her words tumbled out. "Absolutely not! I don't go around accusing people I like of lying. I'm talking about the power of suggestion. That's all. And I don't appreciate your jumping to the worst conclusion!"

"You've a temper. Why am I not surprised?"

"Because nothing surprises you, you're so indifferent and arrogant and superior!"

He flashed her a smile that could have slain a dragon at fifty paces. "And you're so incapable of keeping a single thought to yourself."

"You might be surprised."

"Are you admitting to deep, dark secrets, Billie? Under that utterly adorable exterior, is there a teeming, roiling pit?"

"Why not? Are you trying to corner the market?"

He laughed. For a moment she struggled to hang on to her outrage; then, reluctantly, she smiled in response. "Well, I don't stay angry long."

"And I don't stay indifferent, arrogant and... What was the last?"

"Superior."

"Superior for long, either. In fact, I've never thought I was superior."

"Iain, anyone would look at you and just assume that everything's always come easily to you."

"Then everyone would be wrong."

She leaned back against the seat again. "What did you think of Mara's story? You neatly maneuvered me into a fight so you wouldn't have to comment. *Have* you heard it before? Does it have to do with the curse?"

"It's a story. Nothing more."

"A true story?"

He was silent.

"You believe it, don't you?"

"How can I answer that? I wasn't alive eight hundred years ago. I wasn't there to witness that day or any other."

"But you trust Mara's gifts."

"Let's just say I've seen some surprising results."

"Iain, what *do* you know?"

"I know that we've arrived at Flora's house." Iain stopped the car in front of the little stone cottage. "And she's left a light on for you." He got out before she could answer and came around to open her door.

There was nothing to do except get out. She stood beside the car and faced him. "My visa will expire before I find out anything else, won't it?"

"I don't know."

She admired his face in the moonlight. He had the strong yet refined bone structure of a thousand years of good Highland breeding and the cynical brow of a Regency rake. But it was his eyes that entranced her, eyes that saw everything and mirrored nothing inside him.

Had an ancestor of hers looked at an ancestor of his this same way once upon a time? Had she gazed into eyes as blue and known that their destinies would forever be entwined?

Somehow, at that moment, it didn't seem impossible.

"I'd better go inside." She didn't move.

"I'll walk you to the door."

"That's not—"

"I'll walk you," he said firmly.

They moved quietly through Flora's front garden. The swaying, flowerless stalks of foxglove and delphinium were ghostly outlines against a pale stone fence. Billie stopped beside the door. "If I say thank you, you won't even be sure for what, will you?"

He smiled. "I couldn't follow that."

"There's so much to say thank you about."

"Don't say it at all, and I won't be confused."

She knew she was supposed to go inside. She didn't move. "I'm sorry I snapped at you."

"Billie." He sighed. He reached up to stroke her cheek. She felt the touch in other, less visible parts of her body. "You're an unexpected complication in a very simple life," he said.

"There's nothing complicated about me and nothing simple about you."

"My life is simple. I want nothing from it."

"How odd." She leaned forward. His fingers wove into her hair. She rested her hands on his shoulders. She planned to kiss him on the cheek. It seemed appropriate. It seemed an ordinary thing to do, considering everything they had weathered together that day. She rose on tiptoe. His eyes held hers as she leaned toward him.

She found his lips where his cheek had been. They were cool and dry, and she had never experienced any touch so powerful before. She caught her breath, but she didn't move away. He abandoned her hair and wrapped his arms around her to draw her closer.

The wind caressed her back, but Iain's arms shielded her. He was hard against her, unrepentantly male and unrepentantly aroused. She burrowed what little softness she had against him. His taste was familiar and yet wildly, powerfully new. She had kissed him a million times and never before. Her lips parted, and she knew the sweetest satisfaction of her life when his tongue touched hers.

He drew away from her then, although his arms still encircled her. "Billie." He rested his cheek against her hair.

"I guess this is a little sudden."

"More than a little." He stroked her back, wide, gentle circles that were more arousing than soothing.

She could almost feel regret stealing through him. "By any chance are you wishing that you hadn't jumped into the loch today?"

"I could do no less than Ruaridh."

"Ruaridh?"

He was silent.

"Iain, was Ruaridh your ancestor?"

"It's time for you to go in now. Flora will be worried about you."

"You *have* heard the story before."

"Not exactly as I heard it today." He set her away from him. "I've never heard any part of it that made the Rosses less than perfect."

"Will you tell me what you've heard? Someday?"

"I'll be going away tomorrow. I don't know when I'll be returning."

"Away?"

"Aye."

"I see." His absence had something to do with her. She didn't need to have second sight to know that.

"I'll have a word with Fletcher before I go. He won't trouble you again."

"And you won't, either," she said sadly.

"Do what you have to do here, Billie, then go back home to America. There's always been trouble in Druidheachd for the MacFarlanes."

"And for the Rosses?"

"For the Rosses most of all." He touched her cheek. His fingers lingered for a moment; then he turned.

She watched him walk away. The wind seemed colder by the moment. Even after the sound of his car had faded, she stood in the same spot and watched winter come to Druidheachd.

# Chapter 6

No matter what she was doing, Flora stopped for a cup of tea precisely at eleven o'clock each morning. A week after Billie had begun to board with her, Flora had invited her to partake in the ritual. Billie knew it was a sign of approval. Flora had sons who lived nearby, grandchildren and great-grandchildren and neighbors who frequently stopped in to chat with her or take her to do errands. But she had always taken her tea alone until Billie came to stay.

At the beginning of December Billie came back from the village with freshly baked scones from the Sinclair Hotel and a jar of raspberry jam that Mara had given her that morning. In the past month she and Mara had become good friends, and this morning Billie had news to tell about her.

"Look what I have." She set her booty on the kitchen counter, along with the bottle of fresh cream she had bought at Cameron's, the grocery store-post office-community center that was the heart of all gossip and industry in the village.

Flora lifted the bag of scones and peeked inside. "Just the thing."

Flora weighed all of eighty pounds, but she had the appetite of a weight lifter. Billie imagined that Mr. Daniels had gone to an early grave just trying to keep his wisp of a wife fed.

"I've got more," Billie said.

"Do ye?"

"Gossip." Billie hissed the word slowly, savoring it on her tongue.

"I knew ye'd be good for something, lass, when I agreed to let ye board with me."

"I'm delighted I've fulfilled your expectations."

"Well, sit down and let me pour. Then we'll have at it."

The kitchen was only large enough for two. Billie took her customary seat beside a window rimmed by a stone ledge filled with wintering geraniums. From the window she could see Flora's side garden, a thicket of shrub roses, ivy and evergreens sparkling with snow.

Flora arrived to pour tea into Billie's cup. "First, ye've a letter from home. Steuart's wife brought it with my mail this morning."

"They told me at Cameron's. I'll bet it's from my mother. She still hasn't given up trying to get me home for Christmas."

"But ye will no' be going?"

Billie thought about home, about sunny December days and the close-knit family she hadn't seen for months. "Well, I can't now. I'll be busy a few days before Christmas."

"Will ye, now?"

"Yes. I'm going to be in a wedding."

Flora took her own seat. Her dark eyes snapped with excitement. "A wedding?"

"Now, if I treated you the way you treat me, Flora, I'd smile and lift a brow and say something wonderfully enigmatic. I ought to do that, just to teach you a lesson."

"But yer no' me, lass. So dinna waste another moment."

"Duncan and Mara are getting married, and she's asked me to be her attendant."

"Past time, it is!"

"Apparently Duncan and Mara think so. They're furiously making their plans."

"And yer included."

"It probably seems a little strange, but I feel like I've known Mara all my life. And Duncan's a dear. I feel honored to be asked."

"A few days before Christmas." Flora began on her scone. "Aye, the time's right. A good wedding always takes place bctwccn Martinmas and the New Year."

"This will be a good one." Billie hesitated. "It's going to be at Fearnshader, Flora, or rather, at an old chapel on the grounds."

"Then Iain's back?"

"So they say." Billie tried to ignore the stab of disappointment that accompanied her words. There was no reason to think that Iain Ross should have searched her out now that he was back in Druidheachd. He had made it clear by his month-long absence that she had no hold over him.

"So, he's been back a while, has he?"

Billie shrugged. She told herself it didn't matter. Her days had been full since Iain had left, and she was making headway on her research. "I don't know when he came back. I haven't seen him."

"And ye wish he'd called or come to see ye?"

She gave up the pretense. "Well, we almost drowned together. That's a tie of sorts."

"Our Iain has no ties. Och, Duncan and Andrew are his friends, that's true, but I'd guess that even with them, he keeps a muckle part of himself in rein."

"Why?"

Flora had always avoided Billie's questions about Iain. Now she stirred her tea, gazing at her china cup as if it had answers to give. "Iain's parents died when he was still a bairn. His da first, then his mum. He was sent to England to school, only coming back to Fearnshader for the occasional holiday, when he was tended by servants and an auld uncle of his father's." She stirred harder. "Some in the village said that the uncle was insane. Whether he was or no', it was a terrible way for a lad to grow to maturity."

Billie made a low sound of sympathy, but she was afraid to say a word. She hoped if she remained quiet, Flora would continue. She wasn't disappointed.

"The Rosses' lot is to be unhappy."

This time Flora was silent so long Billie was afraid she had finished. "That seems like a huge waste of cosmic energy, wouldn't you say?" Billie mimicked a deep bass voice. "Let's see, prepare half a million babies for launching today, James, and Peter, get your halo shined up, because there's going to be a rush at the golden gate this afternoon. Oh, and Paul, you see about the Rosses of Druidheachd. Make sure nothing good happens to them, or I'll set you back down on that road to Damascus, and that's not such a great place to be these days."

Flora's eyes sparkled. "Laugh if you will."

"I'm not laughing. Not exactly, anyway. I'm trying to understand."

"There was a curse."

"So I've been told. And that's all I've been told, I might add. Don't you think it's time to enlighten me a little more?"

"It came about because of Ruaridh and Christina."

"Christina." Suddenly Billie's ancestor had a name. "You've known her name all along?"

"Aye. It's a very old story, and I'm a very old woman."

"A very *long* story, I'd guess," Billie said carefully.

"Aye, that it would be."

"One you'd love to share with me."

"Had I only the time." Flora finished her tea and the last crumbs of her scone. "But Steuart's wife is coming back to take me to visit a friend in hospital."

To Billie's knowledge, none of the wives of Flora's sons had first names, though Flora seemed to love them all dearly. "Have you time for any of it?"

"A bit. Yer Christina and Iain's Ruaridh fell in love that day beside the loch, just as Mara MacTavish told you. Separately each vowed they would no' try to see the other again because only tragedy could come from it. But even as they made their vows, in their deepest hearts they were search-

ing for ways to break them.'' She stood and smoothed her
tweed skirt. "And now I must be off. Steuart's wife does no'
like to be kept waiting.''

Billie made a face. "Hey, I can understand her feelings
completely.''

"You must learn patience, lass.''

"Life's so darned short, Flora. Why do I have to waste a
single second of it being patient?''

"Ye've much to learn, Billie. Spend yer time listening to
the things that people dinna say.''

"Well, that gives me a lot of material.''

"Our Iain, for instance.''

"An *awful* lot of material.''

"Would he avoid ye so hard if he had no feelings for ye?''

"I'm afraid so.'' Billie stood, too. "Look, I hardly know
Iain, and I'm not even sure I want to. I'm not a good judge
of character, Flora. I've never learned to see the bad in
anybody. Somebody could steal my wallet and I'd be thinking what clever hands they had or what terrific coordination. People take advantage of me all the time. I don't trust
myself.''

"Ye knew ye did no' like Jeremy Fletcher.''

Billie took their dishes to the sink. Jeremy Fletcher was
now the *absent* Jeremy Fletcher. He had left town the same
day as Iain, not to return. In the end Billie had reported their
encounter to the bobby, but Jeremy had been gone by then,
and no charges had been pressed. "I only took a real dislik-
ing to him after he got nasty. Anyone else would have spotted him for what he was a mile away.''

"The MacFarlane women have always known their destiny. Tell me yer mum did no' know yer da was to be her intended the first day they met.''

Billie couldn't deny it. Her mother and father had married less than six weeks after their first meeting, and to Billie's knowledge there had never been a single regret. The
same had been true for her grandmother. "You seem to
know a lot about the MacFarlane women.''

"Christina knew her destiny, though she fought it.''

"Well, from what little I've been allowed to piece together, Christina would have been better off following somebody else's destiny. I don't think there's a happy ending to that story."

"Sometimes, lass, a happy ending takes a century or twa to come to pass. Sometimes even longer."

Billie was still formulating a response when she realized that she was alone in the kitchen. Flora had slipped away.

Billie had fallen in love with Mara's cottage at first sight. Her own ancestors must once have lived in a home just like it. Built of stone and thatched with rushes, it was as picturesque as its mountain setting.

Billie had learned that Mara had constructed most of it alone. Mara had explained that at the time she'd had her own demons to work off, and she'd chosen hard physical labor and primitive living conditions as her therapy. From nothing she had carved a home and gardens, pastures and a shelter large enough for the small flock of sheep she kept. She was a spinner and a weaver, and she sold her yarn—hand dyed from herbs and flowers she grew and collected—in shops throughout the Highlands.

Until she and Duncan built their dream house farther up the hill above the cottage, Mara intended to live at the hotel with her new husband. In the meantime, she had found a local boy to stay in the cottage during the week and care for the sheep. On weekends she and Duncan and April would use it as their retreat.

On the morning of the wedding Billie warmed her hands in front of Mara's peat fire. The cottage was snug, but central heating was a luxury no one in Scotland seemed to have heard of. After a raucous party at the hotel, attended by nearly every female in Druidheachd, she had spent the night in the cottage with Mara, a last symbolic salute to the single life.

"You must see the cottage in spring," Mara told her as she dressed to go outside and check on her sheep one last time before they left for Fearnshader. She fastened her dark green cloak and pulled on gloves. "I've flowers planted all around the cottage, and the hillside blooms with daffodils.''

''I think I'll still be here in the spring. Flora's introduced me to wonderful people with wonderful stories. I'm gathering quite a collection.''

''I'm glad it's going well.''

''As well as it could, considering that the idea wasn't well thought out before I came. I'd planned to do something else. This was . . . my second choice.''

''Was your other idea turned down, then?''

''No.'' Billie looked up and smiled ruefully. ''But the other idea was one I could have researched closer to home. The advantage of this one was that it was thousands of miles away.''

Mara wrapped a scarf around her neck. ''We have something more in common, then. I came here to escape a man, too.''

Billie had never really discussed her past or her personal life with Mara. There had always been other, happier things to discuss, but somehow, Mara knew about her past anyway. ''Talking to you can be very disconcerting.''

''I dinna see why. Why else does a woman flee across an ocean to a village so remote it's less than a dot on the map?''

''Who was the man you escaped? Your former husband?''

''Aye. His mission in life was to make me doubt myself.''

''And you came here and built this cottage, stone by stone, to prove that there was nothing to doubt?''

''Aye. That I did. And then I met Duncan.''

''And now you're about to be married.''

''But I made very certain, Billie, that Duncan would no' make me doubt myself, too.''

''I'm not sure I'll ever trust myself in exactly the same way.''

''Give yourself time.''

Billie considered that as she stared at the blue smoke curling up from the hearth. Mara whistled for Guiser, her border collie, who was lying near Billie's feet. She heard Mara leave, but she didn't turn as the door closed. When she finally turned to toast a different part of her anatomy, she discovered that she wasn't alone after all. Iain stood beside the door, and he was watching her.

"Well, hi there," she said. "You could have announced yourself."

"Hello, Billie."

She really didn't know what else to say. When she didn't speak, he did. "I came to take you and Mara home with me."

"I thought Andrew was going to be our transportation."

"There were some last minute details to oversee. He asked me to take his place."

"I'm surprised you weren't too busy yourself. Who's checking to be sure all Fearnshader's gargoyles are washed and polished?"

He smiled. "So you're to be Mara's attendant at the wedding."

"That's right."

He crossed the room and joined her at the fireplace. "I half expected to find you back in the States for the holidays."

She really didn't know how to respond. Had he hoped she would be gone? Or was she just imagining that his long stay out of town had involved her in some way? "I half expected *you* to stay away for them. But I'm glad you're back. Fearnshader will be a lovely place for the wedding."

"And that's the only reason why you're glad I've returned? Because I can open my home?"

"I'm not sure why else I should be. You've been back in town three or four times in the past month, but this is the first time I've had the pleasure of your company."

"I've been very busy with business. I apologize."

"Don't. You don't owe me anything, Iain, certainly not your presence. I'm just glad to see you again."

"Are you?"

"Why wouldn't I be? Just because on the one memorable day we spent together I was drowned, stripped, attacked, regaled with tragic visions of my ancestors and soundly kissed? That's no reason to worry about what's coming next."

He didn't smile. "It would be a hard day to top."

She made a wry face, although it felt forced. "So, let's not try. Okay?"

Iain looked as if he wanted to say more, but she suspected he wouldn't. He confirmed it when he turned away. "As soon as Mara comes back, I'll drive you to Fearnshader. I've had a room readied for you, in case the festivities go late into the night. That will be easier than finding a sober driver to take you back to Flora's."

Billie wasn't going to argue, but she had absolutely no intention of staying overnight at Fearnshader. She wasn't sure she could explain why, not even to her own satisfaction.

The door slammed, and Billie looked up to see Mara covered with snowflakes. "I shall stop fussing over the sheep now, I promise. Guiser will watch over them until Danny comes. I'll just get my bag, and we can be off."

"I'm ready, too," Billie said. She reached for the coat she'd thrown over a chair and slipped it on.

Iain watched; then, with a shake of his head, he stepped forward and took the front flaps in his hands. He stood so close that she could smell the subtle, musky scent of his aftershave. His gaze connected to hers. She couldn't have looked away, not even for all the answers to all her questions. His hand brushed her breast as he fastened the top button, then followed the row to the bottom, fastening the buttons one by one.

"I'm a big girl," she said when he'd finished. Her voice emerged low and sultry. "Didn't you know?"

"Aye. There's very little about you I haven't noticed. Including the fact that you don't look after your own welfare."

Billie was afraid he was right. If she really looked after herself, she would make a point of avoiding Iain as stringently as he had avoided her. Sadly, she realized that wasn't going to happen. In the month since she had last seen him she had nearly convinced herself that the attraction between them was all in her overheated imagination. Now Iain was back in her life, even if only temporarily, and she felt as if someone had hot-wired her nervous system and jump-started her heart.

And judging from the flicker in his eyes, Iain was tuned for takeoff, too.

# Chapter 7

Billie wore jeans and sweaters as if they were part of her, so much a part that Iain hadn't been able to imagine her wearing anything else. But when she emerged from the bedroom he'd set aside for her, dressed in wine-colored silk and amethysts, he questioned the scope of his own imagination.

Silk emphasized everything that denim and wool had hidden. She had small, perfect breasts, a tiny waist and narrow hips. He had already noticed that her legs were as long as a dancer's, and just as elegantly shaped. Now they were covered in shimmering stockings designed to make it impossible for a man to look away. As Iain admired her, he had a vision of the day he had held her naked in his arms. He realized just how badly he wanted to do it again, but this time in his bed, with Billie's legs twined around him.

"I gather I pass?" She was staring at him, too. Her voice was husky. "God, *you* certainly do. Great legs, Iain."

"Do you think so?"

"I think you were born to wear a kilt."

"You look particularly bonny."

For a moment she almost seemed embarrassed, a charming and unexpectedly feminine response to his compliment. She looked away. "I feel like I'm in a fairy tale. I'm sure that in the Middle Ages Ruaridh and Christina didn't live this well, but I'll bet they'd have felt at home here."

He wasn't surprised she had learned her ancestor's name. "Ruaridh was born at Ceo Castle."

"And Christina?"

"There's nothing left of the place where she was born."

She didn't ask more, which surprised him. As she studied the staircase that swept down to the hall below them, he tried to see his ancestral home through her eyes. From the outside Fearnshader was a Gothic monstrosity, with castellated towers, soaring parapets and pointed-arch windows. The stone walls were smothered by ivy, which did nothing to soften the harsh angles but somehow added to the air of decaying grandeur.

Inside was little better. The halls were so cavernous that as a small boy he had often passed his parents walking through them and remained hidden. Too many of the fifty rooms were dark and cheerless, in need of a keen eye, a loving touch and the strength to turn over a portion of the relics of past centuries to willing museums. He didn't seem to possess any of the qualities needed to make Fearnshader a home.

"Mara says there's been much unhappiness here," Billie said. "But there's been laughter, too, and that moderates it. Was it good to grow up here, Iain? I mean, when your parents were still alive?"

Unaccountably he thought of evenings in front of the sitting room fire, held tightly against his mother as she read story after story and his father smiled fondly from a nearby armchair. There had been Sunday walks along the loch and into the hills, trailed by his father's hounds and his mother's terriers, afternoons at play with Duncan and Andrew as his mother pruned her rose garden and laughed at their antics.

And then there had been the nights, so many of them just before his father's death, when he had heard sobbing, and voices raised in argument. Sometimes he could still hear his mother crying, even though he knew it was only the wind.

"It was like anyone's childhood," he said. "There were happy times. But no one is supposed to be happy for long, are they?"

"Where on earth did you learn to think like that? I'd swear the damp climate's made a pessimist out of you. Maybe I'm lucky the MacFarlanes were driven out of town."

He saw questions in her eyes, and concern. He could allow neither. "The music will be starting soon. The guests are arriving. Is there anything I can get for you before the chaos really begins?"

Her forehead wrinkled in speculation. He doubted she was capable of having a thought that wasn't visible on her face, and he found that facet of her personality, like so many others, to be completely captivating.

She moved toward him, a rustle of silk, the flash-fire of amethysts and, surprisingly, the fragrance of violets. She touched his cheek, and her fingers were soft against his skin. "I want you to be happy," she said softly. "I want whatever haunts you to go away."

"I think you've read too many fairy tales."

Her voice was light, but her eyes were troubled. "Fairy tales are my business, remember?"

He removed her hand, but he couldn't seem to let it go. He brought her palm to his lips and kissed it before he left her at the top of the stairs.

"Duncan Sinclair, you may kiss your bride." The minister of the village kirk beamed at Duncan and Mara as Duncan took him at his word and swept Mara into his arms.

Billie tamped down the urge to whistle and settled for a sentimental tear instead. Duncan and Mara's wedding was the most beautiful she had ever seen. The ancient stone chapel on Fearnshader's grounds was lit entirely by candles and adorned with cascading swags of evergreens, holly and ivy. A light snow had fallen as the vows were exchanged, and now the world outside the high, narrow windows was a winter wonderland.

A barrel-chested piper had led them along the snow-dusted path to the chapel, and now he began to play again. Duncan and Mara started down the aisle, each holding one of April's hands. Duncan had surprised them—Mara most of all—by wearing a kilt. He swore it was the first and only time he ever would, but Billie thought he wore it proudly, as required. Iain and Andrew had stood beside him at the ceremony, and the three men of midnight, each in full Highland regalia, were a powerful presence, almost as if they had been spirited to the chapel from a day long ago.

Billie had listened carefully to the words of the ceremony; she had rejoiced in the glow of Duncan and Mara's love for each other; she had blinked back tears as seven-year-old April stepped forward to accept Mara as her second mother—Mara's choice of title. But she had also watched Iain throughout the wedding. The flickering candlelight had added mysterious dimensions to his profile. Tonight he was more the warrior, less the disenchanted poet. There was a fierceness that he often hid, but that couldn't be denied. He was a man of strong emotions, and standing among the people he cared most about, those emotions were almost visible.

He moved toward her now and held out his arm. Andrew had been closer. She had expected him to escort her back down the aisle, but she took Iain's arm and walked beside him to the stunning drone of the piper.

"It's done," he said when they were outside.

She shivered, despite the coat someone had handed her for the trip back. The chapel had been cold enough, but now the winter wind tore at her bare wrists and throat. None of the native Scots seemed even to notice. "Are you glad?"

"Without question."

"I've never seen two happier people. Three, counting April."

"April's own mother is trying to give April what she can. But Mara will be her first and most important mother, no matter what she chooses to call herself."

There was a flash of bright blue in front of them, and the little girl in question came back to launch herself into Iain's arms. "Did I do okay?" April wrapped her arms around Iain's neck and held on for dear life.

"You were the absolute hit of the show."

She peeked over his shoulder. Her face was a small, female version of her father's, complete with his serious gray eyes. "What do you think?" she asked Billie.

"I think your Uncle Iain's right. You were terrific."

"Are you going to get married next? Mara says you are."

"Really? Does she say to whom?"

April looked puzzled.

"Never mind," Billie assured her. "I don't think I want to know. It'll spoil the fun."

"Somebody named Ruaridh." April scrambled down to run to Andrew.

"Ruaridh." Billie breathed the name.

Iain didn't look at her. "Obviously she's mistaken."

"Unless we're about to be catapulted back in time. I felt like that had already happened when I was standing in your chapel."

"Did you?"

"I'm sure you'll think I'm crazy... crazier, but that's a very holy place, Iain. I could almost feel the spirits of all the people who've celebrated and mourned there." She flashed her dimples, even though he wasn't looking at her. "Even if they were Rosses."

"Not all of them were Rosses."

"But not MacFarlanes, I'm sure. I've got a feeling that my relatives were never allowed through that door, unless they were delivered there in coffins."

"The Rosses never wasted good wood on MacFarlanes. We weighted them with stones and threw them in the loch."

"Then I'm related to the monster, I suppose. In a roundabout way."

He laughed. "I'm convinced you're related to the devil himself. Is there anything you take seriously?"

"Sure. My quest to discover why my family cursed yours. I'm beginning to think it was for withholding information.

If all the Rosses were as secretive as you are, it's no wonder the MacFarlanes went on the warpath. *Our* curse is a need to know everything."

"Then I'll tell you something you don't know."

"Really?" She wasn't holding her breath.

"Aye."

They were nearing the house, and the many guests who had just come for the reception were a mass of humanity sweeping forward to congratulate the bride and groom. "Tell me quickly," she urged, "before we're trampled."

"No need to worry. It will only take a moment."

"Tell me!"

"Ruaridh and Christina were married in that chapel, too."

There were a hundred candles burning in Fearnshader's rooms and hallways. Iain had hired a man to do nothing but replace them as the evening wore on. Candlelight mellowed the gray stone, and Christmas greenery softened even the most forbidding nooks and crannies. A Scottish country band filled the air with music, and laughter drifted from one room to another. The party threatened to go on all night.

"So, how does it feel to be a married man again?" Iain asked Duncan. He and Andrew had managed to drag Duncan away from his well-wishers. And now that the three men of midnight were standing in a corner together, they were given a wide berth.

"Right," Duncan said.

"Mara's the bonniest bride I've had the fortune to see," Andrew said.

Iain had to agree. Mara, in a dress of cream-colored lace with garlands of freesia and pale yellow roses woven through her hair, could take a man's breath away. His gaze flicked to Billie, who was laughing with Alasdair Melville on the other side of the crowded room. The two women couldn't possibly have been more different. He had always found being with Mara relaxing, almost meditative. They could sit quietly together, and his mind could wander comfortably, safely, to other places.

But there was nothing comfortable about Billie. Where Mara was peace and tranquility, Billie was a plunge into Loch Ceo. She could take a man under so quickly he hardly knew he was in the water.

"Iain?"

Iain realized that Andrew had asked a question. "I'm sorry. My mind's wandered. What did you say?"

"She's quite bonny, is she no'?"

"Aye. Mara is particularly bonny tonight."

"No' Mara. We finished discussing Mara moments ago. I'm talking about Billie."

"Bonny's not the right word."

"What is, then?" Andrew struggled to hide a smile.

"Vivid. Lively." *Enchanting.*

"Have you danced with her?"

Iain hadn't danced with anyone except some of the village's oldest residents. He had escorted Flora Daniels through some of the dances, and his own housekeeper, Gertie Beggs. Skillfully he had avoided any woman young enough to think of him as something other than a son. "Have you?"

"I'm about to, unless someone stops me."

Iain knew that Andrew was prodding him. More than one dewy-eyed village lass sighed over Andrew, but despite his warmth and wit, Andrew avoided serious relationships.

"Would you like me to dance with her?" Iain asked. "Is that what you're trying to say?"

"No' necessarily. I know she confuses you. I would hate to see you confused in your own home, Iain."

"You've not a drop of subtlety anywhere in your blood."

"Of course no'. You've enough for us both."

"Dance with her, Iain," Duncan said. "Everyone will make note of it, and it will give Mara and me a chance to slip away while they're watching you."

"And why will they be watching us?"

"Because it's known far and wide that Billie's a Mac-Farlane," Andrew said. "It's been whispered about all evening."

"What do they think will happen? That I'll take her in my arms and drop dead of a heart attack?"

"Does that worry you? Alasdair's here, after all. He should be able to prevent the worst damage."

Iain raised a brow. "Friend or not, Andrew, you should watch what you say."

Andrew clapped him on the back. "Should I? Are you no' glad that someone has the courage to prod you, Iain? Or should we all bow and scrape?"

"No one in Scotland bows and scrapes, you idiot."

"Go bow to the lady, Iain," Duncan said. "And do it now, before someone else grabs her. I want to take Mara home."

Iain watched the flickering candlelight deepen the rich glow of Billie's hair. She was still talking to Alasdair, who had been her partner more than once. Beside Alasdair's bland good looks she was a fountain of vibrant color and movement. He couldn't look at her without wanting to experience her with his other senses. He was afraid, terribly afraid, that she was everything that had been missing in his life.

He left his friends and crossed the room toward her. He was stopped again and again, and he murmured polite responses, but he was aware of Billie each time, and of a growing distress within him that he was going to miss the chance to dance with her. And suddenly he wanted that very badly.

Alasdair had disappeared when he reached her at last, but he was talking to another man. Iain wondered who had introduced her to Martin Carlton-Jones.

"Are you enjoying yourself, Billie?" he asked. He nodded politely to Martin.

"Yes. It's been lovely." She smiled up at him, and, as always, he felt a sharp tug of attraction.

He turned to Martin Carlton-Jones, whose middle-aged cheeks were heavily flushed from too much whiskey and more exercise than he was obviously used to. "And you, Martin?"

"Yes. It's quite a colorful experience for a Sassenach like myself."

"You're from England?" Billie asked.

"Yes. From just outside London. I enjoy these jaunts to the Highlands. I've been trying to convince Iain, here, to help me make them more permanent."

Billie cocked her head in question.

Iain didn't smile. "Martin and his partner, Nigel Surrey, would like to own Druidheachd, lock, stock and barrel. I've tried to explain there are already people living here, but I'm afraid that neither he nor Nigel is willing to give up easily."

"Own Druidheachd?" Billie turned to Martin. "And where would you put all the villagers?"

"Iain exaggerates immensely. I'd just like to own enough of the village to make it a bit of a holiday spot. But I'm afraid Iain is far too old-fashioned and aristocratic to approve of tourism."

"Iain aristocratic?" Billie smiled again. "How can that be? He's invited us to this party, hasn't he? Quite obviously he's enchanted by the common folk."

Martin Carlton-Jones looked as if he had been struck. Iain wanted to laugh, but he *was* too aristocratic to be that rude. "Martin, will you excuse us? I haven't had the opportunity to dance with Billie yet. And there's one coming up she'll enjoy."

As if on cue, the band, who had been taking a short break, reassembled to begin again. Martin moved away, and Iain held out his hand. She seemed surprised, and her eyes widened. They were a thousand shades of brown, eyes he could gaze into forever without noting every detail.

She gave him her hand. "Well, I wondered if you'd dare be alone with me after dropping that little bombshell on the way back from the chapel."

"You can speak of bombshells after the way you put Carlton-Jones in his place?"

"I rarely dislike anyone on sight. But who is this man to think he can buy Druidheachd?"

"A businessman with a one-track mind."

"I think we should reroute his track."

Iain smiled. "Have you danced The Dashing White Sergeant before?"

"Is that like the Texas Two Step?"

"I'll show you."

"You'll have to. Being a Scot by descent didn't descend to my feet. I've hopelessly snarled every set I've joined. Poor Dr. Melville will have to see an orthopedic colleague."

"That's not true. I've watched you."

"Have you?"

"What you lack in experience you make up for in creativity."

She grinned, and her dimples were a mile deep. "Do they teach you to say those things in lord school, Iain? Could anyone be that charming without years of instruction?"

"I'm absolutely sincere."

"You are absolutely nuts, but I'd love to dance with you, as long as you know what you're getting into."

They formed a circle with the others, a wide circle that threaded all the way around the room. Iain faced Billie and gave a slight bow.

"Is this one of those dances where you leave me immediately and go on to another partner?" she asked. "Is that why you asked me for this one?"

"No. You're mine for the duration."

"That very nearly sounds like a wedding vow. One of those do-it-yourself types penned by a real cynic."

He laughed, and the music started before he could respond. "Just follow along and watch the other women."

"I'd much rather watch you."

Something stirred inside him. It was not a dance where he could hold her close, and suddenly he regretted that. He executed the opening steps, all Highland flourish and style. She made a reasonable stab at holding up her end of the bargain, and he nodded. They circled each other, and he pulled her arm high into position as he put his other arm around her waist.

He understood for the first time the purpose of a dance like this one. It was not good clean fun. It was nothing more

than a mating ritual. They circled each other, but the rules
were strictly enforced. When he was allowed to hold her, it
was only for a brief moment, and then the embrace was
proscribed and controlled. But their eyes never left each
other. And as the pace grew more frenzied, they found ways
to be more intimate. His arm tightened around her waist;
her hip brushed his. She taunted him with her eyes and with
the sinuous sway of her body. When he turned her grace-
fully under his arm, her breast grazed his chest.

By the time the music finished with a flourish, desire had
claimed him as an old friend. Billie's cheeks were flushed
with exertion and excitement, and her eyes smoldered with
something much more elemental. The room seemed to dim.
The candlelight flickered, sending spiraling shadows against
the old stone walls. As Iain blinked to focus, she was transformed. She was Billie, and not Billie. Her hair cascaded
down her back, although it was nearly covered by a linen
headdress, and her gown was longer and of a softer rose.
She lifted her eyes to his, the same warm brown eyes fringed
by dark lashes, and he could see the greatest part of a mil-
lennium in their depths.

He was swept with a wave of dizziness. He leaned toward
her. She leaned toward him.

A hand gripped his shoulder.

Iain whirled. In that moment he felt danger all around
him. He was surrounded by people who wanted vengeance.
He could not protect Christina from what awaited them.
They were doomed by their love.

"Iain."

He was ready to strike. He lifted his hand.

"Iain, have you lost your mind?" Andrew asked softly.

He stared at Andrew. His friend. He muttered an oath.

"Excuse us, Billie," Andrew said. "But I've got to con-
sult your dance partner about rooms for the night." Andrew turned and walked away from the dancers and Billie.

Iain faced her. She looked winded but unaware of what
had just transpired. He knew that something was expected
of him. He floundered for the right thing to say, but his
voice was perfectly normal. "Will I see you later tonight?"

"Sure. I'll still be catching my breath."

He found Andrew in a corner. He stopped just in front of him, but he couldn't speak.

"You look as if you've seen a ghost." Andrew rested his hand on Iain's shoulder.

The dizziness had already receded, but now it had been replaced by fear. "A ghost?"

"Aye. Iain, for a moment back there you looked at me as if you thought I was someone else."

"Aye, I have seen a ghost, Andrew."

Andrew frowned. He gripped Iain's shoulder, as if in comfort.

"I've seen a ghost," Iain said. "The ghost of my father and all the Rosses. I've seen the ghost of what awaits me."

Duncan and Mara had not slipped out of Fearnshader. Mara had decided to change first, then leave by a secluded door in the west wing. Billie found her just as Mara unzipped the small case in which she'd brought her traveling clothes.

"I thought you might need some help." Billie crossed the room and held out her arms. "It was a beautiful wedding and the best party I've ever been to."

Mara hugged her. "The party's still going on, Billie. Are you certain you'd rather no' be dancing than helping me dress?"

"Lord, no. I need a breather, and so do all the poor men who offered me a dance. And I wanted a chance to say goodbye and wish you well on your honeymoon."

"Duncan's quite spoiling me, but I can no' wait to see New York and California."

Billie knew that Duncan and Mara had chosen the United States for their honeymoon because Duncan wanted Mara to meet the family and friends who had not been able to come for the wedding, particularly his sister Fiona, who had been badly injured as a child and was still frightened of travel. "And April's going to England to be with her mother?"

"Aye, for a fortnight. Then Lisa's taking her back to America to join us, so April will no' feel left out of the honeymoon fun. It will give them a chance to strengthen their relationship. And Iain and Andrew will be standing by, in case they're needed."

"Mara, April said the strangest thing after the wedding. She told me that you'd said I was to be married next, and my intended's name was Ruaridh."

Mara turned away. "Will you unfasten this, please?"

Billie obliged. Mara crossed the room and slipped out of the dress. She hung it carefully on a padded hanger, then took the garland of flowers out of her hair before she turned back to Billie. "I dinna know when April heard me say that."

"Then you didn't?"

"Children have a way of hearing the very things we wish they would no'."

"Mara, what *did* you say?"

"No' that, exactly."

"What, then?"

"Billie, you and Iain are caught up in something I dinna understand, no' completely. But long ago your ancestors fell in love, and there were terrible results. Now you and Iain must change that. Nowt more can be said about it except this. I feel the presence of Ruaridh and Christina strongly when you and Iain are together. It's as if they are with you."

"With us?" Billie held up the green wool dress that Mara had brought with her. "You mean ghosts? Iain told me today that they were married in the chapel."

"Nowt so direct as ghosts. I can no' explain, because I dinna understand it myself. But there's something more." She slid the dress over her head and turned for Billie to zip it. "Iain will be facing trouble soon. I wish I could tell you more, but I can no' see clearly the fate of anyone that I love. I only know that I see a black cloud moving toward Druidheachd. I see it in my dreams and when I'm awake. And sometimes recently I see Iain standing before it, his head bared and his face turned toward the sky."

"A black cloud?"

Mara picked up her hairbrush and began to stroke her hair. "I worry that his life..." She stopped and shook her head.

"What? His life's in danger? Is that what you're saying?"

"It's all mixed up in my head. I dinna know when the trouble will start, or if it already has. And there are different kinds of trouble..." She turned, and her eyes were bleak. "But he should be canny. That I know."

"Look, Mara, it's your wedding night. Let go of all this now. Iain's fine, and Lord knows he's careful. He doesn't let anything or anyone get too near him. You're about to fly off to California, where you can't do a thing. I promise I'll keep the good laird out of the loch and fistfights while you're gone."

There was a knock on the door, and it opened before either woman could answer. "Damn," Duncan said. "I hoped I'd catch more of a view."

"You'll have all the views you want later on tonight," Billie said. "She's almost ready."

"She'd better hurry. I heard a commotion downstairs. I think someone's noticed we're gone."

"I'll take care of the dress and everything else," Billie said. "You two scoot." She hugged Mara again, then Duncan, who was in sport clothes, at the doorway. "Have a safe, wonderful honeymoon. And I promise, everything will be exactly the way you left it when you return."

Mara nodded gravely. After another round of hugs she tucked her arm into Duncan's, and in a moment they had vanished down the back stairwell.

The huge house felt empty, even though the shouts from downstairs were audible. Billie shivered. There was no longer a need to put on a happy front. Better than most people, she understood the place of superstition and legend in the lives of the Highlanders. From the beginning she had appreciated the story of the MacFarlane curse as a whopping big folktale to be savored and even, perhaps, to be studied for what it said about the people who had passed it along for hundreds of years.

But now the scholarly part of her was still, and the part that seemed to be the newest link in a remarkable chain of events was begging to be heard.

"Billie?"

She actually jumped. She didn't know what she had expected, but it was not Iain's voice. She turned and found him standing an arm's length away.

"You were a million miles from here. Thinking about Mara and Duncan?"

"I was thinking that I need to go home."

"Home?"

"Back to Flora's."

"But I have a room for you here. You don't need to go anywhere. You can go to bed right now, if you like."

She didn't want to argue. She most certainly didn't want to tell him that she was spooked, she who relished ghost stories and bloody legends as more grist for her intellectual mill. She simply begged. "Look, will you please find me a ride home? I'm completely exhausted, and I'll sleep much better in my own bed. I'll owe you one if you do this for me."

Shouts and cheers echoed from below. Billie suspected that Mara and Duncan had just driven away. Iain shook his head. "Those who are still left are a merry lot. I can't trust a one of them to drive you back to the village."

Mentally she found and discarded half a dozen potential rides. Flora had gone home several hours ago, and so had everyone else she knew well enough to ask. Even Alasdair Melville, who had been politely attentive all evening, had been called away on an emergency. "I know. What about Andrew? I'll ask him myself."

"He's gone already. He's driving Duncan's car with a woman who looks a bit like Mara in the seat beside him, to throw off the men who'll be bound to chase them. Duncan and Mara are in Andrew's car going off in the opposite direction."

"Clever."

"Not clever enough by half, but we tried." He paused. "I'll drive you."

"You can't do that. You're having the party of the century."

"I can be gone a bit. The fresh air will be welcome."

"Don't try to fool me. There's enough fresh air sweeping through these drafty old halls to pump up a million pairs of lungs."

"I'll drive you."

She realized he was absolutely determined. It was too late to say she'd changed her mind. In full dress kilt, complete with *sgian dubh* in a sheath strapped to his leg, he had the look of a man who would throw her over his shoulder and carry her to the car. "All right. If you're sure."

He didn't deign to answer. "Get your things. I'll wait in the kitchen." He pointed to the back stairwell that Mara and Duncan had taken.

He was exactly where he'd said he would be a few minutes later, arguing with a stern-faced woman old enough to be his grandmother. Billie had seen her from a distance stalking back and forth and giving orders throughout the evening.

"Billie, have you met Gertie Beggs, my housekeeper?"

"No." Billie held out her hand. Gertie's eyes narrowed. "You're the one staying with Flora?" She shook Billie's hand and dropped it abruptly.

"That's right."

"She's told me of you."

"Don't believe a word she says. I'm as docile as a lamb."

"You'll be trouble for Master Iain."

"Gertie!" Iain frowned. "That's absolutely not appropriate."

"She's a MacFarlane, can you no' ken what that means?"

"It means I don't judge people on anything as foolish as ancient ancestors," Billie said.

"I'm no' judging you, lass. I've nowt against you. I'm just afraid." To Billie's surprise, Gertie's eyes filled with tears.

Iain put his hand on Billie's shoulder. "Come on, Billie. Let me get you home."

Billie was upset by Gertie's very real distress, but she knew there was nothing she could say or do to alleviate it. "That's sounding better all the time."

It was snowing harder outside, and she held Iain's arm as they walked to the garage, which was nearly hidden in a thicket of trees. Under different circumstances she would have been enchanted by the snow. Now she was merely chilled. She slipped gratefully into the passenger seat of Iain's Jaguar and under a wool blanket that covered it.

"It was a wonderful party," she said as he started down the drive. She wanted to dispel the gloom generated by Gertie's warning and her own private encounter with Mara. "You've made the wedding a memorable event. Stories about it will probably be handed down for generations."

"It turned out well. They deserved a party. Neither of them has had an easy time of it."

"Mara's..." She struggled for the right word. "Predictions? Visions? I don't know what to call them. But whatever they are, they must take a terrible toll. She seems to feel other people's pain."

"Aye."

"Iain, how much credence do you put in them?"

"Is this an exam?"

"Please, just give me your opinion."

"There's magic here. There always has been, and there will continue to be long after you and I are dust. I took my degree at Oxford. I studied philosophy and logic as well as other more practical subjects, and nothing I learned there could begin to explain some of the things that Mara's seen or some of the things that have happened in Druid-heachd."

"Then you believe she can see the future?"

"I've been personal witness to it."

"Is she always right?"

"There is always some truth in what she sees."

Billie shivered and told herself it was the cold. "She's worried about you."

He didn't answer.

"Iain, do you think she has reason to be?"

Again he didn't answer.

"Is there anything I can do? Do you really think this has something to do with me? Because if you think it does, I'll stay as far away from you as I can. I don't want to be accused of bringing some ancient curse to conclusion. I came to do research, not to start you on the path to doom and destruction."

"What led you here, Billie?"

This time she didn't answer. She was still ashamed of the reason she had fled her own country.

"Why here and not somewhere else? There are a hundred picturesque Highland villages where you could have settled in and listened for stories."

"My family came from this one."

"And that called you here, didn't it? In some curious way, that was the factor that made you choose Druidheachd. Your family has been gone from this place for a century, yet somehow you knew that a long time ago they had come from this wee dot on the British map. And so you came back."

"That doesn't seem odd to me. It was a connection of sorts, and I had no other connections to guide me. Druidheachd seemed to have everything I needed. It's remote. In many ways it's hardly progressed into the twentieth century. Legend and superstition are still a part of the fabric of daily life. It turned out to be a perfect choice."

Falling snow shone in the beam of the Jaguar's headlights as they continued along the narrow road that wound beside Loch Ceo. They were on a downward slope, moving slowly and carefully but still making good time. There was a mesmerizing crunch of snow under the tires, and the perfectly tuned purr of the engine, but otherwise the night was silent. Billie pulled the blanket tighter around her and stared out the window. There was nothing to see. The snow curtained off the shadows of mountains and the glistening waters of the loch. She and Iain were alone, in a world that seemed suddenly devoid of all other life. She couldn't resist her next sentence.

"Iain, Mara told me that when you and I are together she feels the presence of Ruaridh and Christina."

He turned to her, taking his eyes off the road for only a moment. But it was at that precise second that the car began to spin. He bit off an oath in an accent as broad as Andrew's and began to wrestle with the steering wheel. "Hold on!"

Billie grabbed an armrest and watched him struggle. Her own experience driving on snow was limited to none, but she knew the rules and, obviously, so did he. He steered into the spin without braking. She knew what awaited them just off the road. Together they'd already been baptized in the waters of the loch, and this time their chances of emerging were nil. The car shuddered and the tires squealed as they bounced off the road, then just as the loch loomed in front of them, Iain regained control. Carefully he edged back onto the road. Then and only then did he gently tap the brakes.

Nothing happened except that the car picked up speed. The hill was steeper here, and the ice covering the road was thicker. Despite Iain's efforts, the car sped faster down the hill. He tapped the brakes once more, but nothing happened. The car fishtailed again and slid sideways, turned, picked up more speed and began to careen from one side of the road to the other.

"Arms over your neck and duck your head," Iain shouted.

Billie didn't have time to think about what Iain planned to do. She did exactly as he'd ordered. A million thoughts roared through her head at once, but only one was perfectly clear.

Somehow, she and a medieval seductress named Christina were responsible for this.

# Chapter 8

He had a bruise where his forehead had slammed against the steering wheel and a shoulder that throbbed unmercifully every time he raised his left arm. The Jaguar, which had been a gift to his father as a young man, was in worse shape and now resided in Edinburgh in the care of a vintage automobile expert who promised it would be better than new when he'd finished with it.

And then there was Billie.

Iain woke up on Christmas morning to an empty house, images of the woman he had almost deposited in the loch and a flagrant arousal. He had been dreaming that Billie was sleeping beside him. He could still feel the slender length of a leg curved over his, the soft pressure of her breasts against his side, the silky tickle of her hair against his shoulder. He could imagine what it felt like to trail his hand down the swell of her hips and bottom before he slowly turned her onto her back and savored the welcome that awaited him.

Merry Christmas.

Fearnshader was as still as a tomb. His household staff was small, and because of the wedding they had worked particularly hard in the past weeks. Now they were scattered around Scotland and beyond on a well-deserved holiday, and he was completely alone. He had celebrated Christmas by himself for years, ever since he had finished his course at Oxford and returned to take over the family estate. He had not been able to bear the institution of new Christmas traditions when memories of holidays spent with his parents were still deeply entrenched within Fearnshader's stone walls. So he had done nothing, and now nothing was a tradition itself.

Snow had fallen through the night, and frost webbed the multipaned windows of his bedroom. He rose and hoped that the chill would chase away thoughts of Billie, but instead he found himself imagining what it would be like to have her rising with him, to stand in this room together, wrapped in each other's arms for a good-morning kiss.

Merry Christmas.

An hour later, after a breakfast so silent that even the ghosts of Christmases past could not be heard, he found himself in the Land Rover that had been his gift to himself on his twenty-first birthday, driving down the loch road that had nearly been the scene of his death, to check on the woman who had nearly died with him. Hollyhock yapped at every passing car from the back seat but did nothing to distract Iain's thoughts.

He had tried ringing Billie, but there was something wrong with the lines in the village, a not uncommon occurrence. Once in the car he was glad that he hadn't been able to speak to her on the phone. He wanted more, even though he knew how dangerous it was. He wanted to see for himself that she was really all right. He wanted to know that she was not suffering, that she was not lonely, that whatever had brought her to Druidheachd was not haunting her as he was haunted.

The village was storybook lovely, with snow etching stones as old as the earth itself and blue smoke curling from ancient chimneys. He passed children in brand-new Christmas coats riding down the mellow slope of High Street on brand-new Christmas sledges.

He parked on the street and walked up the hill toward Flora's cottage, where an elaborate wreath hung from the door. He suspected Billie's handiwork immediately, since the wreath was nearly as large as Flora herself. He knocked before he could change his mind and promised himself that he would only stay long enough to be certain that she was fine.

Billie answered the door. Her red blouse was a bright contrast to the pallor of her skin. A bruise adorned her jaw and another her cheekbone. She was an independent woman, with a brain that worked like lightning and more courage than a modern major general. And still he wanted to put his arms around her, hold her close and keep her safe forever—along with the thousand others things he could think of to do to her.

"Iain." She stepped outside and closed the door behind her. She reached up and touched his forehead. Lightly. Gently. And desire roared through him. "It's worse than I thought it would be. How's the shoulder?"

He told himself she was just being kind. He told himself he needed to practice self-control. "Fine, if I'm careful. But I came to find out about you."

"Did you?" She smiled, and there was a shyness about it that enchanted him. "I'm fine. Perfect. Thanks to you."

"Thanks to me you were in a rather serious accident."

"Thanks to you I survived it. You were brilliant. I don't know how you managed to slide into that tree instead of the loch, but we almost took our last swim together." Her fingertips brushed his cheek as she dropped her hand. "Iain, I'm sorry. I really am. I shouldn't have been so pigheaded and insisted you bring me back here that night."

"You've apologized ten times, Billie. And you didn't insist that I bring you home. I volunteered, and I chose the wrong car to drive. It's behind us now. We're still here discussing it, aren't we?"

"But your Jaguar isn't."

"It can be fixed. It needed some bodywork anyway."

"You're just trying to make me feel better."

He smiled. How could he not smile at her despite every warning voice inside him? "Is it working?"

"Yes." Her eyes searched his. Standing so close to her he was powerless. He relived his dream, the magical feel of her body against his, the warm glide of his hand over her skin. He wanted to look away, but he couldn't have, not for any reason. "I bet you have plans for the day, don't you?" she said at last.

"Actually, this was as far as I'd planned."

"Flora's son Steuart and his wife invited me to their house for tea. Flora's going."

"Then I won't keep you." He didn't move.

"I said no."

"Did you?"

"I'm not sure why."

A day of hiking on Bein Domhain flashed through Iain's mind. He had taken one step like thousands of others, and suddenly there had been nothing beneath his boot except two hundred feet of air. He remembered that feeling of being suspended, of time stopping, and then the terrifying struggle to regain his balance before he plunged to his death.

He was poised on the edge of a chasm again.

This time he couldn't stop the fall. "Come home with me." He reached for her hand. "Let's celebrate the remainder of the day together."

"Hey, you don't have to do that." Her eyes were troubled. "I'm not your problem, Iain. I'll be fine. I've got a good book to read and a thousand letters to write."

"You *are* my problem. More of one than you can guess. And I seem to be yours."

She didn't pretend not to understand. "You could end this now, before it's a problem that gets totally out of hand."

She was giving him one last opportunity to do what was right, what was safe. And he wasn't strong enough to accept. "I'll take my chances."

She covered his hand with hers. "I'll get my coat."

Billie was all too aware of the man beside her. Only rarely could she concentrate on one thing at a time, but since the moment she had stepped onto Flora's porch, she had thought of nothing except Iain.

There was an inevitability about being with him today. Somehow she had known that they would spend the day together. She had none of Mara's second sight, but since she had awakened that morning, she had known that Iain himself would be her very finest Christmas present.

She looked away to try to maintain a little distance. On one side of the road glimpses of Loch Ceo flashed between snow-covered evergreens. On the other the landscape was steeper, leading into the hills and eventually to Bein Domhain, where Mara had her croft. She had never seen a more beautiful landscape. She could understand why, centuries ago, Iain's kinsmen had claimed it as their own.

She wanted to see even more.

"Iain, stop." Billie put her hand on Iain's arm as they turned the bend that would lead to the best view of Ceo Castle.

"What for?"

"I've never been through the castle. I've wanted a tour since the first day I came to the village."

"It's closed to the public."

She gazed at him from under her lashes. "Oh? And am I just the public? I believe it was the honorable Lord Ross himself who informed me that our ancestors were married on these very grounds. I believe that makes me a family member of sorts."

He slowed but didn't stop. "The walkways are slippery under better conditions. With this latest snow, it'll be icy, as well."

"I promise I'll be careful." She grinned at his expression of polite disbelief. "Really, Iain, I can be careful when I choose to be. And don't you need a walk? Hollyhock certainly does. It's cold, but it's glorious. There's even sun, and it won't stay out much past two. If we're going to do it, we should do it now."

Hollyhock barked from the back seat and tried to vault into Billie's lap. She sternly reprimanded him, and he stretched out contritely with his head on his paws.

"See? You're outnumbered," she told Iain. "I can't vouch for your safety if you pass up this chance. Even I can't control a thoroughly frustrated dog with the jaws of a wolf and the heart of a lion.''

"A short tour.''

"Agreed. In the spring you can give me a full-blown one. We'll hit the highlights today.''

He drove a short distance and pulled onto a bumpy track. At one point he stopped and got out to unfasten a massive padlock barring a gate across the road. Then he got back in and continued another two hundred yards or so, finally stopping a short distance from the castle.

He came around to open her door. "Take your expectations well in hand. There are no knights and ladies in full-dress costume, no halls of armor or tartan exhibitions here. There aren't even any displays of ancient torture devices. Ceo Castle isn't much more than a heap of stone.''

"I can supply the rest.''

"Aye. And I suspect you will.''

Hollyhock bounded toward the castle, and Iain and Billie followed at a slower pace. "Did you play here as a little boy?'' she asked.

"Sometimes.''

"Just think, while my brothers and I were making forts with rotting pine logs and vines, you were pretending to be king.''

"Duncan and Andrew and I camped and played here as often as we could. But for the record, I rarely got to be king. More often I was a mortally wounded messenger or royal bodyguard who had given his life for his sovereign.''

"How'd you get stuck with that?''

"I had a flair for the dramatic. Neither of the others could die half so well.''

"This is an act I'd prefer not to see.''

"You've no idea what you'll be missing.''

She slipped her hand inside his. It seemed awkward not to, even though he hadn't touched her since they'd left Flora's. She swung their arms back and forth as they walked down through what must once have been a wide defensive ditch. It had been filled in centuries ago, so that it was now only a shallow depression.

"What do you know about castles?" he asked. "Is this one of your many areas of expertise?"

"Absolutely not. I've always preferred to study the common folk. But I've done some reading since I arrived. I visited several castles on my journey north to Druidheachd. Stirling, St. Andrews, Urquhart on Loch Ness."

"They're all elaborate in comparison, I'm afraid."

She knew that was saying quite a bit, since Urquhart and St. Andrews were little more than well preserved and documented ruins. "I've come across very little information on Ceo Castle, or on Druidheachd and the surrounding area, for that matter. It's almost as if the rest of Scotland went about its historical business while Druidheachd was lost to view. Of course, it was remote and never a particularly strategic location for any war or skirmish, but I guess I'm still surprised."

"See the stones piled over there?"

She nodded. He was pointing to an area just yards away.

"Most likely they're what's left of the stone causeway that crossed this ditch. There would have been a gap in the middle that had to be crossed by a drawbridge. The stones that are left are broken up and useless, which is why they're still here. The good ones were probably carted away for use in local buildings."

"What a shame."

"I suspect Fearnshader has its share of castle stone in the foundation."

"Another mark against your ancestors, Iain."

"Just spare me another MacFarlane curse." He pointed farther along, in the direction they were walking. "The causeway probably ended there. The lowest of the walls that you see would have been the gatehouse. The best estimate is that in its heyday it was three stories tall, with rooms for the castle keeper, and a room just above the portcullis—the iron grate that protected the entry—where it could be raised or lowered. There was probably a prison cell or two, possibly a storehouse for grain. We don't really know for certain. There's been a bit of archaeological excavation from time to time. There's sure to be more in the future."

"You approve?"

"Absolutely, if it's done well. Ceo Castle belongs to all of Scotland."

"Yet you own it still, when most historical monuments have been given over to organizations to preserve them."

"I'll do the same someday. When the time is right."

She wanted to know more but realized it wasn't her place to ask. "And what about the highest walls? And the tower?"

"We'll walk the walls. Come on."

By the time they had reached their final destination, the best preserved and navigable of two circular towers, Billie's imagination had taken flight. She had become reacquainted with upper baileys and water gates, nether baileys and great halls. So little had survived of the once proud castle, but every bit that was left resounded with history and legend.

She wanted to know it all, every last story, every tear that had been shed and laugh that had echoed here. "It's so wonderful. So astounding. Do you know what you have here? We've been walking through rooms that are centuries older than European civilization in the Americas. There's so much history here!"

"Rooms without walls or roofs, most of them. And so much of the history's lost."

"Then it has to be reclaimed. Somebody has to do it. You've got to make sure of it."

"Do you know your eyes sparkle when you're excited? I've heard that expression a thousand times, but I've never really witnessed it before."

His words stirred something deep inside her, and she smiled. "Don't you feel it, Iain? This is a powerful place. I can almost see the ghosts of your ancestors going about their business. Ruaridh was born here. And how many more?"

"We'll probably never know."

"Let's climb the tower."

He held her back. "Not today, Billie."

"Why not? It's a perfect day for it. I know we could see every bit of the loch. I'll bet we could see for miles. The vilage, the mountains. And then I'll be a good girl and go back to Fearnshader without another word."

"The stairs will be icy."

She looked up. "Why? There appears to be a roof."

"A very old one, and the steps are worn and slick even when they're dry."

"Can we try? I promise if it gets too bad, I'll come down without an argument. It would just be so wonderful to go up here."

Now there was no expression in his eyes except resignation. She realized she had pushed too hard, but before she could withdraw her request, he started toward the tower. "Let's get it over with, then."

She followed, at a loss for how to apologize. She had the feeling that whatever she said now would make things worse. He waited in the doorway. "You first," he said. "There are handholds. Be certain to use them, and step carefully. It's narrow and winding, very close quarters. I'll be right behind you."

She hadn't realized just how narrow it would be. She gazed up and saw an endless spiral of steep steps. For a moment she wasn't sure she could do it. Her aversion to enclosed places was like a hand choking off her breath.

"We don't have to do this," he said from behind her. "It was your idea."

It was as much of a dare as she needed. She had broken bones for less. "I'm on my way. See if you can keep up." She put one foot in front of the other and began. One foot, then the next. There were handholds, but thousands of clawing, grasping hands had smoothed them nearly away. Her only consolation was that there wasn't a trace of ice on the steps.

She made herself think of other things as she climbed. Exactly what she would say in her next report to the faculty committee that was overseeing her dissertation. Who she could interview for more information about the ghost that was said to warn village residents of impending danger. Why she was falling in love with a man who kept more secrets than the CIA.

Her concentration and her foot slipped, and strong arms steadied her from behind. "We're halfway there," Iain assured her.

She could feel the warmth of his arms against her hips and his palms against her abdomen. "I suppose that means it would take just as long to go back as to keep going."

"You're not afraid, are you? I'm sorry if I frightened you. The steps seem fine after all."

She had no intention of discussing the revelation that had nearly sent her tumbling. And even less intention of standing enclosed in the intimate warmth of his arms. "I'm fine. Terrific. I'm just a little spooked by closed-in places. I got stuck once hiding from my brothers in a storm culvert. I was there for an hour before they could pry me loose."

She began to count steps, reminding herself that each one took her closer to fresh air and open space. She ignored trembling knees and sweaty hands and climbed. And she tried desperately to ignore the fact that the man behind her was beginning to mean too much to her.

She knew she had reached the top when cold air ruffled her hair. Sunshine poured through the opening, and she emerged again into the prettiest winter day of the year. The air was as clear as high summer. On one side of the walkway connecting the towers the loch shone like a polished silver coin. On the other a narrow strip of forest bordered a rolling moor that stretched toward the mountains. "It was worth it." She waited for Iain to appear. "It's every bit as beautiful as I thought it would be. Is it safe to walk over to the edge?"

"This area is perfectly safe, except for the places where pieces of the walls are missing. I'd trust the rest of it over anything built by contemporary hands."

She wandered from one end of the walkway to the other. The greatest part of the battlements was intact, complete with narrow arrow loops for wily medieval archers. There were a few places where the stone had crumbled or perhaps been removed, but she carefully avoided those.

When she had paced the whole distance she stood looking over the countryside she had already come to love. "I didn't know it was so beautiful. Until now the country-side's been like the pieces of a skillfully designed jigsaw puzzle. But here's the finished picture. And I love it."

She turned, and Iain was right behind her. "It's in your blood, and it appears that centuries haven't diluted it."

"You love it, too, don't you?"

"That's why I always return. No matter where I go, I always come back. No matter what waits here for me."

The words were perfectly innocent, but there was something about the way he said them that made her shiver.

"You're frozen." He put his hands on her arms. "And you should be. Have you finally seen enough? Can the rest wait?"

She almost expected him to kiss her. There was more than concern in his eyes. There was something as old as the castle. He didn't move for a moment; he just stood there holding her at arm's length. Then he dropped his hands and turned.

She watched his face as they walked back to the stairwell. She might have missed the carving on the battlement nearest the stairs if she hadn't stumbled on a raised stone. She caught herself quickly, but as she looked down, she saw what she hadn't noticed before.

"Iain, what's this?"

He didn't answer for a moment. When he did, his voice held no hint of why not. "It's an inscription."

She moved closer, squatting in front of it so that it was at eye level. "It looks very old." She traced the letters with her fingers. "I can't read any of it."

"That's because it's in Gaelic."

"Actually, I understand a little Gaelic when it's spoken, but I've never tried to read or write it. I plan to work on that while I'm here."

"Why do you understand it?"

"My mother always swore at us in Gaelic. And believe it or not, her father spoke it fluently. He could recite poems and tell stories he'd learned from his father. I've got folktales in my genes, and Gaelic, too, I suppose." She turned to him. "What does it say?"

"Not as much as it should. Look at the stone carefully."

She examined the stone, and she saw what he meant. "It's only half here. The other half of the block is missing." She frowned. "This is odd, Iain. It looks as if it were put in place this way. Do you know the story?"

"It's difficult to tell anything from half an inscription, especially one so faded by time."

"Have experts looked at it?"

"To my knowledge no scholar has found it particularly noteworthy."

"I love a good mystery." Reluctantly she got back to her feet.

He held out his hand. "I love a warm fire and a good woman."

The expression in his eyes made her forget everything else. She linked her fingers with his. "I think the trip down will be easier than the one up."

"Oh? Why?"

"Because this time I get to watch you."

"But your view won't be nearly as interesting as mine was."

They made the trip down the stairs and the rest of the drive in comfortable silence, but the moment they pulled up to the front of Fearnshader, Billie was anything but comfortable.

The old house, so warm and welcoming on the evening of Duncan and Mara's wedding, was forbidding on this sunny winter afternoon. Inside, it was no better. The halls were cold and gloomy, and the rooms were shrouded in indifference. Iain didn't seem to notice, but Billie was consumed with the loneliness that seemed like a living entity. She was happier than ever that they were going to spend the day together, because she couldn't endure the thought of his being alone here on Christmas day.

"It's so quiet, so profoundly silent," she said as they walked through the house. "I've been in empty churches that were noisy in comparison."

"The stone absorbs all noise."

"I think I'd give anything to hear a bird sing or a baby gurgle."

"We'll go into the sitting room and make a fire. It's the homiest room in the whole place. I'll turn on the stereo."

She took his arm. "Let's go."

Iain might think that the sitting room was comfortable, but Billie was immediately appalled. There wasn't a speck of dust anywhere, but it looked as if no one had looked at the room with an eye for comfort or beauty in a decade.

She busied herself rectifying that. "First we open all the curtains. Then we build a huge fire in the fireplace. We turn on all the lamps. Iain, there are a dozen lamps in this room, and only one is on! And if that's not enough light, we'll find some candles left over from the wedding and light those." Billie fluttered around the room like a moth looking for a flame.

"I gather you think this room is gloomy, too."

"Good lord—and I'm not talking about you—yes! Don't you?"

He looked around, and a frown puckered his elegant forehead. She nearly caught her breath. At all times Iain was magnificent. But slouching against his own fireplace, surveying his private kingdom with the aristocratic demeanor of a storybook prince, he was even more.

"I suppose it could use a wee change or two."

"It could use a U-Haul truck and four strong men!"

"I thought you'd have more respect for tradition."

"Look, I don't want to alarm you, but a lot of what's in here is junk, pure and simple. And with my background, I should know. Maybe some of it's valuable junk, and maybe some of what isn't would appeal to collectors of kitsch, but it badly needs sorting, and the rest needs carting away. The room deserves better."

"Then you don't think I should demolish the house stone by stone?"

"I'm sure the house is perfect. It just needs some attention."

"Translated, that means it needs half a million pounds poured into it?"

"Nothing so grand or expensive. Just a loving eye and a little elbow grease. And a big, burly man to trim the ivy and the hedges."

"My mother once told my father she wanted to do a wee bit of work on the gardens. He had to sell prime Edinburgh property to fund it."

"And I'll bet it was worth every penny—pence he paid."

"He thought everything she did was worth a fortune."

Billie heard something in Iain's voice. Yearning? Pride? She wasn't sure. "This is the first time I've been away from my family at Christmastime, and I miss them more than I can say. But you haven't had yours for a very long time, have you? I bet you miss them terribly."

"I miss them."

She knew better than to pry any further. She had learned that Iain would tell her what he wanted, when he wanted, and not one moment before. "I think we owe them all, your parents and mine, a wonderful Christmas day. Not a one of them would want us to sit around and mope. So, let's get busy."

"Are we about to renovate the house?"

"Just this room. Let's pull that sofa—it looks comfortable, at least—closer to the fire and put that table in front of it so we can have dinner in here."

"Dinner." He strung out the word as if he had never heard it.

"Iain, you have to feed me. It's standard procedure." The expression on his face was a mixture of bewilderment and humiliation, and he wore it with charm. "Wedding leftovers?" she coaxed.

"I'm afraid they went to the shut-ins who couldn't come to the party."

"And I'll bet you don't cook, do you?"

"I'm certain that the Sinclair Hotel must be serving today. I'll take you there."

"Yuck. You will not. Is there food in the house?"

"There's a refrigerator, a freezer and cabinets filled to overflowing with groceries, none of which I have the faintest idea how to prepare for a guest."

"Oh, so you cook, but not for guests."

"Rather like that."

She had stayed far away from him, busying herself with the lights. Now she moved closer. "Well, like I told you before, *I* cook, and I'll admit to being wonderful at it. I worked under some of the best cooks in the fleet. I'll train you."

"Your tramp steamer days?"

"Exactly."

His arms shot out, and he pulled her close before she could flutter away again. "Billie, I didn't invite you here to work. We'll go to the hotel."

She could feel the warmth of his hands through her blouse. "Overcooked carrots and lamb so well done it could have died of old age in the time it took to cook it? We deserve better."

"Frances Gunn is one of the finest cooks in Scotland."

He was kneading her arms, and her heart was pounding to the rhythm. "Frances Gunn isn't going to be working on Christmas day."

"And neither should you."

"Cooking with you will be a pleasure."

He lowered his face to hers, and his arms circled her. She bent like a willow branch into the curve of his body. The gloomy old room seemed lit with a new and softer light. "Then I'll be a willing recipient of any pleasure you want to give me," he said.

She knew better than this. There seemed to be a thousand secrets between them, and she had a long history of thinking the best of the worst people. Yet she couldn't break away. She was mesmerized by the look in his eyes. There was nothing evil in this man. She would stake anything on that. But there was so much that was wrong with his life, and she seemed to be caught up in it.

She was caught up in *him*. She couldn't move away, and she couldn't stop her arms from pulling him closer. Touching him was a feast of sensation. She had yearned all her days for the touch of his body against her but never known she yearned. Everything about him seemed so intimately familiar, yet new and powerful.

"I think I could get hooked on giving you pleasure," she whispered.

"And taking it?"

"Particularly that." She relaxed into his kiss. And for long moments there was nothing else to say.


Dinner was roast duck stuffed with leeks and mushrooms and glazed with orange and ginger. There were potatoes whipped with fresh cream and butter, and carrots and cabbage sauteed with fresh herbs from Gertie's windowsill pots. Stale bread was transformed into bread pudding with a potent whiskey sauce, and Billie fed bite after bite to a protesting Iain until he begged for mercy.

"Leave the dishes," he insisted, when she tried to get up from the sofa to clear away the table.

"Wouldn't you rather look at the fire?"

"Fine. I'll take the dishes in the kitchen as soon as I can move. But you're not allowed to set foot in there again."

"Are you afraid I'll cook something else?"

"Terrified."

"I saw some truly gorgeous Camembert in the back of the refrigerator."

"Which is exactly where it stays."

"If the medieval Rosses ate as little as you do, I can't understand where they found the strength to keep their estates. My brothers would consider that meal an appetizer."

He pulled her to rest against him. "Describe your brothers to me."

"Three mean and ugly junkyard dogs."

He laughed. His arms slipped around her. There wasn't an ounce of fat on her anywhere, but she had eaten more than he had. He had a suspicion the Camembert was going to disappear, too, as soon as she could get to it. She moved closer, fitting herself against him as if she knew his body intimately. He knew better than to let this happen, but he rested his cheek against her hair, and one hand slid up her neck to play with the wisps that adorned it.

There was something remarkably sensuous about those silky tendrils. They were a hint that the woman in the no-nonsense, practical hair had a seductive alter ego hidden just under the surface. There were other hints, too. Her penchant for fabrics that felt good to the touch, the surprising and lushly romantic scent of violets that she favored. She was not exactly what she seemed.

But neither was he.

Billie looked up at him through her eyelashes. His heart beat double-time, and he realized just how fast he was getting in over his head. And this time he wasn't in the loch.

"I'll bet you prefer women with hair down to their waists and curves like a Highland road map," she said.

"What brought that on?"

"An attack of utter hopelessness."

He touched her face. His hands weren't quite steady. "Do you see anyone like that in this room?"

"I see the ghosts of a dozen women just like it."

"Who's been talking to you?"

"Iain, you have a reputation as towering as your family tree."

"Do you believe everything you hear?"

"Tell me it's not true."

He was caught completely off guard. No other woman of his acquaintance would have faced him down this way. "Are we both going to talk about our romantic pasts? If you're liberated enough to ask, you're liberated enough to answer."

"I don't have much to tell."

He thought about his own response carefully. "I have a lot to tell," he said at last. "And none of it is worth mentioning."

She continued to stare up at him. He thought she was reading the nuances of his answer and weighing them. Then she nodded. "You make short forays out from behind your castle walls, then you go back inside, pull up the drawbridge and settle in for the siege."

He didn't know how she had already learned to know him so well. "And you? Why don't you have much to tell?"

"I've thought I was in love twice. The second time was a particularly terrible mistake."

He could see that mistake in her eyes. She was still suffering for it. Anger started somewhere deep inside him for the man who had hurt her. "Do you want to talk about it?" he asked, careful to keep emotion from his voice.

"Want to? No. But maybe you ought to know what an idiot I can be."

She didn't need exposure. She needed comfort, even if she didn't know it. He shrugged. "Then go ahead and tell me."

"Dave was one of my fellow graduate students, and he was nothing short of a con man. The thing is, I couldn't see it, even though friends warned me. I always see the best in people, even when it's not there. And I thought Dave was just misunderstood because he was so brilliant."

"Was he brilliant?"

"At using people? Absolutely. He sure drained every drop he could from me. He was attentive and passionate, and I mistook that for love. I was caught up in the romance of it. We were two starving graduate students fighting our way through academia together. I refused to see that I was doing all the fighting, and that he was taking my ideas, my research, my hard work, and using it for his own advancement. I think I realized after a while that I wasn't really in love with him, but I was loyal right up to the bitter end. I thought he needed me, so I gave him everything. And when I should have realized he didn't deserve it, I kept on giving. I'm a fool, pure and simple, without the gift to tell the truth from a lie."

"You're not a fool."

"I am, but not as much of one as he played me for. I was working on an idea for my dissertation. I'd spent months researching it and preparing to submit it to my committee. I discovered that Dave had taken everything I'd done, added a few touches of his own and submitted a nearly identical idea to his committee first. I guess he was sure that when I found out, I would be much too humiliated to blow the whistle. But I did, and even though it was largely his word against mine, I was the one that the faculty believed. Dave was dismissed from the university, but before he left he managed to destroy all my notes and make off with my entire collection of reference books, a good number of which were irreplaceable. He even wiped out all my computer files so I'd be forced to start over.''

Iain's response was profane and exactly to the point.

She smiled sadly. "When Dave finished with me, I wasn't sure what was left. I decided to leave the country to find out—and get farther away from him in the process. At the end he made vague threats against my safety, and while I didn't really believe he was serious, I didn't want to be looking behind me every minute, either. The worst part of all this is that I don't trust my own judgment anymore."

"Have you ever considered tattooing crosshairs over your heart?"

"What do you mean?"

"You've just told me how vulnerable you are and exactly where. If I were a man who enjoyed hurting women, I'd be thrilled, even motivated, by your honesty."

"You're not a man who enjoys hurting women."

"Oh? You can tell that?"

"Of course I can! What do you think—" She stopped herself. Her eyes grew wary. "All right. You've made your point."

"What point is that?"

"That I was absolutely right. I haven't really changed."

"No." He stroked her hair back from her face. "That's not the point at all. I'm *not* a man who enjoys hurting women, so your judgment is correct. But you're also feeling cautious, and you've a right to. You don't know me—"

"Iain." She touched his cheek. "You don't let anyone know you."

He saw the questions in her eyes. Instead of answering, he lowered his lips to hers. There were years to tell her about, but not an hour of them could he really share with her. There was half an inscription at Ceo Castle that he should translate for her, but he didn't dare translate a word. His burdens were his own and not to be carried by anyone else.

He felt her move in his arms. Her breasts strained against his chest, perfect small mounds that begged for his touch. He moved from consolation to lust in the space of a heartbeat. He was as famed for his self-control as for the many women who had shared small portions of his life, but now there was nothing of control in his response. A moment ago he had thought he would never be hungry again. Now he was ravenous.

Her lips opened, and her arms circled his neck. She was lying half on top of him, and each time she moved he could feel the repercussions. Even as an adolescent he had never felt this desperate need, this passion to obliterate all conscious thought and sink into a woman forever.

His hands settled at her waist, but only for a moment. He had planned to hold her away, to give himself room to gain control. Instead, he jerked her blouse from the waistband of her skirt and slid his hands up her rib cage. If she'd worn a bra, he might have been able to stop. But she hadn't, and he had never felt anything as soft, as pliant, as her breasts. He groaned as she moved against his hand. Her nipples were as hard as pebbles; nothing had ever had the power to excite him more.

She threw her head back and moaned. Her skin was flushed and her eyes half-closed. He could feel the rapid pounding of her heart, the ragged surge of her breath. He kissed her throat, her cheek, her earlobe. He considered the trip to his bedroom, the trip to the rug in front of the roaring fire, the seconds it would take to undress her and make love to her right there.

And then he considered what any of that might do to her.

For a moment he was unsure whether he had the fortitude to move his hands, to stop kissing her, to turn so that the length of her leg, the cradle of her hips, didn't mold so perfectly to his. He had always done what he knew to be best, no matter how hard it had been. It was the one thing on which he could pride himself.

For a moment he had no pride.

Then, from somewhere, he found the strength. He did all those things. Slowly, gently, murmuring assurances as he did. "This is going too fast. I'm sorry. I have no right."

She didn't argue. She moaned, as if mourning a loss. He felt the moan deep inside him.

"I want you. Don't think that I don't." He brushed kisses across her hair.

"You don't have to apologize."

He laughed. Even to his own ears he sounded like a man who was strangling. "Lord, Billie." He took her hand and placed it where it was guaranteed to make him lose control immediately and entirely. "Do you have any doubts?"

Something rumbled through her, and he realized it was a variation of his laugh. "Iain." She laughed again, and it was a little less strangled. "Shall I explore, just to make sure I understand?"

This time he pushed her hand away. And then they were both laughing, and watching each other warily as they did.

"It's growing late. I'd better take you home." Iain disengaged himself from her entirely. In a moment he was on his feet, holding out his hand.

"You're sure that's what you want to do?"

"You know what I want to do. But you're going home."

He almost expected her to argue, or at least to ask for an explanation. Instead, she took his hand and stood.

She lifted her chin. There was still a spark of defiance in her eyes, something wonderfully feminine that had probably come straight down through her genes from another MacFarlane woman.

"Tuck in your blouse," he said.

She made a swipe at it. Her southern drawl was more pronounced than he had ever heard it. "I seem to be all thumbs."

"You seem to be asking for trouble."

Her eyes sparkled, and her dimples flashed. "You were the one who created the problem."

His eyes didn't leave hers as he tucked in the blouse. "You realize you're absolutely heartless."

"Absolutely not. I'm all heart. That's exactly my trouble."

"You are exactly the kind of woman every man needs in his life."

Defiance disappeared. For a moment she was so vulnerable he saw straight to the core of her, to the center of a soul badly shaken by the man who had squandered the treasure she'd given him. He watched her recover slowly. "What a lovely thing to say."

He knew he had to warn her yet reassure her at the same time. He hoped that somehow she would understand his next words. "Billie, nothing that happens between us will be your fault."

She frowned. "I don't understand."

He didn't know how to tell her anything without telling her everything. He tried to smile. "It's only that I think you *are* all heart, and you would blame yourself for every problem in the world if you thought it might help."

"Iain, what is it that frightens you?"

"I'm not frightened." He touched her hair, because he couldn't help himself. "I haven't been frightened of anything for a long, long time."

"Then what are you resigned to?"

She was as astute as he had guessed. "A life alone. And there's nothing either of us can do to change it. It can never be any different for me."

# Chapter 9

Mid-January was exactly as Billie had expected it to be. For a woman used to Florida's nearly constant sunshine, the nearly constant gloom of the Highlands was worse than depressing. She was cold all the time, and long thermal underwear had become a second skin. Despite the picturesque setting of Flora's cottage and its tiny, charming rooms, Billie would have abandoned it gladly for a plain cardboard box with central heating and storm windows.

To make matters worse, Iain had disappeared from her life again. She didn't know where he had gone, since he had neglected to say goodbye. She had phoned him several days after Christmas, only to find out from Gertie Beggs that "Lord Ross was gone, had no' left any messages for her and would no' be back for some time." Iain's message was clear anyway. The intimacy of Christmas day had sent him running again. He had told her in no uncertain terms that he had to live his life alone.

He had just neglected to explain why.

"Lassie, ye come from sturdy Highland stock. Ye've no cause to let a wee turn of bad weather get ye down." Flora thumped her china cup on the table and narrowed her eyes.

She had lectured Billie throughout their traditional morning tea, and Billie had ceased trying to defend herself.

"What shall I do, then?" Billie asked.

"Ye need to get out. Ye need to go visiting."

Billie had already considered that. There were several friends of Flora's who had proved to be fountains of folklore, all of which they doled out a drop at a time to make sure that Billie would continue her visits. Mara had left her car at Billie's disposal, but it was old and unreliable in cold weather, and not one of the women lived within easy walking distance.

"I suppose you're right," Billie said. "I've been cooped up with my notes and my computer for too long."

"Ye've been cooped up with yer thoughts. And gloomy ones they be."

Billie ignored that. "Maybe I'll see if Mrs. Fairmow would like some company. If Mara's car won't start, I suppose I can get there on foot."

"T'would be better to accept young Dr. Melville's offer of a ride into the country."

Billie set her cup down. "What offer is that?"

"He rang early, while ye were at Cameron's. I told him ye'd be ready at half past eleven. Which gives ye only a wee spot of time."

"For Pete's sake, why didn't you tell me earlier?"

"I thought ye might say no."

"Why? It sounds like a great idea. Where's he going, and why?"

"He has a patient or two out beyond Bein Domhain. He travels there weekly to check on them. He thought ye might like a change, that ye might like to have a look."

Billie got to her feet. "Well, I'd better get ready. And next time, you don't have to walk on tiptoe. I'd have said yes without all this plotting and maneuvering, Flora."

"He seems a fine lad."

He was a fine lad, and although Alasdair was a year or two older than she was, that was the way Billie thought of him, too. Since their first meeting they had become friends. He was intelligent, enthusiastic about his work and easy to talk to. Several times they had eaten together at the hotel, and once they had driven to Inverness to take in a movie. He regaled her with stories of his patients, and she told him about the material she was collecting for her dissertation. But there was nothing romantic in their friendship. He was a mellow and congenial man who couldn't begin to fill the gap that Iain's disappearance had left in her life.

And that was too bad.

By the time Alasdair arrived she had changed into a presentable black sweater and tan wool pants. He greeted her with a casual kiss on the cheek. "Does this mean you're coming?"

She stepped back to examine him. He was the quintessential Scottish country doctor making rounds in a tweed coat, deerstalker hat and a bright tie that was slightly askew. "Of course. I'm looking forward to it."

"The weather's no' so good," he warned.

"I know. I walked down to Cameron's for the mail. Do you have a rash of suicides this time of year?"

"Are you joking?"

"Nope. You know, there's that thing about light deprivation and depression. I find myself not wanting to get out of bed in the mornings."

"And is it just for the lack of sunlight, Billie?"

She grimaced. "Who knows? Anyway, I'm ready to go soak up what light there is." She called a last goodbye to Flora and closed the door behind her.

"Have you been out this way before?" he asked on the way to his car.

"Not as far as we're going."

"Then you'll particularly enjoy the ride."

She did enjoy it. The sun didn't peek out from behind the thick cloud cover, but the heater in Alasdair's car worked perfectly and kept her toasty warm. He told her funny stories about his days as a houseman at an Edinburgh hospital, and she found the malaise that had settled over her lifting.

"I'm surprised you've no' been out this way," he said, when they had driven for half an hour or more.

Once over the hump of Bein Domhain, they had passed nothing but rocky farmland and clumps of grazing sheep. There was an austere beauty to the land, even under the thick cloud cover of winter, but she hadn't been possessed by any desire to stop the car and explore. "Why? Is there something out here that I should see?"

"If I'm no' mistaken, this is the homeplace of your ancestors."

She sat very still. "My ancestors?"

"You're a MacFarlane, are you no'? Did you no' say once that's what brought you here?"

"Are you saying that this is where my family lived?"

"Oh, it's no' quite so straightforward, as you must know by now. There were no surnames in Scotland for centuries. But later, when kinsmen and their supporters began to group themselves that way, this is said to be where the MacFarlanes of Bein Domhain had their lands."

"I wonder why no one's mentioned that before."

"I'm surprised no one has. I only mentioned it in passing."

Iain had told Billie that the place where Christina had been born no longer existed, but now she wondered. "How do you happen to know so much, Alasdair?"

"Well, I grew up here, remember? As did my father and his father before him." He shook his head. "My father may have been a simple gamekeeper, but he was a man who remembered everything he'd ever heard about Druidheachd and the lands around the loch and Bein Domhain."

She wondered how many other people knew that these had once been MacFarlane lands. She had a gut feeling that Iain knew and had just decided not to mention it. "Is anything left of the MacFarlanes? Any structures? Ruins?" She watched him shake his head each time. She slapped her knees in frustration. "Circles of standing stones where they sacrificed whatever Rosses they could get hold of?"

"If it's Stonehenge you want, Billie, it's a bit to the south."

"So, there's nothing? Iain Ross has a castle, a mansion and a sizable chunk of Scotland, and the poor old Mac-

Farlanes have some tortured trees and a few pitiful sheep to remember them by?''

"How about this? My first patient is Annie MacBean, an old woman who's lived here since the dawn of time. Why do you no' ask her if there's any bit of a memorial to your family here? If there is, Annie will know.''

Twenty minutes later, Billie knelt in front of Annie and let the old woman's hands play over her face. She was a hundred years old, and her eyes were nearly opaque from cataracts. She lived alone except for a well-fattened cat, although there was a granddaughter up the road who looked in on her twice a day.

Annie was ancient, but there was nothing wrong with her long-term memory. "Aye, ye have the strong bones of the North. Yer a Scot, through and through, lass, no matter where ye were born.''

"Well, I've been told I look like my mother, and she's been told she's MacFarlane through and through.''

"Yer people are here no more.''

"I know. But is there anything of them? Any structure? Church? House? Ruin? Cemetery? I'd love to see something that was part of them, Annie.''

Annie nodded. She was silent, as if she were thinking. "Have ye seen the stone?'' she asked at last.

"This is the first time I've been this far west, so I haven't seen anything.''

"It's no' far. Ye could walk there.''

"Great.'' Billie stood. "I'll take a walk while Dr. Melville examines you. Where should I go? And what should I look for?''

Annie gave directions that seemed easy enough to follow. The walk sounded pleasant and shorter than half a mile if she took the required shortcuts. "Ye'll come upon a stone fence with a stile crossing it. Just over the stile will be a large stone, no' well shaped or extraordinary. T'was carved by an ancestor of yers.''

"Carved?''

"Go and find it,'' Annie said. "And see for yerself.''

"Go ahead, if you'd like," Alasdair said. "If I've finished by then, I'll bring the car and meet you there."

Billie bundled up against the cold and the cruel wind sweeping across the treeless moor that bordered Annie's cottage. Annie's directions had been explicit, and Billie looked for landmarks as she hiked down the road in the opposite direction from the way she and Alasdair had come. She walked along a hedgerow, and at a wide division, she ventured into a field. Ignoring the black-faced sheep and one ram who watched her intently, she headed for a clump of trees at the border.

The walk reminded her of childhood games when she and her brothers had made treasure maps. She followed Annie's directions and hoped that what waited for her at the end was more worthwhile than the Monopoly money and dime store jewelry she'd dug up as a child.

About twenty minutes later she came to the stone fence and the stile, which was nothing more than rickety wooden steps that crossed it. At first she didn't see the stone. She had expected something at least the size of Plymouth Rock. The stone in question sat at the base of a cluster of stunted hazel trees, and a strong man who'd wanted it badly enough could have found a way to haul it home.

Lichen crusted the surface, and a thicket of brambles, dried broom and gorse surrounded it. Billie stooped and cleared a place to kneel. At first she thought she had found the wrong stone after all. There was nothing of interest here. But as she rubbed her fingers across it, indentations became evident. Words had been carved into the surface. She wasn't sure what she had expected. A statue, perhaps, or at least a monument of sorts. This was a simple fieldstone, a broken one at that, with something inscribed in its surface. A suspicion began to form.

"So, you found it."

She turned and discovered Alasdair behind her. "You made good time."

"It's far simpler by car. Annie was as fit as a fiddle and no' in need of my services today."

"If this is all that's left of the MacFarlanes, I'd say we're in pretty bad shape."

Alasdair squatted beside her. "You're certain this is what she meant?"

She didn't share her suspicions with him. "I don't know what else she could have. And there *is* writing on it, though I can't tell what it says."

He stood. "Let's clean it up and see."

A few minutes of careful scrubbing with alcohol and gauze pads from Alasdair's well-equipped bag revealed deeply chiseled letters. Billie stared at half a Gaelic inscription as Alasdair read what words there were with a properly guttural accent. "Too bad it's no' all there," he said. "It's missing too much to make any sense."

"Then you can translate?"

"Aye, I speak Gaelic so I might be able to, if the text was complete."

She contemplated the stone. "Do you have paper with you? I think I have a pencil in my purse."

"You want to make a rubbing?"

"Why not? It's something, anyway." She didn't add that she would be making another rubbing of the matching half, which was firmly embedded in a battlement of Ceo Castle. Until she translated and understood the whole text, she didn't intend to share it with anyone. She smiled up at him. "Half a family memento is better than none."

"Let's see what we can do."

As he went back to the car for paper, she traced the letters with her fingertips. The wind whistled across the field and rattled the hazel branches. She was cold down to her wool-shrouded toes, but the stone felt almost warm.

The tower steps seemed more forbidding than Billie remembered them. Despite a burning desire to make a rubbing of the tower stone, she had not driven to Ceo Castle yesterday after Alasdair had dropped her back at Flora's cottage. What passed for sunlight had already disappeared, and she had resigned herself to waiting until the morning.

But the morning had arrived with so little sun that now, at ten o'clock, it seemed like dusk.

The tower had been intimidating on a sunny day with Iain climbing right behind her. Now she stood at the bottom and gave herself a pep talk, but her feet weren't listening.

She had parked Mara's car at the edge of Cumhann Moor some distance away and hiked to the castle. Iain had made it clear that the ruins weren't open to the public, and signs on the grounds emphasized it. If she was going to trespass—and she certainly was—she hadn't wanted to advertise the fact. Now she wondered whether anyone would find her before spring if she made it to the top and lacked the courage to climb back down.

All the way up she imagined that spectacle, visualizing ridiculous pictures of herself as a short-haired Rapunzel waiting for rescue from the tower. Only this particular princess would demand a helicopter before she gave her heart to any prince.

Despite sweating hands and shaking legs she reached the top without mishap and emerged into a friendlier gloom. She was less interested in the view than she'd been on her first visit, but she spared a glance for Loch Ceo, the moor and the mountains in the distance. Wind whipped across the walkway and whistled through the arrow slits in an unfriendly, atonal symphony. She unfolded one of the large sheets of paper she'd carried in her pocket, took out a charcoal stick and settled in front of the inscription.

There was no doubt in her mind that this was the other half of the "MacFarlane stone." How it had gotten here was the real mystery, along with why no one had ever brought the other half to the castle. If Annie MacBean had known the stone's whereabouts, surely dozens of other people knew it, too.

Perhaps even Iain.

She traced the letters with her fingers. Had one of her own ancestors chiseled this inscription? Had he sent a message into the future for his kinsman to find? It was a fanciful thought, not a scholar's thought at all, but it appealed to her on a hundred different levels. And if it was true, it excused her trespassing as a necessary evil.

The stone seemed strangely alive to her, as if it vibrated with a special power. That wasn't a scholar's thought, either, and she knew that the source of power wasn't the stone but her own imagination. Still, she felt a definite pull from it, and her hand wasn't quite steady as she placed the paper over the stone and began to rub the charcoal across it.

"Do you need someone to hold the paper for you?"

Billie dropped the charcoal, and the paper fluttered to the stone floor. She turned and found Jeremy Fletcher leaning against the wall not ten feet away, his arms crossed over his chest. His expensive cashmere coat looked as warm as July sunshine, but his thin-lipped smile was as cold as the ice on Loch Ceo's shore.

The wind had blocked the sound of his approach. A dozen curses came to mind as Billie got to her feet. "You're back."

"Don't let me disturb you, Billie. I'll just watch for a bit."

"Did you follow me here?"

"What would make you think so?"

"Look, Jeremy, I don't want any trouble. Why don't you just go away and I'll forget you were trespassing?"

"And you, of course, are not?"

"I have permission to be here," she lied. "We both know you can't say the same."

He pretended to look around. "There doesn't seem to be anyone about who might care."

"Why did you follow me?"

"Follow you? I'm just here for the view."

"Take a good look, then leave, please."

He didn't move. Billie knew there was no chance she could get past him and down the stairs. Even with a decent head start, given the way her fears slowed her down, he would catch her almost immediately.

"What's your interest in that stone?" he asked.

"Local history."

"That's right. I'd nearly forgotten. And, of course, the history of the Rosses interests you most of all."

"I don't remember saying that."

"Perhaps not, but as I understand it, Iain Ross interests you a great deal. Would you like to be the next Lady Ross, Billie?"

"I'd like you to leave so I can finish up here."

Jeremy stripped off gloves that exactly matched the gray of his coat and examined his nails. "There are better things to aspire to, you know, than marriage to Iain. The last Lady Ross found that marrying into the family was no bargain. They've always been cursed. No one who's living today can remember a time when it was otherwise."

"Thanks for the warning. Are you leaving now?"

"You do know there's insanity in the family, don't you?"

Billie was silent. She didn't want to betray a single thought, so her eyes didn't flick from Jeremy's. But she remembered an early conversation with Flora. Iain had been sent away to school, but on holidays he had returned to Fearnshader and a great-uncle who was said to be mad.

"Every generation," Jeremy said.

"I don't see what any of this has to do with me."

"I would hate to see history repeat itself." He smiled. "Try to imagine marriage to a lunatic. One can hardly imagine the strain of such a thing, can one? Watching the person one loves most deteriorate day by day until the choices become too horrible to contemplate."

"If you don't go, I will." Billie stooped and picked up her paper and charcoal, but she didn't take her eyes off Jeremy. "Please get out of my way."

He stepped in front of the stairs. "What would you do, do you suppose, were you in that situation? Can you imagine watching the man you love lose his mind, bit by bit? And it's not just the mind, you know. There's much, much more. One day he reaches for something and finds that his hand refuses to do his bidding. It starts simply at first. Headaches. Memory loss. Difficulties with coordination. Then it progresses a bit at a time, but so slowly that there's always a question that it's really happening."

She was beginning to feel something very much like fear. "Jeremy, stop! I don't want to hear this."

Another voice sounded from behind Jeremy. "You would have had to hear it sooner or later, Billie."

Billie watched Iain emerge from the stairs. His head was bare, and his black hair was tossed by the wind. Despite the cold, his dark leather jacket was thrown open.

Jeremy whirled and faced Iain. His fists came up, as if to ward off an attacker, but Iain shook his head. "Leave, Fletcher, and leave now, while you still can."

"You don't want her to hear the rest, do you?" Jeremy inched backward as Iain climbed the last few steps. "You don't want Billie to know what kind of family you come from?"

"Is there more you'd like to tell her? If you prefer, I'll wait until you've finished before I throw you down these steps."

"You're the son of a bloody madman and a murderer!"

"And you're the extortionist who caused the death of the finest woman in the world." Iain advanced on Jeremy. "And I have the documents to prove it. Maybe I should mete out a bit of justice now, the way I didn't twelve years ago."

"Stop it!" Billie moved forward. "Iain, don't. Get out of here, Jeremy." She put her hand on Iain's arm.

Iain shook it off, but he stopped just short of grabbing Jeremy. "What's it to be, Fletcher?"

Jeremy straightened, and his hands fell to his side. "I already have what I came for. Now she knows enough to find out the rest on her own."

"Then I'm afraid you've wasted your time. I'd have told her myself."

Jeremy barked out a counterfeit laugh. "Just the way you've told everyone else?"

"Right now certain papers bearing your signature are in the hands of my solicitors. When they've examined them, it will be up to them whom I tell and what the consequences will be for you. But were I you, Fletcher, I would leave Scotland before any more of this comes to light."

Jeremy narrowed his eyes. "You're bluffing."

"Am I? What have I to lose? My wife? My children? A life worth living?"

"You're a Ross! You don't want the world to know the things I do!"

"On the contrary. Perhaps it's past time."

Billie watched indecision play across Jeremy's face.

"Do you need more to convince you?" Iain asked. "Actually, I have more. I've proof that the brakes on my Jaguar were tampered with the night of Duncan Sinclair's wedding. And I've proof that you were seen on Fearnshader's grounds that night."

"Brakes? I had nothing to do with your brakes!"

"No? Coupled with everything else I have on you, your word won't be worth much."

"I was nowhere near your car!"

"I would choose a country far away," Iain said. "One without an extradition treaty."

Jeremy circled, giving Iain a wide berth. At the stairs he turned and fled.

Billie realized her knees were weak. She stared at Iain. His blue eyes were hooded. For all the passion in the things he had said, not a bit of it was evident on his face. The wind rumpled his hair, but his expression was that of a man who wasn't touched by anything. "Are you all right?" he asked.

She nodded, although it wasn't true. "How did you know...?"

"That you were here? I saw Mara's car. I'd already guessed it would only be a matter of time before you came up here to inspect the stone."

"I thought you were out of town."

"I learned that Jeremy was on his way back. I beat him by an hour or so. I've known where he was every second since."

"You've had him followed?"

"I was afraid he might go after you again."

"You weren't far from wrong." She approached him slowly. "So, you waited until he did, and then you showed yourself? What am I, the bait in a trap?" She stopped just in front of him. "Couldn't you play your little games with Jeremy without me?"

"How much of what we said did you understand?"

"I haven't had much time to put it together!"

"He's been using you."

"I've got to hand it to him. He really knows how to pick 'em. Or maybe I just have a sign on my forehead."

"It's not you he was after. He wanted to get revenge on me."

"Then why use me? And why does he want revenge?" She was torn between wanting to shake him and wanting to give him comfort. He showed signs of needing neither, but she sensed despair behind his tight control.

"Billie." For a moment his guard slipped. She saw deep sorrow in his eyes. "Everything he said was true."

She was afraid to touch him. "Explain it to me, so I can understand."

He didn't respond.

"Iain, was your father a murderer? Is that what Jeremy was saying? Did he go insane and kill somebody?"

"My father killed no one."

"Then what?"

"My mother did."

For a moment she couldn't breathe. She stared at him and wished she had never asked.

"My mother helped my father die, Billie, long before there were controversial doctors to do it. My father had slipped into madness. Both he and my mother had known for some time that it was happening. Fletcher was right. The Rosses have been cursed for centuries. We're victims of a neurological disease so rare that it doesn't even have a name you'd recognize. But the symptoms appear in middle age, and by then it's already been passed on to the next generation. The disease has gone through our family for centuries. Sometimes we were foolish enough to believe it had ended, then another family member succumbed. My father wasn't the eldest son. By all rights he shouldn't even have inherited all this."

He swept his hand in an arc. It was the saddest thing Billie had ever seen, because now she knew that nothing Iain owned mattered at all. "Did he have a brother who died?" she asked.

"Two of them. One in the war, another at birth. His own father died in an accident before he was old enough to show any symptoms, although *his* brother, my great-uncle, was diagnosed late in life. By then, after centuries of superstition, the genetics of the disease were just beginning to be understood. The hope was that my grandfather had never been afflicted, and so my father would be free of the disease, too, as well as all his descendants. Despite that, Father was nearly forty by the time I was conceived. He waited that long, just to be certain. And then, when there was still no evidence of symptoms, he made a leap of faith."

Billie felt tears well in her eyes. But she couldn't comfort him, because she knew he wouldn't accept it.

He turned and stared out at the loch. His back was rigid. "I don't know when he realized the truth. But I remember well the final year of his life. He went from a healthy, hardy man to a shell of what he'd been. He would seem almost normal one day, then the next he wouldn't recognize me. He believed I was his brother come back to haunt him, or one of the servants. Sometimes he couldn't control his own body. He sat beside the window, refusing a wheelchair. And when he could speak, he said terrible things, primarily that he wanted to die. He begged us to kill him."

He faced her again. His eyes were carefully blank. "One night he became very ill. There was no time to get him to a large medical center. The best my mother could do was take him to the hospital in Druidheachd. Dr. Sutherland was the only person in the village who knew about Father's illness and exactly what it meant. He made my father as comfortable as he could, then he left the room for a few minutes. My mother had been a nurse. The sedative Dr. Sutherland had given Father was in easy reach. There was a fresh supply of hypodermics in the cabinet."

He looked away.

"Iain." Billie didn't have to be told the rest. Tears slipped down her cheeks now as she imagined the horror of that night.

"It was over swiftly. She put an end to what could have been years of deterioration and suffering. If Dr. Sutherland suspected what she'd done, he never let on. But somebody else suspected. Jeremy Fletcher was a young man of twenty then. He'd been in a brawl at the hotel pub that night, and he'd come into the hospital for some patching up. He was in the next room when he heard my mother wish my father farewell and heard her sobbing. He was still there when Dr. Sutherland came back into the room and found that my father was dead."

"And he blackmailed her?"

"Aye. Until the day she died. She was still a young woman, but the strain of what she'd been forced to do and the terrible fear of exposure robbed her of what strength she had left. She caught a pneumonia that was easily treatable, but she didn't respond. She died just a year after my father. And the day I turned eighteen and came into my inheritance, Fletcher came to me and told me everything. Then he demanded that I give him money, too, or he would expose my mother's actions and my own potential illness."

"You didn't . . ."

"No! I went through all my mother's papers, and I found proof that he'd been blackmailing her. He's not particularly intelligent. He had sent her threatening notes, and fortunately she had kept them. There were bank drafts and canceled cheques. All the proof I needed. I convinced him that if he tried to expose my mother or blackmail me, I'd make his extortion public. It's been a standoff since then. I've never reported him to the authorities, and he's never exposed my family's secrets."

"Until now."

"He's been waiting until he could hurt me the most."

For a moment she didn't understand. Iain obviously saw her confusion. "Jeremy believed that if you knew the truth, you'd leave me."

"Leave you?"

"He isn't especially bright, our Jeremy, but he has an unerring sense of who and what matters to people."

There was nothing Iain had said that had shaken Billie more.

"Only this time, he was wrong," Iain continued softly. "Because I've known from the beginning that there couldn't be anything between us, Billie. I watched the hell my mother went through, and later I watched my grandfather's brother go mad and die by slow degrees. I couldn't put a woman through that. Not any woman. Particularly not one I loved."

"Do you have the disease, Iain?"

He shrugged.

"There's no test to determine whether you do?"

"Aye. There is a test for those at risk, a recent innovation that isn't yet perfected. Right now it can absolutely rule out the chromosomal defect in only about thirty percent of all those who take it."

"But it didn't rule it out in yours?"

"I haven't had the test."

"Why not?"

"It's not infallible. It's only conclusive in one of every three or four possible cases. The others still have to live with uncertainty, knowing that without a true negative they may or may not be destined to succumb. So there's only one way to end this curse. I have to end my days alone. No wife. No children. Then, and only then, can I be certain that no more Rosses will have to suffer the way my parents and ancestors did."

She tried to digest everything he'd said. But only one word stood out. "Curse? Don't tell me you think that this terrible disease is the MacFarlane curse? Tell me you don't think this is some medieval legacy from my family to yours."

"Only a madman would believe in curses." He smiled, and it was the saddest thing she had ever seen.

"No!"

"Does it matter?" He took her hands, but there was reluctance in the way he held them. "There have been centuries of suffering in my family. There won't be any more after I've died. Call it a curse, or call it genetics. It's up to me to see that it ends."

"What does the stone say, Iain? Because I've found the other half, and I'll put the two inscriptions together."

"Leave it alone. Leave it all alone. I've told you everything you have to know. Go back to America. Forget everything you've learned here."

Her mind was whirling too fast. She was vaguely aware that he was gripping her hands too tightly. "What did you mean about the brakes on your car? That's what you said to Jeremy, wasn't it? Did someone really tamper with them?"

"Go home! Haven't you heard what I've been telling you? There can't be anything for you here."

"Iain, you're in trouble, and you want me to leave you?"

"More than anything. Leave while you can."

"Tell me the rest of it!"

He dropped her hands. "There's nothing for you here. There's no reason for you to stay." He walked over to the inscription and lifted the paper off the floor. He ripped it into a dozen pieces and sent them sailing in the wind.

He turned at the doorway and stared at her. She couldn't read the expression in his eyes, and she was mute. He had already started down the stairs before she found her voice.

"You think this is the end of it, Iain? Well, this is just the beginning. I'm not leaving." She ran to the stairwell and shouted after him. "Do you hear me? I'm not leaving Druidheachd!"

Her own words echoed back to her. Even the sound of Iain's footsteps had died away.

# Chapter 10

Like most of Druidheachd, the cottage hospital was gray stone and charming, although in the gloom of a winter morning even the smoke frothing from the chimney and the warm glow of lights through the windows failed to make it seem welcoming.

Billie stepped inside and closed the door securely behind her. A woman in her seventies sat in the tiny reception area shuffling papers at a long table. She spared Billie one glance before she returned to her work. "You've come to see young Dr. Melville?"

"Yes. But I'm not a patient. I just need to talk to him, if he's not too busy."

"I'm certain he's no'. You're the American? Billie Harper?"

Billie wasn't even surprised her identity was known. "That's right."

"I'm Jeanne Sutherland. Just dinna think you can persuade Alasdair to leave his employment here. My husband could no' find another to replace him." She looked up. "He's the third young doctor that's come, you know. No' a one of the others could get along with Angus."

Since the entire conversation was preposterous, Billie ignored the majority of it. "And Alasdair does?"

"Aye. He knows what to say and when to say it." She did a quick visual examination that made Billie feel as if she'd just had her annual physical. "You'll find him at the end of the corridor."

Billie passed two large rooms with hospital beds. Iain's father had probably died in one of them. She kept her eyes averted.

There was a small room at the end of the hallway with a battered metal desk and a wall crammed with filing cabinets. Alasdair sat at the desk, reviewing a folder. She paused in the doorway. "Alasdair?"

He looked up, and his smile lit the morning. "Billie." He stood. "Come in and close the door."

She did. "Alasdair, who's the Rottweiler at the front desk?"

"Jeanne? Why she's the very heart of this hospital."

"I think she believes I'm going to capture you, drag you back to America and lock you in a room until you marry me."

"There would be only a wee bit of dragging, I ken," he said gallantly.

She smiled, but it faded quickly. She was here now, clutching the satchel she'd used to protect her reason for coming. And she didn't know where to begin.

"This is no' a social call, is it?"

"I've brought you something. I need this translated, Alasdair, and you're the only person I can trust to do it."

"Would you like to have a seat?"

She shook her head. She thought she should probably face the next few minutes on her feet.

"I'll be pleased to help if I can."

Billie reached inside the satchel and took out a piece of paper. "You remember the stone we found, and the inscription?"

"Aye."

"Well, I've found the other half. It's imbedded in Ceo Castle. I've put the rubbings together and copied the letters. It's so old that some of it was a little hard to decipher. This was the best I could do."

Alasdair reached inside his pocket and pulled out glasses. Billie handed him the paper, and he studied it intently.

She thought about Jeanne's insinuation as she watched him. She was not and would never be in love with Alasdair Melville. She was much too flawed. She didn't fall in love with men who were uncomplicated and good-natured. Last year she had believed herself in love with a man who possessed no values or morals. This year she was in love, hopelessly and totally, with a man consumed by terrible secrets.

Alasdair looked up at her. "It's no' a bonny thing, Billie. Are you certain you want to know?"

"I'm sure."

With an expression of total resignation he began to read. "On the blood of my daughter, Christina, I swear an oath of vengeance. May the descendants of Uchtred macRoss of Druidheachd forever be cursed, as the wild swan that flies from the shores of the firth to the lonely mountain tarn. May his descendants never know home and never know peace. May the children of his blood forever live in fear for their lives. May they always be forced to look behind them for the children of mine."

He looked up again. "And if this curse falters and our families are united again, may they who commit this blasphemy writhe in agony and terror for the remainder of their days."

She was silent for a few moments, absorbing what she had just heard. When she spoke, her mouth was dry. "Good old Grandpa didn't pull any punches, did he?"

"This must have been inscribed many years after his death. It may have been passed down and embroidered from son to son, or even invented by a fanciful MacFarlane hundreds of years later."

"You're trying to make me feel better because the curse inscribed on that stone may not have been set down exactly the way it was first uttered? You're giving credence to the possibility that one bitter old man's ravings could affect people for centuries?"

He set the paper on his desk. "I give it no credence. But I will admit to trying to make you feel better."

"It's a terrible thing, whether I believe a word of it or not. So much hatred carved into a stone for eternity." She took the paper and put it back in her satchel. "Do you know how the stone was broken? And why part of it's at Ceo Castle? That seems like the last place anyone would want it. Did Annie MacBean say anything to you after I left?"

He looked as if he were debating whether to tell her the truth.

"Please, Alasdair."

"Aye. She said that many years after the stone was carved there was a battle for possession of it between the MacFarlanes, who had it, and the Rosses, who wanted it. The Rosses believed that if they could destroy the stone, they could also abolish the curse. Somehow, in the raid, the stone was broken. The Rosses captured only a portion, but their chieftain refused to destroy it, saying that unless it was destroyed in its entirety, the curse would no' be lifted. He was never able to obtain the second piece, so before he died, he had his portion added to the battlements at Ceo Castle as a reminder to his kinsmen that they should be ever vigilant."

"Was he mad, Alasdair? Was that why he had it put there?"

He looked away. "Why do you ask?"

From the carefully blank expression on his face, Billie realized that Alasdair knew about the real curse in Iain's family. It wasn't surprising. Iain's father had died in this hospital, and judging from the bevy of filing cabinets, all records from the inception of the hospital were probably still accessible. For all she knew, Iain's own records made note of the possible fate that awaited him. It would only make sense, since this was the first place he would be brought in a medical emergency.

She hedged her answer. "Only a madman would want to display the evidence of the hatred directed toward his family."

"The times were different. Even sensible men were gripped by superstition."

"You know, it didn't take me long to find the second part of the stone. Now anyone who wanted to could dig it out of that field and throw it in Loch Ceo, along with the one from the castle—if they could get it out of the wall."

"Modern men realize that problems can no' be solved so easily."

She stretched out her hand, and he took it. "Thank you for translating for me."

"I would say it was my pleasure, but it was no'."

She turned as if to leave, but at the doorway she faced him again. "One more thing."

"Anything, Billie."

"This is a question to the physician, not the translator."

He nodded.

"I've discovered that a close friend of mine has a hereditary neurological disease in his family."

Alasdair's expression betrayed nothing.

"He feels his only recourse is to live the rest of his life alone. He's afraid that if he takes a wife, she'll be forced to watch him suffer, and that if he has children, they may suffer from the disease themselves."

"It sounds as if he's given it muckle thought."

"I think so, yes. But there's a test that can rule out the disease at least some of the time, and he refuses to take it."

"That's certainly his right."

"I can't understand it."

He smiled sadly. "Put yourself in your friend's place, Billie. Without the test he still has hope. With an inconclusive response on the test, his hope narrows considerably. Would you want to know the hour of your own death, or that you faced a terrible ordeal at the end of your life? It's not cowardice that keeps your friend from seeking answers. Living with uncertainty takes a special kind of courage."

Fearnshader, with all its rooms and endless vistas, often seemed like a prison to Iain. He had one true retreat within its walls, one where he never invited even his closest friends. The conservatory had been added to the house by his mother, who had ordered a more utilitarian version torn down to make way for it. She hadn't been a fanciful woman, or a greedy one. Her desires had been remarkably simple and her lifestyle modest, despite his father's wealth. The conservatory and the gardens surrounding it had been her only extravagances. She had yearned for her childhood home in Sussex, with its moderate climate and longer growing season, and the conservatory had assuaged her loss.

Iain's father had spared no expense when having the conservatory constructed, and it had become a luxurious, pampered retreat from gloomy Scottish winters. It was a room for gala parties, with Japanese lanterns strung from the rafters and profusions of exotic blossoms scenting the air. During his childhood, the conservatory had often seemed like the heart of his home.

After his parents' deaths, Iain had returned from his years at school to find the conservatory badly neglected. The lush tropical plantings that his mother had so loved had either vanished or badly deteriorated after her death. He had hired a gardener immediately to salvage what he could, but without his mother's tender care and devotion, the conservatory seemed doomed.

Until he had taken it over himself.

Iain had not relished the idea of doing the work. As a child he had potted plants beside his mother and, with her careful guidance, learned proper names and growing habits. As a young man he had remembered nothing from those days except their mutual joy when a tenderly nurtured plant had flourished and grown. But faced with the prospect of losing this last potent link with his mother, he had begun to read and experiment.

Now, years later, he had returned dying specimens to health and replaced others with the identical varieties that his mother had listed in her gardening journal. He had added his own favorites, camellias and passion flowers and a magnolia tree so rare that he had been forced to wager for it in a poker game. Now there was a fountain in the center that emptied into a water garden of iris, lilies and goldfish. Somewhere along the way the conservatory had become his

passion and, possibly, his salvation. Today it was neither.
He had risen from bed, put on faded blue jeans and an old
rugby shirt, and come to the conservatory before breakfast. It was now afternoon, and he hadn't left its glass walls.
He had tried to lose himself in his work and to reestablish
the fragile peace he often found here, but he hadn't succeeded.

The words of the MacFarlane curse continued to run
through his head like a litany. When he heard Billie call his
name from the doorway, it almost seemed as if he had con-
jured her from the ashes of dying hopes.

He turned and gazed at her for a moment, but he was
careful that his face registered no expression. Then he turned
back to his work.

Obviously she hadn't expected a welcome. She crossed the
room and stood beside him. "I had no idea you were a gardener."

He was pruning with wickedly sharp shears. He chopped
off a shoot he had considered keeping. "I'm not."

"You could fool me."

"It's just something that has to be done."

"And there's no one else in the whole of Scotland who
you could hire to do it?"

He looked up again. He wondered if all the things he felt
shone somewhere deep in his eyes. "Why are you here?"

"Somebody with a little white cap and a dust mop let me
in. Gertie's gone, I take it, or I'm sure I would have had to
fight her tooth and nail to find you. You'd have had to
sweep up the pieces."

"She knows I prefer not to be bothered when I'm here."

She registered no hurt, although he knew her well enough
to be certain he had wounded her. "Did you have the conservatory built yourself?" she asked.

"No."

"Then it's been here for a while?"

"Aye."

"It's almost too wonderful to be real." As if her sole
purpose were casual, meaningless conversation, she fin-

gered a tendril of the vine he was pruning. "I think I know this one. What do you call it?"

*"Campsis radicans."*

"We call it trumpet vine at home. But I've never seen one with a variegated leaf."

He took another whack, then started destroying another useful arm of the vine. "Did you come to discuss horticulture, Billie?"

"I'd love to see this in bloom. How do you suppose someone bred this incredible specimen?"

He didn't, couldn't, answer without saying a million other things.

"I have an uncle with a nursery, and his passion is hybridizing new varieties of impatiens. I think you call them busy lizzies here, don't you?" She was too smart to wait for a response that wasn't going to come. "For years Uncle Phil's purpose in life was to create a deep scarlet impatiens with double blossoms. After years of experimentation and failure and more experimentation, he finally succeeded. He got one perfect plant. Exactly what he wanted."

Iain stopped mutilating the vine and leaned against the stone planter. The shears dangled from one clenched fist. Framed against a row of blossoming orange trees, Billie had never looked more appealing. She wore blue today, a blue so vibrant it seemed to crackle with electricity, and her cheeks were already flushed from the moist heat of the room.

"But there was just one problem." Billie could probably see him from the corner of her eye, but she didn't turn. She continued to finger the vine. "After the plant bloomed, it began to shrivel. He took cuttings before it died and rooted them, but they bloomed and began to shrivel, too. So he took cuttings from those. The same thing happened. Finally, generations of cuttings later, years after anyone with a lick of sense would have quit, Uncle Phil took another batch. There were only a dozen little plants left by then, and he was getting tired of trying, but he's a stubborn man, a real Harper, so he just refused to give up. The plants bloomed and started to shrivel, too, just like all the others.

Except one. One of them didn't. It was as healthy as could be. Perfect and healthy and fabulously beautiful. And now that one perfect plant is patented, and my uncle is selling its progeny for a small fortune to specialty nurseries.''

She touched one of the largest leaves, stroking it with her fingertip. For a moment he could almost feel her touching him the same way. "Do you suppose the same thing happened here? That someone refused to give up after failures and more failures? That someone just kept trying until they got one vine like this?''

She was breaking his heart, but Iain's tone was sardonic. "Subtlety is not your strong suit.''

"True.'' She tried to smile and failed. "Honesty is. I know that taking cuttings from flowers and gambling that you have a future are two very different things, Iain. But I also know that sometimes things come right for no good reason at all. You have one chance in two that you'll live to be a healthy and happy old man. And I can't bear the thought that you're going to throw that chance away. Because the way you've chosen to live isn't going to make you happy, even if you live to be ninety.''

"Do you really believe I haven't considered this on my own?''

She faced him, hands at her side. "I believe you've considered it. By yourself. Without giving anyone else a chance to say their piece. I'll bet that even Duncan and Andrew don't know about this, do they?''

She must have seen from some faint change in his expression that she was correct. She touched his arm, fingers resting lightly there. "Don't the people who care the most about you deserve a place in your life and in your decisions?''

"The people who care the most are the ones who will suffer the most.''

"Isn't that their choice? Or will you leave Druidheachd in five or ten years and settle somewhere far away while you wait for the disease to show itself?''

"And if I did?''

"Those of us who care would search the ends of the earth to find you.''

He closed his eyes. Just for the briefest moment. But he was afraid she saw his despair anyway. "Some of us would take our chances, Iain," she said softly. "Some of us would feel blessed to share whatever good time is yours, whether it's an hour or the rest of a long, healthy life."

He shook off her hand. "You have no idea what you're offering to risk."

"Risk? Because I'm a MacFarlane and that dooms the relationship between us? I know the curse. I know every bit of it now. It's nothing but words. Vile, hateful words. And it can't mean a thing if we don't let it."

"This is about genetics, not curses!"

"It's about choosing between fear and hope, and I don't care what anyone says! You've chosen fear!"

"It's about risks, Billie, and what can happen if the gamble fails."

She no longer pretended she was talking about Duncan and Andrew. "But isn't that my choice?"

The pruning shears clanged to the ground, but he hardly noticed. "Let me tell *you* a story. I turned ten just a few months before my father died. There had always been a special celebration on my birthday, but obviously there was no cause for celebration that year. I suppose you might say it was a relatively good day for my father, because he knew who my mother and I were. He called us both to his bedside, and he tried to talk to us. By then forming words had become almost impossible, because he couldn't control his lips or tongue. When he couldn't make himself understood we tried to calm him, but he grew more agitated. I finally realized what he was saying. He was trying to tell me that I should never have been born. I was much older before I found out what he had meant, but I've never forgotten that birthday. My father battled incredible obstacles to make me understand that it was up to me to be sure that no other Ross suffered the way he had. And the way that I probably would in the future."

Billie was struggling with tears. He could see them gleaming unshed. "I know I have no right to criticize your choices. No one has that right. But I'm telling you that I'm willing to stand by you." She reached out and rested her hands on his shoulders. "Please, let me."

He covered her hands with his, pushed them to her sides and held them there. "And then what? Would you stay with me out of pity when I started to forget who you were? Look at this, Billie. Do you know why I wear this ring?" He held up his right hand, where he wore the band of twisted white and yellow gold on his little finger. "It was my mother's wedding ring. I wear it to remind myself what she endured."

"Iain—"

"Would you sit beside my bed when I could no longer move on my own, or swallow, or speak? Or what if I show no signs of illness? What if we have ten wonderful years and I still seem perfectly healthy? Would you begin to push me to reconsider my decision to remain childless? Would you start talking about the odds of having a healthy child, or about adoption? Because we could never conceive a child together, and we couldn't adopt one, either. I won't bring children into a hell like the one I endured."

"We don't need to have children."

"You weren't born to be my nurse."

"You're taking my choices away from me."

He struggled to harden his expression and seal off his heart. "You have no choices. You're a wonderful woman, a breath of fresh air, but I don't want you in my life. I've never wanted anything except to be left alone with my problem, and I still don't. I hope you'll believe me and do just that."

"I don't believe you."

He folded his arms to keep from reaching for her. "That's one choice I'll leave you."

Her eyes were drowning in tears. "I love you, Iain. I don't know how it happened, or when or why, but I know we were meant to be together. I've danced around it through this whole conversation, but there it is. I don't know how, but I fell in love with you the first time we met, exactly the way Christina must have fallen in love with Ruaridh."

"But I will not die in your arms the way that Ruaridh died in Christina's!"

"Tell me. For God's sake, tell me how and why they died and let's be done with it! Because it's haunting us both!"

He saw he was going to have to hurt her more. "It's not a bonny tale. There's nothing for either of us to be proud of in it."

"Tell me anyway."

"Against all odds Christina and Ruaridh were married in secret by a sympathetic priest who believed, like a fool, that their parents would become reconciled and forge new ties. But when the marriage was discovered, Christina was locked away by her father, the priest was put to death, and an emissary was sent to the pope to request an annulment. Ruaridh and some of his loyal kinsmen came to rescue her, despite his own father's command that he denounce her. They managed, in the dead of night, to find and release Christina, but the following morning when they neared Ceo Castle they realized they were under pursuit."

He paused, but there was no way to avoid the rest. He plunged on. "As they rode toward the castle, they called for the drawbridge to be released, but Ruaridh's father refused. He left Ruaridh and Christina to the mercy of both the Ross and MacFarlane men. The MacFarlanes were led by the cousin to whom Christina had been betrothed, and he was particularly vigilant. Ruaridh retreated to Cumhann Moor, hoping, I suppose, to make it into the hills, where they stood a better chance of fighting off their pursuers. But once on the moor Ruaridh was wounded immediately. As Christina cradled Ruaridh in her arms, her cousin plunged a sword into his heart. Then he turned on her."

"It's just a story! It has nothing to do with us."

He grabbed her and held her away from him. "You of all people know the power of legends. Maybe this one doesn't have anything to do with us, but I will not have it repeated more closely than it has been already. I will not sacrifice you on the altar of my family's curse. I will not put you in danger, Billie, nor will I allow you to suffer because of me."

"Do you love me, Iain?"

"What I feel doesn't matter!"

"Of course it does. If you love me, too, then we can face this together."

"There's no hope of that."

"You said you don't want to put me in danger. What danger? Does it have something to do with Jeremy? Were your brakes really tampered with?"

He wished he had never revealed that fact in her presence. "It's simply something I said to make Fletcher leave."

"You wouldn't lie for the sake of convenience."

"I'm having him watched. He won't hurt either of us. You have no reason to be concerned."

"Do you love me, Iain?"

He dropped his hands. "No."

She was silent, but she didn't move away. Her eyes frantically searched his face. He struggled to shut himself away from her, somewhere far away where she couldn't sense what he was feeling.

At last she shook her head. "I was wrong about you."

He wanted to respond but couldn't find the words.

"I was wrong. You *can* lie for the sake of convenience. And right now it's convenient to protect me and keep me safe. But you do love me."

"You've told me yourself that you're not a good judge of other people's feelings."

For a moment she looked uncertain. He despised himself for playing on her deepest fears. But then she shook her head again. "You love me. And you want me in your life. All you have to do is open the door a little, Iain, and I'll be there."

He knew that if he spoke, he would regret forever what he said. He turned away and picked up his shears. And when the last tendril of the trumpet vine had been tamed, he looked behind him and found she had gone.

# Chapter 11

Cumhann Moor was a desolate place in the winter. The heather and bracken, so scenic in late summer, were dead-leaf brown, and the profuse wildflowers were nothing more than stalks against the pewter-hued sky. Since Duncan and Mara's wedding there had been neither snow nor rain, and the thirsty earth crackled under Billie's feet.

She wasn't sure why she had come here after seeing Iain. She had walked for nearly half a mile, and it was growing darker quickly, although it was only midafternoon. As if to convince her to turn back, a cruel wind whipped across the treeless expanse and flayed every inch of exposed skin, but she walked on.

Christina and Ruaridh had died here, or so the story was told. In the course of her research into genealogical records, Billie had found no proof that either of the young lovers had ever lived, but somehow it didn't seem to matter. Here they had died, at the mercy of those who should have loved them the most.

And there had been no mercy.

Her thoughts whirled faster than the wind. She didn't envy Mara her second sight, but this once she wished that she, too, could see the past, no matter what pain it brought. She had come to study the stories of Druidheachd and instead she had become immersed in one. Her life was entwined with ancient clan hatreds, with betrayals and tragic lost love. She could no longer separate her own life from that of Christina, or Iain's from Ruaridh's. A terrible illness explained by straightforward genetics had become a medieval curse; the man she loved had become a martyr to it.

She loved Iain Ross. A realization that should have filled her with joy filled her with terror instead. She hardly knew him. Their hours together had been few, and she'd had reason to be wary and insecure. But despite that, despite every reason she had *not* to fall in love, she had. She was bonded to Iain in a way she had never conceived possible. She knew things about him that she couldn't know, but she had no doubt that if she asked, she would discover she was right.

*She knew what it would be like to make love to him.*

Billie stood on a low rise staring toward the mountains and considered that revelation. She and Iain had never made love, but not because of her own caution. She had been ready to give herself to him on Christmas day, not because she found giving herself to be a simple thing, but because it had seemed so right. When Iain touched her it was miraculously new, yet as old and changeless as time itself.

She knew what it would be like to make love to him. She could almost feel her body melt against his, feel the way he would move his hands over her, the way he would draw his lips over her breasts. She knew that the moment when they became one would be a moment of such completeness that she would never feel whole again unless he was near. She, the confirmed—but perhaps all too theoretical— feminist.

She almost believed that Iain loved her, too. She read emotions in his eyes that he never communicated. She had seen his expression change when she'd asked him if he loved her. She had seen him steel himself to hurt her. He cared too much about her to cause her pain. He wasn't a man who would take what he needed at anyone else's expense, but he was a man who found it easy to be charming, yet distant

She knew he was perfectly capable of taking comfort in a woman while still communicating that their liaison was temporary.

There had never been any thought of that with her. He was afraid that if he made love to her, he would never let her go.

And perhaps it was true.

There was no sound on Cumhann Moor except the keening of the wind. It was a woman's wail, haunting, piercing, and it shattered Billie's concentration. She folded her arms and rubbed her gloved hands over them. More than ever she knew that she should start back. But something called to her.

Christina had died here. Her life had been short and tragic, but she had known the full scope of Ruaridh's love. Billie didn't envy Christina, but she envied the love that had been so sorely tested on this moor. From the beginning Christina and Ruaridh had known how small was their chance of happiness, yet they had chosen love and hope despite the odds against a happy ending.

Iain had abandoned both. And still, there was no possibility of a happy ending for either of them.

She picked her way down the rise, straining to see where to place each foot. There was another rise ahead, a higher one that was part of a series of land ripples that eventually would lead into foothills. She knew better than to go any farther, but she pushed on. She would climb this rise and see what lay ahead; then she would turn and find her way back to Mara's car. She wasn't ready to return to Flora's, to warmth and cheer and Druidheachd gossip. The moor seemed appropriate somehow, despite bitter wind and thickening gloom.

Or because of it.

She didn't know how long she walked. She stumbled once on the uneven ground, and once she stopped to look behind her to be sure that she wouldn't lose her way. She had almost reached her destination when she stopped again.

There was a pile of stones—what the Scots called a cairn—just ahead of her. The cairn hadn't been visible until she was nearly on it, because the stones were blanketed by vegetation and feathered with fronds of winter-slumbering bracken. There was nothing accidental about it. The stones were neatly piled in a wide circle, several feet high, and they were of different sizes and shapes. She stared at the pile and remembered a superstition that Flora had once related. In the Highlands there had always been strict guidelines about where the body of a suicide was allowed to rest. Often such bodies were not allowed in the churchyard, and when they were, they were placed on the north side at such an angle that no one, particularly a pregnant woman, could step over the grave and court bad luck.

"Nowt will grow where a suicide is buried," Flora had added. "Or where a murder has been committed, for that matter. If we passed such a grave, we tossed a stone upon it."

Billie, who had been taking notes, had been careful to be sure she understood. "And the site of a murder?"

"Aye, that too, lass. That, too."

"Are there places like that in or near Druidheachd that I could visit?"

"Aye, but t'would be terrible luck to tell ye where. Terrible. Dinna even ask."

Now Billie stared at the cairn and shudders ran up her spine. There had been thousands of people living in this area since the Middle Ages, but she was as certain as she had ever been of anything that this was where Christina and Ruaridh had met their deaths. She moved forward and knelt beside the cairn. The ground was cold against her denim-clad legs, but she hardly noticed. She stripped off a glove and touched a stone, then another. She had the same sensation she had experienced when touching the inscribed stone in the field near Annie MacBean's cottage. The stones were warm.

She hadn't cried since her confrontation with Iain. Her sorrow had been too fresh. Now tears streamed down her cheeks, but she wasn't even sure for whom she wept. She squeezed her eyes closed and heard the sound of horse's hooves. A woman screamed, and a man shouted to her. She heard the storm of weeping, the clashing of swords.

She opened her eyes in horror. The wind keened louder, the bitter Highland wind. A twentieth century wind. "Christina," she whispered.

She felt the other woman's agony as profoundly as if it were her own.

Billie stood and stumbled away from the cairn. The sky was nearly dark, and she was trembling from the cold. She was frightened now, as she had not been before, not even when Iain had told her that she could be in danger. She was filled with such a sense of foreboding that for a moment she couldn't start back the way she had come. She was paralyzed, caught somewhere between the past and a future that seemed to press down on her and choke off her breath. She coughed, and as she gulped helplessly, air rushed into her lungs.

It was tinged with smoke.

She whirled, but nothing greeted her except darkness. She knew the direction she should go; she could still see the outline of the rise she had just crossed. She sniffed the air again, and again it seemed tainted. She was reminded of crisp Thanksgiving evenings at her Kentucky grandmother's, and bonfires of autumn leaves scenting the air. But there was nothing festive about this.

*"Run, Billie."*

She heard a woman's voice as plainly as if someone were standing beside her, but there was no one there. She didn't have to turn; she didn't have to search. She knew who had spoken.

She began to move. Slowly at first, then faster, until she was running in the direction from which she had come. The air grew smokier, but still she ran.

*"Teich! Luathaich! Run! Danger!"*

Iain stood at the top of Ceo Castle and surveyed his own private kingdom. He knew men like himself who had inherited lands and titles and believed they were better for it. But he had never considered himself better than any other resident of Druidheachd. He was different, marked forever by land grants to long departed ancestors, by favors to kings who now adorned the pages of history books, and wars that he himself would have refused to fight.

He could see for miles; he had title to it all. And what was any of it worth?

Iain didn't know why he had come to the castle. He had found himself here soon after Billie's departure. He had gazed at Loch Ceo and remembered the day he had seen her struggling there. Perhaps he had come to reestablish that tenuous bond. Or perhaps he had come because he couldn't abide the voices echoing through Fearnshader's halls. Whatever the reason, he had grown chilled here as evening fell. And still he hadn't left.

He went to the other side of the walkway and gazed out over the narrow forest that was the gateway to Cumhann Moor. As a boy he had hiked the moor with his father, but he had always been reluctant. The first time they had come upon the stone cairn his father had put his hands on Iain's shoulders and forced him to stand beside it.

"Remember this place," Malcolm Ross had said. "For it was here that a terrible crime was committed against our family."

Iain had only learned the whole story of the moor when he was a man. But from the moment his father had forced him to face the cairn, he had begun to hate Cumhann Moor. In his father's day there had been shooting parties there, but Iain had always found a way to avoid them. With the help of keepers and underkeepers, the moor had supported a wealth of grouse and pheasants, but for Iain there had only been a stone cairn and a wind that wailed sorrowfully no matter what the time of day or year.

Now the moor was a dark stretch of land rising toward mountains nearly shrouded by evening mists. He wondered if Billie had believed the story of Christina and Ruaridh's deaths. Or had she seen it as one more Highland legend, one more folktale to be related in her dissertation? Would she ever understand how the story of their deaths had rung through the centuries, haunting every Ross who had lived in this castle or, later, at Fearnshader? Would she understand how it haunted him?

Chimney swifts darted in the deepening twilight, and out on the loch, a lone boat whistled its last farewell to day. Iain realized he had to go back home whether he was ready or not. He moved away from the battlements, but just as he was about to turn toward the steps, he glimpsed something in the distance that stopped him. The mists rising from the moor were no thicker than usual, but they were denser, and they billowed strangely.

He narrowed his eyes and stared out at them.

The mists weren't mists at all.

By the time he was on the ground below, running toward his car, the smell of smoke was tangible. He owned a medieval castle, a vast Gothic estate and a twentieth century state-of-the-art cellular car phone because he was so often on the road. He prayed that this once, despite mountains and poor weather, he would get the reception he needed.

He called in his plea for help without serious difficulty, then drove toward the road that ran beside the moor. It was little more than a track, erratically maintained since the days of hunting weekends and rarely driven. It had been used today, though. He saw the proof as he rounded a curve. Mara's car was parked in the midst of a stand of evergreens bordering the road. He hadn't seen it from the castle because it was so well hidden.

Billie was here.

The smoke was thicker now, thick enough to tickle his throat when he sprang from the car. He drew in what air he could and shouted for her, but there was no reply.

He didn't bother asking himself why she had come. He knew. He hadn't told her about the cairn, but she had gone to walk the moor alone, perhaps to experience what she could of her own family's tragedy. He shouted again, and again there was no reply.

He looked for a break in the trees, assuming that she would have done the same so that she could approach the moor from the nearest point to the car. He found one and cut through the forest, shouting as he went. He reached the moor and started across it. The land wasn't flat; there were tufts of vegetation, pits where peat had once been dug, wee hills and valleys that kept him occupied as he moved forward.

"Billie! Answer me!"

The smoke was visible here, although with the wind lashing around him, he couldn't determine its source. He thought it must be some distance away, but he couldn't be sure. He'd had no time to closely examine how a fire might have started in this desolate and abandoned place. It was the wrong season for lightning storms or careless campers. Some land owners routinely burned strips of their moorland to encourage the proper ground cover for game, but Iain had never been convinced that was good ecology. And the season was wrong for *that*, too.

He began to run. He shouted Billie's name, but the wind whipped it away. The smoke was growing thicker, but he still hadn't seen flames. He ran farther into it, because there was no other choice. "Billie!"

Smoke clouded his lungs and choked off his shouts. He slowed his pace, but he kept moving. Between the darkness and the smoke, visibility was minimal. He wondered how he would find her unless he stumbled upon her. The moor was vast, the terrain deceitful. He could pass just meters from her and never know she was there.

"Billie!"

He heard something beyond the impenetrable wall of darkness in front of him. A gasp, a choked cry. He tried to focus on it and head in that direction. "Billie? Say something, damn it. Guide me."

"Iain."

Relief was cut short by the first glimpse of flames. He came down the far side of a low rise and saw a red glow on the horizon. "Billie!"

"Here." She materialized out of the darkness, limping but moving on her own. "I'm here."

He didn't have time to think. He covered the distance between them and clasped her to his chest. "You're hurt." He kissed her hair. His hands moved over her back, testing, confirming, supporting. "Billie." He lifted her face and kissed her hard; then he pulled away. "We've got to get out of here."

"Do you know how?"

"Aye."

"I've hurt my foot. I can't move fast."

"I'll support you. Come on."

He put his arm around her waist and pulled her along beside him. He could feel her struggle to keep pace, but she didn't complain. All the things that were wrong between them seemed immaterial now.

She stumbled, and he caught her. "Careful. I don't want you hurt worse," he said.

"It's moving so fast. One minute it was smoke, then a glow, then I could see the flames."

"We'll move faster."

"Who could have set it?"

He'd found time to ask himself the same. "No one. It's a freak of nature or an accident. How did you injure your foot?"

"I twisted my ankle in a hole." She suddenly stopped moving. "Iain, look!"

He raised his head and peered into the distance. Flame shot like living fountains into the air. "Bloody hell, we've made a wrong turn."

"No! I don't think so. It's circling us."

It couldn't be true, yet he was afraid she was right. He pulled her in another direction. They could still get back to the road this way, although it was farther, and he didn't know how much longer Billie could continue walking. "Just stay with me," he said.

She was limping badly, but she was making a valiant effort to keep up. He could feel her straining at his side. Her body against his seemed so delicate. For all her quicksilver energy and lionhearted courage, she was still a small woman and now an injured one. "I'm not going to let anything happen to you. I'm going to get you out of this," he promised.

"We'll be okay."

He wanted to believe his own words, but just beyond them on the horizon, he saw flames. They were cut off again. The air was smothering now. He heard her coughing just before he began to cough himself.

He realized they might be in more danger from the smoke than the fire. Unless the flames reached the forest strip that bordered the moor, there was little to feed them once they'd devoured the heather. The flames would die on their own. He had only to find a safe place to cross to the road.

But first they had to survive the smoke.

He stopped for a moment and unwound the scarf at his neck, then he wrapped it around hers, bringing it up around her mouth. "This will help." She tried to protest, but he silenced her. "Do it. We'll move faster... if you're not coughing."

He flipped up the collar of his coat and buried his chin inside it. It wasn't much of a filter, but it was better than nothing. "Come on."

He aimed for the edge of the flames, adjusting and readjusting his position as he guided her toward the road. She was hopping on one foot now, dragging the injured one behind her, but somehow she managed to keep going. He was afraid to carry her, afraid that with the added strain his lungs wouldn't do their job and they would both die of the smoke.

The flames were moving fast, faster than they had any right to. It was winter, and despite an unusual lack of rain or snow, the low temperatures should have hindered the fire's growth. Iain could no longer deny that the fire had been set.

He could see the trees, outlined behind the flames, which were still a safe distance from them. There was a space for them to cross, but it was narrowing dangerously as they drew closer. If they could run for it, they had every chance, but at their slower pace, it was going to be touch and go.

Obviously Billie had drawn the same conclusion. "Iain, you can't make it in time... dragging me!" She was racked with coughing.

"Do you think I'd leave you?"

"Yes! Do it!"

"There's a precedent, isn't there... for dying in your arms."

"You aren't Ruaridh!"

He wasn't. He had denied his love for Billie as Ruaridh had never denied his for Christina. If they died together here on the moor, she wouldn't even have the comfort of knowing what he felt for her.

He scooped her up in his arms and damned the consequences. "I'm *not* Ruaridh. I'm going to... get us out of this."

She struggled, but her thrashing brought on another fit of coughing. He was coughing harder, too, and it slowed his steps. Their safety zone was narrowing. For a moment he considered retreat, but it was too late to find another path out of the moor. Even if he was that lucky, it could be devoured by flames before he reached it.

"Billie..."

She pounded on his shoulders, but she was too weak from coughing to answer him.

"Stop it. I love you. Stop it!"

She began to cry. He could feel her tears inside him. For a moment he thought he was losing his mind at last, just as he had always feared he would. He had held her this way before and felt her tears. He had embraced her exactly this way.

He stumbled on. One foot, then another. Time seemed suspended, and the fire seemed to roar through his head. He could feel her body against his and then the powerful muscles of a horse racing beneath them. There were shouts and the thunder of horse's hooves.

And there was a feeling of such desolation.

The trees loomed ahead of him. He stumbled in their direction, coughing and gasping, but the flames were racing from each side to complete the fire circle. He wasn't moving fast enough. No matter how fast he moved now, it wouldn't be fast enough.

He heard screams and the clash of swords. He clutched Billie to his chest to protect her.

"Iain!"

He heard a man's voice call his name. For a moment he
thought he truly had lapsed into insanity. Then he peered
through the choking, smothering smoke, and men appeared. They were attempting to beat back the fire. Someone ran through the narrow gap and grabbed Billie from his
arms. Someone else offered him a shoulder to lean on.

"Damn it, Iain, what a fine moment you chose for an
evening stroll!"

Through streaming eyes Iain looked up and saw Andrew.

And with his friend's help he crossed safely to the other
side of the flames.

# Chapter 12

"It's a glaikit man who will no' take telling, Iain. You've heard the constable and the firemen, too. Will you no' show a bit of sense and let me stay the night?" Andrew extended a hand in plea, but his fingers were clenched into a frustrated fist.

"I don't need another guard. I've alerted my grounds keeper and the staff that's here, and this house is as sturdy as a fortress. Everything's bolted down and shut. Besides, Hollyhock's installed himself by the front door to trip intruders. We'll be safe."

Billie lay cuddled under a woolen blanket on the sofa in front of the sitting room fire and watched Andrew, who seemed ready to pounce on Iain and bolt him down, too. Of the crowd that had thronged through Fearnshader in the hours since their rescue from Cumhann Moor, he was the last to leave. And he wasn't going to leave easily.

"It's that skellum, Jeremy Fletcher, who's done this," Andrew said.

"I don't think so." Iain's gaze flicked to Billie. She met it with a raised brow. Until now Iain had been absolutely silent about his own theories concerning the fire.

Andrew shoved his hands into pockets too small to contain them. With his shoulders hunched forward and his weight balanced on the balls of his feet, he looked like a warrior just waiting for a battle cry. "Then who?"

"Martin Carlton-Jones. And Nigel, too, perhaps."

Andrew stood absolutely still, but Billie had rarely seen anything so deceptive as Andrew motionless. "And why would they destroy the very land they covet?" he asked.

"But it's not destroyed. It'll come back, and they know it. The fire will encourage new growth. Eventually there will be better cover for game. Imagine the autumn shooting parties. They found a particularly clever way to threaten me and mine without hurting their future prospects."

"Have they prospects, Iain? Duncan refused them the hotel, and as yet no one else in the village has sold property to them, but once they've a foot in the door..." His voice trailed off and he shrugged.

"Need you ask?"

Andrew lowered his voice, but Billie could still hear his next words. "Aye. Do you no' think I can see your life, Iain? Nowt you have has brought you happiness. Perhaps you think you'd be better rid of it all?"

Iain's mouth thinned into an angry line. "I can't believe you said that."

"The sentiments are no' my own but ones I've heard in Druidheachd."

"I see."

"Do you? Martin and Nigel are a thrawn pair, ruthless exploiters, both of them, for all their fine manners. If they've set this fire, it's a sign they intend to pursue you hard. And there are those in Druidheachd who believe you'll succumb."

"Then there are those in Druidheachd who are wrong."

"Can you keep all you own, Iain? Have you the resources to fight them?"

Billie suspected that if anyone but Andrew had asked that question, Iain would have exploded. Instead he gave the slightest nod. "The resources *and* the will."

"Then the people of the village have the will to protect *you* and keep you safe. Duncan and I most of all."

"There's no need. I can and do take care of what's mine." Iain turned his face to Billie. His eyes revealed nothing, but she knew that in some way he had included her in what belonged to him.

Andrew looked at her, too. "You have much to protect."

"Vigilance increases with value."

"You know where I live."

Iain clapped Andrew on the back with an easy affection that Billie had only rarely seen him display. The bond between the two men was almost visible. "Just as I always have."

Iain remained silent after Andrew kissed Billie's cheek and left. She watched him stir the coals in the fireplace, and she drew a small measure of consolation from that time-honored domestic ritual. Fire could destroy, or fire could comfort.

When he was apparently satisfied, he added more wood and rearranged the logs. His hair was still damp from a shower, and it waved against the high neck of his dark sweater. She thought it might dry completely before he turned to face her.

"Iain." She wanted to go to him, but she could only call his name. She called it a second time. "Iain..."

He turned. He looked completely composed, as if nothing had passed between them today. "Are you warm enough yet?"

"Good God, yes. If you took my temperature, you'd think I had a fever."

"Dr. Sutherland said you should take special care tonight."

"He said we both should. Stop fiddling with the fire and come over here."

He took his time replacing the poker. His eyes were shuttered when he stood before her.

Billie threw off her cover and sat forward. She would have stood, except that she wasn't sure she could. Her injured ankle had been pronounced sprained, but not seriously so, and securely taped. She was supposed to stay off it for the next week.

"I could have gone home with Andrew or the constable." She looked up at him. "I don't know why you insisted I stay here. You're ignoring me."

"You're in no condition to travel."

"A ride into Druidheachd isn't exactly a voyage to Mars." She paused. "At least, not if we're just talking about distance. Sometimes I think I'd have better luck understanding Martians. Maybe that's where I should have gone to do my dissertation."

"Billie . . ."

She waved away his response. "You jumped down the throat of everybody who offered to take me home. After it was clear we were both going to be all right, you shooed everybody except Andrew out of here like they were contagious. You gave our fine local bobby the short shrift. You even neglected to mention your suspicions about the brakes on your Jaguar. There's somebody out there wreaking havoc with our lives, but you told him an investigation could wait until tomorrow. Now I find you have a pretty good suspicion who might be at fault. I want to know what's going on."

"We've both been through an ordeal. You didn't need to answer more questions tonight, and, for that matter, neither did I. You didn't need a car ride or a trip back into the winter air. You needed quiet and a good night's sleep in a safe place, and I thought this was the best possibility. There'll be time to deal with Martin and Nigel."

"I see." She wished she could jump to her feet and throttle him, but she settled for a voice dripping icicles. "Then why don't I just mosey on upstairs to one of the forty or so bedrooms in this museum and do just that? Then in the morning you can have one of your staff drive me home in an armored car. You won't even have to see me again. That way you won't have to spend the evening pretending to poke logs so you can avoid me."

"You're obviously angry."

"Right! I darned well am!" She hurled the blanket at his feet. "Damn it, Iain, take your lordly manners and your raised aristocratic brow and use them on someone else tonight! We almost died together! We nearly repeated history out on that moor! We came within inches of perishing in each other's arms, just like Christina and Ruaridh. So if I'm feeling angry, I have a reason or two for it. *Comprende?*"

"Perfectly."

"Is that all you're going to say?"

His jaw was clenched so tightly that only one word escaped. "Probably."

"I see." She took a deep breath. A cough started somewhere in her chest. She'd been warned to expect, even welcome, coughing tonight as a way to clear her lungs of residual smoke. She choked this one back. "By any chance were you told as a child that talking about your feelings was a bad idea?"

"Are we indulging in stereotypes here?"

"Sure. Absolutely. Stiff upper lip and all that? Because we've been through hell together today, and except for some concern about my health, you're pretending that none of it even happened."

"The important thing is that you're safe."

"I'm miserable. You're miserable. And we have it in our power to change that, but you refuse."

"Billie, don't do this."

"You told me out there that you loved me."

He didn't deny it, he just didn't respond.

"Was it true?" she prodded.

"Don't do this."

"I'm going to do it." She stood. Pain shot through her right leg, and she shifted her weight to her left. "Do you love me or not, Iain? Were you lying because you wanted my last moments to be happy ones? That's absolutely ridiculous, of course, but I can't think of any other reason you'd lie."

He moved forward to steady her. She slapped his hands away. "Answer me!" A raised voice was too much for her. She began to cough again.

He grabbed her hands and held them. "This is no time for a tantrum."

"I'm going home. Either you call somebody to take me or I call them myself. But I'm getting out of here." She jerked her hands from his with such vehemence that her weight shifted. Pain jolted through her right leg, and a wave of dizziness assailed her. She stumbled as she tried to regain her balance.

Iain caught her against his chest. His arms came around her waist. "What in the bloody hell are you doing, woman? You're not supposed to be standing. We're not supposed to be fighting!"

"By God, I'll do both! What kind of women are you used to, anyway? Well, I'm not one of them. I stand *and* I fight. I don't give up." She pushed against his chest, but he held her tighter.

"Is that what you think I'm doing?"

"Isn't it?" Her eyes were just inches from his, but she refused to read emotions in them. "You know, somebody told me that it takes a special kind of courage to live with uncertainty. For a little while I almost bought that, Iain. I almost believed you were courageous for living with yours. But I was wrong. There are no uncertainties in your life. You're certain of everything. Certain the very worst is going to happen. Certain you're not allowed to grab whatever happiness you can. Certain you have to protect me. Certain you know what's right for everybody. Well, I'm certain, too. I'm certain that you're going to die one heck of a lonely martyr! And whether you do it at fifty or ninety, you could have so much more."

He stiffened. She expected him to thrust her away, but his grip was like a noose tightening. "How dare you speak for me? Do you know what it's like to want something so badly you die a little every time you realize it can't be yours?"

"No! Because I would find a way to have it or die trying. It would be a quicker and prouder death."

"Is it so simple, then? Love conquers all? Well, it doesn't. Love can doom you to destruction."

"Do you think love destroyed Christina and Ruaridh? Hatred destroyed them. And at least they died knowing they had reached for all they could."

He shuddered. She felt it go through her, as well, cell by cell. She felt his agony, his despair. She rested her hands on his cheeks and stared into his eyes. "I love you, Iain Ross. And I don't believe in curses. Every second we waste is a second we could have had together."

"Every second we spend together is a second that brings us closer to destruction."

"I...don't...care!" His arms tightened around her, and she leaned against him. Her lips were just inches from his. "It's my choice. And I choose you."

He shuddered again. There was a war going on inside him; she could feel every individual battle. Defeat shone from his eyes, and her own were bright with tears. "There's nothing I can say, is there?" he asked.

"You can say you love me."

He didn't say it. He kissed her in surrender. He had kissed her before, but never like this. His mouth devoured hers. He was consumed by all the passion he had withheld, all the emotion from which he had protected her. Her head dipped backwards with the ferocity of the kiss. Her lips parted, and he answered with a groan of pure need. Tongue glided over tongue, and she clung to him, answering his need with her own. A dam had burst, but she wasn't in danger of drowning. She was in danger of riding the rushing current so far that she could never return to this place.

She didn't want to return. Not ever.

His lips bathed her chin, the hollow of her throat. Her palm rested against his chest, and she could feel his heart thundering against her fingertips. "If you can't say you love me, make love to me. Show me," she gasped.

"You're out of choices, Billie. Just this once we're going to do something my way." His voice was rough. His hands were rougher. She could feel his fingers digging into her flesh in sweet torture. His movements were restless, frustrated, as if he needed to know all of her at once. She yielded gratefully to him, knowing that he could no more stop what they

had started than he could change eight hundred years o
history.

After her bath she had donned an Oxford shirt belong
ing to him. Now the familiar buttons slid through his fin
gers and he spread the shirt wide. Her breasts were bare, an
she moaned when he covered one. There was sweet tortur
here, too. He had a sorcerer's hands. His palm glide
roughly over her, an incantation by touch alone, and hi
long fingers worked a stunning enchantment. He pressed he
farther back, and his hips mated with hers. She could fee
the heat of his arousal and the moist, answering warmth o
her own.

"Do you think this has been easy?" He kissed her agai
before she could respond. His lips were fierce and demand
ing, a step from punishing. "Do you know how many night
I've lain awake thinking about this?"

She knew. She had lain awake and dreamed of him, too

"I've touched you this way." His hand travelled to he
other breast. "I've made you mine in a thousand differen
ways."

She moaned as his thumb claimed its prize. "I hope ther
are... some surprises left."

His laugh was tormented. "Shall we find out?"

The shirt fell to the floor, and his sweater joined it. Hi
chest was broad and brushed with dark hair. She smoothe
a hand over it in mindless, tremulous fascination before h
lifted her off her feet. As she clung to him, he carried her t
the sofa.

"We're fortunate this is here, aren't we?" There was sa
casm in his voice, distress at his own lack of dignity.

"I'd make love to you on a bed of stones."

"You may very well get that opportunity." He knelt be
side her, and his hands slid under the fabric of the swea
pants she'd borrowed. He jerked them roughly over he
hips, and as he did his fingers brushed over her abdome
"Because I can't seem to keep my hands off you no matt
what pain it might cause." His hands were shaking. He wa
angry with himself; it was in his voice, but his hands wer
still shaking with need.

"You'll only cause me pain if you don't make love to e."

"God knows, I hope you believe that forever."

She felt his hands gliding over her hips, her legs, and fially the tug of the fabric as he freed her from it. His belt uckle clanged as he undid it, and a small explosion announced that he had unsnapped his jeans. There was nothg graceful or seductive about the way he stripped them off. hey were in the way, and then they weren't.

Billie's breath caught at the sight of Iain completely unothed. He was lean and beautifully formed. He only stood ill long enough to gaze back at her, as if he needed that one ngering look but was too impatient for more. She could el her body flush under his scrutiny, but not from shyness r fear. Heat suffused her skin and erupted through the lost sensitive parts of her body. Then she was experiencg him in a different way. He was beside her, and they were ace-to-face. He flung a muscular leg over hers and edged er closer. Her breasts flattened against his chest. The sweet gony of patience dissolved; thought dissolved. She burowed against him, mindlessly seeking pleasure and rease.

"Oh, no, we have a bit more self-control than that." He irned her to her back and half covered her. "We're going make this last for a moment, anyway."

She let her eyes plead with him. "There'll be other mounts."

"Not nearly enough." He kissed her as his hand moved owly, mercilessly, over her. She arched against him, seekg all the magic his talented, elegant fingers could wield. "I ish I could give you all the moments a man can give a oman."

She was melting inside, melting too fast. "I'll just settle r you."

"Settle, is it?" His blue eyes were the dark of midnight, ut his hands poured sunlight through her and told her evything she needed to know. He touched her as if she were treasure he had lost and reclaimed. He murmured sounds at told her his pleasure was as great as hers.

She shifted restlessly and became the magician. On h
side she draped her arms around his neck, and then, as h
turned to accommodate her, she eased over him, leg to leg
hip to hip. "Will you settle for me?"

"Woman, what are you doing?"

She kissed his forehead, pushing his hair back as she dic
She graduated to his nose, then brushed his lips with her
His lips were moist and greedy, but she gave him only a hir
of sustenance before she kissed a trail along his jawline an
the base of his throat. His chest was warm under her lip:
She could feel his heart thrumming unevenly, and she li
gered there.

The firelight danced on the walls and expanded until th
room seemed as bright as the sunshine expanding inside he
From somewhere she heard the fluting of songbirds and th
shrill call of an eagle. She could feel Iain's hands slidin
along her spine, nipping at the sides of her breasts, urgin
her against him. The feelings cascading inside her were olde
than time.

So much older.

*He was so dearly familiar. She knew what he wante
what he loved best. She had explored him this way befor
He had been the one to teach her how a man showed his lo
for a woman. In a secluded glen, beside a thicket of bla
berries and under the scented shade of a hundred pines.*

He was as hard as iron; she was velvet and silk in con
parison. She rocked against him, and her mouth traile
lower. She possessed the fierce heat of him with her hand
cradling him and moving to his own inner rhythm. "Yo
like this, don't you?" she whispered. "I know. I remen
ber."

The eagle called again. A breeze wafted over them, wari
and fragrant with blooming heather. His voice was hardl
more than a growl. "You've bewitched me again."

*Again. Aye, again. Just as she had once before. In a s
cluded glen, where bees buzzed among the wildflowers, an
birds sang as they stripped the blaeberry bushes of the
fruit.*

Her mouth moved lower. She whispered against his abomen. "And why not? You've bewitched me. Why else would I be here?"

He groaned and with one mighty effort turned her to her back again. He settled over her. Her heartbeat was like the roll of drums. "You're here because you love me," he said.

"Your fault entirely."

"Fate's."

She could feel his smile, his voice cutting through her like the sunshine that surrounded them. He lifted her chin and touched her lips with his. The gentleness of the kiss was almost her undoing.

"Now," she whispered. "The moment has ended."

Still holding her chin in his hands and staring into her eyes, he lifted his hips and thrust into her triumphantly.

*It had been this way from the first. Gentle strength. Quiet power. A mating of minds and spirits and bodies. She could feel herself dissolving against him. Just as she had once before. From the beginning, in the scented shade of a hundred pines.*

"*Mo boirionnach boidheach!*" he cried.

She *was* his woman. His beautiful woman. She was his. She called his name and moved against him. And all the moments left to them merged into forever.

She didn't want to come back to earth, to time and the limitations of the flesh.

The flesh. The magnificent, soul-expanding flesh.

Billie opened her eyes and watched the way the firelight played over Iain's body. The flames shifted, grew brighter and dimmed, and with each flicker, each liquid burst of brilliance, the shape of him seemed to change.

"You called me Ruaridh."

She let her gaze travel to Iain's eyes and saw that he was awake. Slowly she gathered her forces to respond. "No. I didn't. I couldn't have."

"You called me Ruaridh."

"*Mo boirionnach boidheach.*"

"What does that mean?"

"That's what you called me. Your beautiful woman. Billie tried to sit up, but Iain was warm against her, and he body fit his too perfectly. She contented herself with na rowing her eyes. She was so boneless, nerveless, that it too moments to achieve. "I did not call you Ruaridh."

"Aye, you did. At the end, Billie. And you misunde stood. I don't speak Gaelic."

She managed a smile, but her heart felt tight in her ches The boneless inertia of complete satisfaction was stiffenin into fear. "You are Iain Ross. I am Billie Harper. We f nally made love."

He managed a smile, too, but his eyes were clouded. "B it can't happen this way again. I almost forgot to prote you."

"But you did. Primitively, but definitely."

"I am never careless. My God, I could have given you child."

She saw a thousand torments in his eyes. She smoothe her fingers over his eyelids and watched them close. "Yc weren't careless. You took care of me, of both of us. Yc had more presence of mind than I did. Much more. I cou only think of..." She hesitated. "You."

He rested his face against her shoulder. She could feel t even whisper of his breath against her breast. He was sile: for a long time, such a long time that she believed he h fallen asleep. She couldn't concentrate on her doubts ar fears while he held her in his arms. She found herself dri ing, too, to a place where the sunlight was warm and be hummed in a grove of scented pines. She was nearly aslec herself when he spoke again. "You called me Ruaridh, B lie."

She could no longer deny it. She could think of only o explanation. She lifted her head. "I suppose, just for th moment, I was thinking of Ruaridh and Christina."

He shifted and pulled her to rest in his arms. "Perhap: was thinking of them, too."

# Chapter 13

Dwarfed in the center of Iain's huge and ancient bed, Billie looked like a particularly fetching china doll. She had crawled in that position all night—or at least the part of the night when he had allowed her to shut her eyes. She was an energetic sleeper, who staked a claim to more than her own half of the mattress and defended it with vigor. She was also a cuddler, who even when immersed in the deepest dreams had entwined her legs with his and splayed her fingers against his chest. Until now he had preferred distance and measured affection.

Until now.

Iain's parents had slept in this bed together. After the worst of his early childhood nightmares, he had sometimes slept here with them, despite the outraged warnings of his starched and proper nanny. When he had moved back to Fearnshader after his years at Oxford he had considered choosing another room or simply getting rid of the bed. But he didn't put a seventeenth century state bed on the rubbish heap. And even though he could have sold it for a fortune, he hadn't been able to bear the thought of strangers sleeping in it. So he had custom-ordered a new mattress to

fit the bed's outrageous proportions and installed himself i
the room.

And until last night, no woman had ever slept there wit
him.

Billie murmured something. Iain was too far away to hea
what it was, but he had already learned that she talked in he
sleep, as if days were too short and sleep too wasteful. H
wanted to go to her, to smooth back the hair feathere
against her forehead and kiss her awake. He knew that he
arms would slip around his neck, and she would open to hi
with sweet, passionate generosity, despite a similar encour
ter in the night. The human male might have physical lim
tations, but the human female had none—and a certai
human female named Billie Harper was perfectly capable o
convincing Iain that his own limitations were easily ove
come.

Instead, and regretfully, he turned away from the bec
The night had been enchanted, but the sun had risen an hou
ago. In the light of day he was plagued once more by fea
that he had destroyed her life. In the bed where generatior
of Rosses had slept and loved, he had promised her thing
with his body that his heart believed were impossible.

He shaved in the bathroom just off his bedroom an
stepped into the shower. He ached in ways he never had be
fore, in places where he had never truly been touched. No
the way Billie had touched him. She held nothing of herse
back, and she had demanded the same from him. He was
passionate man, but he had never begun to explore the dept
of his passions until last night.

He loved her. It was so clear, so simple. He was ashame
at how easily it had happened, and how powerfully. For s
many years he had steeled himself against love. He had is
lated himself in all the essential ways, schooled himself t
remain distant. But all that had been possible only becaus
he hadn't yet met Billie.

He thrust his whole body under the shower, as if it mig
help wash away his fears. Water sluiced over his head an
beat down on his shoulders. He didn't hear the first scream
or rather, he didn't recognize it for what it was. The secon

sent him shooting out of the water and straight through the connecting door.

"It can no' be!"

Billie sat up in bed and tried desperately to remember where she was. She came awake by leaps and bounds, but still not fast enough. She could only manage to pull a sheet over her naked breasts before the woman screamed again.

"You'll both be destroyed now, both you and Master Iain. Have you no' heard the curse? Do you no' see what you've done? You've brought destruction into this house, Billie Harper, and terrible, terrible torment!"

Billie stared at the woman, then at the shattered teapot forming puddles at the woman's feet. "I'm sorry. Did I order tea?"

"Gertie, what in the bloody hell are you doing?" Iain came out of the bathroom, wrapping a towel around his waist. Billie fixed her eyes on him. The sight was infinitely more pleasurable than Gertie's fury. She watched his gaze dip to the floor, then back up to Gertie's face. "Oh, I see," he said. "I thought you were visiting your son until Friday. I didn't expect you back."

"What is it you've done, Master Iain?"

Billie watched some close relative of humor creep into Iain's eyes. "I think what I've done is perfectly apparent. But I'm sorry you didn't know not to bring me my tea the way you always do."

Gertie would not be put off. "You've summoned the curse! The two of you have summoned it together. Did you no' think of that when you brought this woman here?"

"I believe I was thinking of other things."

"You can no' laugh in the face of the devil, and it is the devil's messenger—" she inclined her head toward Billie "—her very own ancestor at whom you're laughing!"

"That's enough." The hint of a smile died in Iain's eyes. "We're not laughing at anyone. What we feel for each other has nothing to do with anyone *except* us. Now I'll expect you to show some discretion and keep this to yourself. Understood?"

Gertie's eyes blazed. She turned to Billie. "What is it you did, lass, to bewitch him?"

Billie remembered Iain's words as they had made love last night. *You've bewitched me. Why else would I be here?* Memories of a grove of pines and the drifting fragrance of blooming heather tugged at her. Unsuccessfully, she tried to push them away. "Gertie," she said, as the memory played on in her mind, "this is the twentieth century. We don't believe in ghosts or witches or curses anymore, remember? I have no control over who my ancestors were, but it doesn't matter. *They* don't matter."

"Leave us alone," Iain told Gertie. "And for God's sake, don't bring us any more tea."

"Aye, I'll go. But I'm leaving Fearnshader, too. I will no' stay here and be a party to your destruction."

Billie knew that Iain was fond of the old woman. She tried to soothe her. "Gertie, please don't go because of me."

"No, lass. I will no' stay. How can I stand by and watch as a strong, proud family falls to its knees?"

"Oh, look, you've got the wrong lass there. I couldn't bring down a nest of starlings."

"I will no' be back!" Gertie stalked to the door, flung it open, then slammed it behind her.

"And some people think Scotland is a relaxing place to visit. A few tunes on the old bagpipe, a peek at the Loch Ness monster..." Billie rested her chin on her hands. The sheet slipped just low enough to be enticing. "Maybe somebody will do me a favor and revoke my passport."

"You're upset."

Billie looked up at Iain, who had come to stand beside the bed. "I'd apologize, but I can't summon a reason why I should. I was asleep, and then the next moment I was Satan in a nightgown." She looked down. "Out of a nightgown. I suppose that was the problem."

"Gertie's an old woman, and she's seen more than her share of troubles."

"Actually, now she's seen more than her share of me." She held the sheet a little higher. "Was she here when your father died?"

He nodded curtly.

That explained a lot, but Billie didn't want to talk about Gertie anymore. "Did you think about the MacFarlane curse last night when we made love?"

He didn't answer, and by now she knew what that meant. "What part of you resides in the twentieth century, Iain? On a scale of one to ten. One being prehistoric."

"Aye. I thought of the curse. Would you like to know what I thought?"

"What did you?"

"That had I been Ruaridh, and you Christina, I would not have been able to deny myself the pleasures of being with you. Even if I had known what horrors waited for me in the future."

Something smoldered in his eyes, behind the torment, the questions and fears. She lifted her head and her hands. The sheet fell to her lap. "And had I been Christina, I would have pledged to die a thousand deaths for the privilege of sharing just a part of your life."

He didn't want to come to her. She saw his struggle. She held out her arms.

And with a helpless groan, he struggled no more.


Iain was gone when Billie awoke again. Late morning sunlight made a drab attempt to pierce the gloom of the bedroom. She wrapped a blanket around her breasts and limped to the window to pull back the heavy draperies, only to discover why they were closed. Cold air streamed through cracks around the ancient windows. The draperies were primitive insulation.

She shivered and ran her hands up and down her bare arms. She hadn't noticed how cold the room was last night because Iain had kept her warm. Now she wondered where he had gone. She pictured him having breakfast alone in Fearnshader's gargantuan dining room, sitting at the end of a table long enough to seat half the village.

She was looking through his wardrobe for something to wear when there was a polite knock at the door. The young apple-cheeked woman who had instructed her yesterday on the proper route to the conservatory appeared in the doorway. "Pardon, Miss Harper, am I intruding?"

Billie was balanced on one leg, wrapped in a blanket in an unfamiliar bedroom, and the young woman had walked right in. It seemed the definition of intrusion. "Umm... nope."

"These were delivered here for you this morning." She held out a pair of well-worn crutches. "From Dr. Sutherland. And I've your clothes. They've been washed and pressed, and the smell of smoke is gone."

"Darn, and I was going to sell them to a Manhattan bistro. Heather smoke could very well be the next craze in haute barbecue."

"Aye, Miss Harper. I'm sorry."

Billie took pity on her. "I'm teasing. I appreciate your work on the clothes. I was just about to take a shower, and I was wondering what to wear."

"Would you like your breakfast up here?"

"No. I'm going to look for Iain. It would be more fun to eat with him."

The young woman looked uncomfortable. "Pardon, Miss Harper, but Lord Ross is gone. Left about an hour ago, he did. Said he left you a note. I'll be driving you home when you're ready to leave."

Billie stared at her. "Gone?"

"Aye. Did you no' get his note?"

"No. I'll look for it."

"I could help."

"No." Billie was still trying to digest the fact that Iain had left without telling her directly. "No. I'll find it myself."

"And breakfast?"

"Just coffee. Up here, if you don't mind."

Billie waited until she was alone again before she began to search. She ignored the crutches and limped around the bedroom looking for the note with no success. She finally found it on the bathroom sink. Iain had gone to find Martin Carlton-Jones. She was to go back to Flora's and not to worry. He would be certain she came to no harm.

She had read grocery lists written with more warmth.

Billie told herself not to read more or less into the note than was there. Iain was concerned with protecting her.

*Just as Ruaridh must have tried to protect Christina.*

"No." She shook her head. Last night was already a stunning memory, but there were spaces in it, distant, fragrant wisps that made no sense to her. She had made love to Iain on a sofa in front of a smoking fireplace.

*And he had whispered endearments in Gaelic, a language he didn't speak or understand.*

Something like fear edged along her spine. At the very height of pleasure, she had called out Ruaridh's name. The legends of star-crossed lovers and the curse had seeped so far into her consciousness that at that moment of total fulfillment, both she and Iain had stepped over the line between reality and fantasy.

There could be no other explanation.

She clutched Iain's note in her hands and prayed that history would not continue to repeat itself.

After a night at Fearnshader, Flora's cottage seemed like a dollhouse, but a warm and welcoming one. Flora took one look at Billie, sat her down at the kitchen table and plugged in the electric kettle for tea. "Ye'll drink it strong and sweet, and ye'll drink plenty of it."

"You won't get an argument from me." Drinking tea with Flora seemed like such a normal, natural thing to do. Billie reminded herself that most people spent their days this way, going about their daily lives without curses or crises to fuel them.

"Ye're certain that Dr. Sutherland said you could be out and about?"

"As long as I don't put weight on my foot or get too tired." She watched Flora busying herself with the tea tray. There would be scones and fresh fruit as well as the usual pot of Earl Grey tea. She hadn't realized she was hungry until now.

"T'was a close call ye had, lass. Far too close, to my way of thinking."

"There's no doubt the fire was set. And by somebody who knew exactly what he was doing. I don't think I would have gotten out alive if Iain hadn't rescued me."

"But it's the next time, Billie, that must concern ye."

For a moment Billie didn't understand. Then she realized that Flora wasn't looking at her, Flora who could meet the eyes of the devil and send him cringing back into the bowels of the earth.

The door buzzed before she could respond. "More for tea," Flora said. "Practice with yer crutches, lass, and go answer it for me."

Billie got to her one good foot and reached for the crutches, which Flora had stationed close by. She swung her way to the front door with distaste. The crutches were easy to manage, but she hated anything that slowed her down. Balancing precariously, she opened the door. Mara and a giggling April were waiting on the other side.

Hugs were exchanged, and explanations. "Aye, it was a glorious holiday," Mara explained. "But we thought it was time to be back."

"And you, April?" Billie asked.

"I missed Uncle Iain and Uncle Andrew!"

"They spoil her at every opportunity," Mara said with an indulgent smile. "It's no wonder she misses them."

"Mum said you hurt your ankle running from a fire," April said.

"Mum?"

"Because Mara's my Scottish mommy."

"Terrific choice, short stuff." Billie ruffled April's hair before she turned to Mara. "How did you hear about my ankle? Is the gossip that detailed already?"

"I did no' hear about it from anyone." Mara made her statement with no subterfuge or apologies. "I had Duncan drop us here so we could check on you. He would be here, too, but I asked him to leave us alone."

"I see." Billie knew where Mara's information had come from. She was beginning to accept things that would curl the hair of the very proper scholars on her doctoral committee. "You have something to tell me, don't you?"

Flora spoke from the kitchen doorway. "April, I've seed for the birds. If ye spread it on the ground, then sit as quiet as can be on the bench in my garden, ye can watch them fly up and take it."

Mara bent and fastened the top button of April's coat. "Pull your hat over your ears. That's right."

"I've a scone for ye, as well," Flora said. "To eat while ye're watching."

April let Flora guide her into the garden. Mara and Billie followed and installed themselves at the kitchen table. "What I have to say, Flora can hear," Mara said. "Although I suspect that nowt I say will surprise her."

"Why not? Is it common knowledge? One of those things I'm always the last to know?"

"No' common knowledge at all. But I think that Flora knows more than she tells."

"Ye would be the one to know, Mara Sinclair," Flora said, coming in through the kitchen door. Billie could see April huddled motionlessly on the stone bench under Flora's willow tree. Accustomed to Flora's generosity, the birds had already begun to find the seed.

"I don't understand," Billie said. "What are you two talking about?"

"Flora's mum was Margaret Henley."

The name meant something. Billie had heard it mentioned before, but the nearly total recall that had always been her greatest gift seemed fogged by the events of the past weeks. "Margaret Henley," she repeated, hoping it would trigger a chord.

"Aye. She was known far and wide for her visions," Flora said. She brought the tray to the table and set cups in front of each of them.

"Bingo." Billie was flooded with references now. Margaret Henley had been dead for two decades, at least, but the villagers, particularly the older ones, still spoke of her. Only no one had ever mentioned that Flora was her daughter.

Billie turned to Flora. "Why didn't you tell me?"

Flora poured tea into each of their cups. "And what would have been the point?"

Billie considered that. There was more here than just Flora's Scottish reticence.

"I believe that Flora has no' told you because she remembers certain things her mum said before she died, and she did no' want you to suspect. Is that right, Flora?"

Flora smiled and set the fruit and scones on the table.

"Let me see if I've got this straight. Flora's mother could see the future. You can see the future. I'm getting flashes of the past...." Billie's voice trailed off. She hadn't intended to reveal that.

"Aye," Mara said. "I know."

"Any moment now I'll wake up and find myself back in Kansas, my ruby slippers mysteriously turned into tennis shoes...."

"There's a long tradition in the Highlands of peeking through the veil that separates the present from that which has passed before and that which has no' yet passed."

"Einstein would have had a field day here. Hand in hand with Freud." But Billie's mind was seriously whirling, despite her words.

"I dinna think that we have more people inclined this way, only that it's more accepted here that such a thing is possible," Flora said.

"Would a Perlman or a Heifetz have excelled if no' for the recognition and reverence of musical talent by their families and teachers?" Mara asked.

"You've spent your entire life learning to cope. There's been little respect for your abilities," Billie reminded her.

"There is respect here. And understanding. It's just taken time for me to find it."

"Tell me what all this has to do with me."

Flora was the first to speak. "I've kept things from ye, lass. I've been afraid to tell ye what I know. I had to be certain...."

"Of what?"

"Certain that you were committed to staying, Billie, to seeing this through," Mara said.

"Are we talking about the MacFarlane curse?"

Mara sat back in her chair. "Then you've learned of it?"

"She does no' ken it all," Flora warned Mara.

Billie frowned. "Alasdair translated exactly what was on the stone."

"There's more."

"What?" Billie hesitated, then she held up her hand. "You know, I'm not sure I want to hear the rest. If it gets worse..."

Flora shifted in her seat, as if she were settling in. "The stone was inscribed hundreds of years after the curse was first uttered. Christina's father, in his grief and despair, uttered the words and sealed them for centuries. But later, when he realized that he might have doomed his own future kin, just as he had shamefully doomed his beloved daughter, he added a bit."

"He could no' change his words," Mara said. "So he added some. But that addition was never inscribed on the stone."

"Why? What was it?"

"As to why? We dinna know. As to what? There is no record," Mara said.

"None," Flora agreed.

Billie sat quietly for a moment. "But you know? One or both of you knows anyway?"

"On the day that Iain Ross was born, my mother had a vision," Flora said. "She told me that Iain's birth would be the end of the curse that had haunted the Ross family for eight hundred years."

"How?"

"That she did no' say."

"A rather important omission," Billie said.

"The future can be glimpsed but never exactly predicted," Mara said. "Nowt is set in stone."

"Especially the end of the MacFarlane curse," Billie said. "Too bad."

Mara smiled sadly. "Especially that."

Billie leaned forward in her chair. Her tea was untouched. "So far you've both told me pieces of a legend, pieces I hadn't yet heard. What do you know that others don't? What does the sight tell you?"

"I could no' share this with ye before," Flora said. "Because I did no' know if ye were the one...."

"The one to help put an end to the curse," Mara continued.

Billie was torn by how preposterous all of this was, and despite that, how much respect she held for these two women. "And now?"

"Do ye love Iain Ross, Billie?" Flora asked. "And does he love ye?"

Strangely, Billie felt that Flora had a right to know. "Yes."

"Despite the curse and despite the danger?"

"Yes." *And despite a genetic inheritance that might destroy his life and hers.* "Yes, I love Iain Ross. And I think he loves me."

"When Christina fell in love with Ruaridh, he protected her from that love," Mara said. Her green eyes were almost translucent. They were fixed on Billie, but Mara seemed to be looking far into the past. "Their families were enemies, as you know, and Ruaridh was certain that an alliance between them was impossible. Christina was to be married to a distant cousin, and Ruaridh was about to be betrothed to a woman with property that adjoined his own. Despite his feelings for Christina, he made certain no' to see her again. He traveled Scotland and beyond to avoid her."

Flora took up the story. "But one day, despite his great care, Christina and Ruaridh met by chance in the woods that bordered their lands. When Christina realized who the lone man on horseback was, she managed to escape her escort to be with Ruaridh, and in good conscience, he could no leave her alone without protection. Thrown together, the spark between them kindled."

*In a secluded glen, beside a thicket of blaeberries and under the scented shade of a hundred pines.*

"Billie, are you all right?" Mara asked. She leaned forward, concern shining from her eyes, and touched Billie' arm.

The shrill whistle of Roman candles exploded in Billie's ears. Her hands tingled, and her eyesight dimmed momentarily.

"Put your head down." Flora stood and pushed Billie's head toward her lap, narrowly missing the table's edge.

"I know the rest," Billie whispered. "You don't have to tell me." She rested her head on her hands and closed her eyes. She clearly saw a man who almost exactly resembled Iain, but a man from another era.

She knew the rest. In more of a flash than a vision, it had become as clear to her as if she had lived it herself. She saw a woman with hair the color of her own. Long, braided hair and brown eyes, just like Billie's, shining with love. She wanted to deny it all; she wanted a one-way ticket back to the United States. Tears clutched at her throat and denial at her heart. But she could not deny what she knew.

Her voice was wooden. "They made love and pledged themselves to each other. They were married that night by a kindly old priest who bypassed all ecclesiastical authority and tradition. And then Christina went alone to tell her father, believing that as much as he loved her, he would not harm her for her disobedience. Ruaridh insisted that she not go, but she believed that she knew what was best. She believed that she could reconcile the two families, and that they could live peacefully the rest of their days. So she slipped away, while he was sleeping...."

"Aye." Mara stroked Billie's hair.

Iain had told Billie the rest of it, but it was clearer to her now, as clear as a video unfolding. She shuddered and sat up, despite the dizziness. "Their ghosts still haunt Cumann Moor."

"They must be put to rest," Mara said.

"How?"

"The legend is being played out again. Can you no' see that?"

Billie didn't know what she saw. Everything she'd thought and felt could be attributed to an acute suggestibility. And yet...

"There have been two attempts on Iain's life . . . or mine. But I can't see a connection to the story of Christina and Ruaridh. We survived the fire on Cumhann Moor. We were in the very place where Christina and Ruaridh died, but we survived."

"Ye've yet to meet your final test," Flora said.

"Is that what you meant earlier, when you said that it's the next time that should concern me?"

"Yer love must be strong."

"And how do I accomplish that for both of us? I love Iain, and I think . . . know he loves me. But he's so afraid I'll be hurt. There is a curse in his family, and whether or not it has anything to do with the Middle Ages and some ancestor of mine, it's still very real. And he wants to spare me pain." A tear slid down her cheeks, even though she was angry for allowing it.

Flora didn't attempt to comfort her. "Yer love must be strong."

"What was the last part of the MacFarlane curse? You both know more than you're telling, don't you?"

"It established a way to end the curse forever," Mara said.

"How?"

Flora shook her head. "Yer love must be strong."

"My love is strong." Billie looked from woman to woman. Their expressions were as tortured as she knew her own to be. "But I'm afraid that Iain's fears are stronger."

# Chapter 14

Martin Carlton-Jones and Nigel Surrey owned an office building in London's fashionable West End. Built of granite in chunky, matronly lines, the building had settled into the role of stately dowager well before the arrival of Queen Victoria.

On his first visit Iain had expected something brash and contemporary, or at least something inappropriately pompous. Instead, the building guaranteed respectability and confidence before the two men even shook the hands of potential clients.

Iain had neither confidence nor respect for either of the men or what they intended to do. Both Martin and Nigel considered themselves magicians who could transform their chosen corners of the globe into playgrounds for the rich and famous. They had already been astonishingly successful. They owned a Maharajah's palace in Jaipur, a cattle station in Queensland, and an expansive chateau and vineyard in Bordeaux. Now they wanted something closer to home, something British, but suitably quaint and distinctive. They had first contacted him nearly a year ago, and slowly over the past months they had revealed their plan for the future of Druidheachd. He had purposely led them on, even courted them, because enemies without secrets were far less dangerous.

But they were dangerous still.

It was late in the afternoon before he walked through the door of Martin's private offices. He had driven to Prestwick, flown to Heathrow and driven a rental car to the West End. Had Martin known he was on his way, he would have sent a limousine, but Iain wanted no part of that. The game had ended, and when he walked back out the door, he wanted his own car at his disposal.

Martin's offices whispered proper British taste. Leather chairs just old enough to be interesting rested in quiet conversational groupings. Rosewood panelling harbored a series of hunting prints, most of which were variations of a setter holding a bloody pheasant between its teeth. Martin's secretary was a porcelain blonde whose dark red lipstick outlined a haughty smile. The smile softened to something vaguely come-hither when she realized who had entered the room. "Lord Ross, is Mr. Carlton-Jones expecting you?"

"No, but I suspect he'll see me anyway."

When Iain didn't smile, hers faltered. "Well, I'll have to check, you know. He's not always available, even to you."

"He had better be."

Her complexion grew paler. "I'll just check."

"Aye. Do that."

He waited in front of her desk, arms folded and eyes wide open. The door to the inner sanctum creaked, and a sweating Martin walked through it, arm extended. "Iain, my good man, what brings you here?"

"The need for a discussion."

Martin clapped him on the back. "I'm always ready to have a discussion with you, Iain. Any time of the day or evening."

"Delighted to hear it." Iain allowed himself to be ushered into Martin's office. He refused tea, brandy and port, but he took a corner wing chair flanked by two overfed ferns, and Martin pulled up another chair to join him. The room was unbearably stuffy.

"So tell me, what are we discussing?"

Iain leaned back in his chair and tapped his fingers against the wooden arm. "How badly do you want my property, Martin?"

Martin was in his fifties, at least fifty pounds overweight and fifty points higher on the intelligence scale than any casual observer might suppose. "Badly enough to crawl."

"Describe crawling for me, would you?"

"What do you want, Iain? Tell me where to start, and I'll describe anything." He leaned back, too. "Anything within reason."

"Then why don't you tell me what I have that you want most."

"Truthfully?" Martin began to sweat more profusely. He took out a handkerchief and wiped his forehead. "Fearnshader. The castle. The moor and all the property extending on each side of it. Your holdings in the village—"

"All of them? I own a great part of it, you know." Iain was sure that Martin could tell him exactly what he owned, right down to the millimeter. "And some of what I have, a lot, really, would be difficult to sell to you, because like most historic properties, there are so many legal restrictions on my estate."

"We have some of the finest lawyers in the world on our staff."

Iain nodded. "I imagine your staff is extensive."

"We have the finest of the finest. But I'm certain that by now you're familiar with every aspect of what we do."

"Particularly familiar with some of it."

For the first time Martin looked confused. "I apologize, but I'm afraid I've lost the train of thought here."

"You mentioned the moor. I presume you meant Cumhann Moor?"

"The moor nearest your house, yes."

"Cumhann Moor." Iain leaned forward. "The moor that nearly burned to the ground just yesterday."

"No..." Martin looked genuinely distressed. "But how?"

"A question I also find interesting. The answer, of course, is arson. Attempted murder, too, for that matter, since I was caught there while it was burning, as was a friend of mine."

"You're all right? You weren't injured?"

"I'm sitting here with you, Martin."

The room grew stuffier. Martin wiped his forehead again. "Well, Iain, now I'm beginning to wonder why."

"Nothing I have will ever belong to you. Nothing. Not a dust mote, not a drop of water, not a molecule of air. My ancestors were not the only ones capable of entailing property. I can and have done the same. If anything should happen to me, you will never be able to touch a thing that belonged to me. Is that clear enough?"

"Have you lost your mind? Are you implying that I had something to do with the fire yesterday?"

"Of course not. I just believe it's time to show my hand. And here it is. I will fight you and Nigel with every breath left in my body. I'll use every bit of influence I have in Druidheachd and the surrounding villages to be certain that no one sells so much as a blade of grass to you. I'll use my influence in Parliament and with every politician in Great Britain." He stood. "I'll use every scrap of the considerable information I've been able to glean about your holdings internationally and the deceitful means by which you acquired them. And if all that fails, Martin, and you come after what's precious to me, I'll come after *you* in the dead of night. You will never be safe again."

Sweat ran like a river from Martin's forehead. "What have I done to deserve this from you, Iain? I thought we had become friends."

"Then you thought I was a fool." Iain started for the door.

"What have I done?"

Iain turned in the doorway. "You've coveted Paradise, Martin. But I'm afraid it can never be yours."

Jeremy Fletcher was gone. There was nothing left at his residence on the edge of the village except a sign in the win-

dow advertising it for rent. Constable Terrill assured Billie
that no one had seen Jeremy near Druidheachd in weeks; in
fact, the rumor was that he had left Britain entirely.

"Iain believes someone else started the fire," Billie told
Mara, as they walked toward the Sinclair Hotel from the
policeman's office, "but I think Jeremy was behind it. Iain's
bested him in every encounter, and I think Jeremy's a man
with a real need to get even."

"Suppose you're right. What do you think he'll do
now?"

Billie considered. "I think if Jeremy set the fire or hired
someone else to do it, it might be his last stand. He would
see the outcome as a draw, which might be good enough. No
one died, but the moor will be a reminder to Iain for a long
time that not everything is in his control."

"And the brakes?"

"Now that's exactly the sort of thing he would do. Wreak
havoc, then walk away." They were nearly at the hotel before Billie spoke again. "All right. I'm prepared. Tell me
what you see."

"Nowt. The people I love most are the one's I can no'
help. But I'm afraid."

"I know. You think that something else will happen."

"Have you spoken to Iain?"

"No." A week had passed since Billie had awakened in
Iain's bed; seven days since he had disappeared off the face
of the earth. Her ankle still throbbed occasionally, but as
each day had passed without hearing from him, her heart
throbbed more painfully.

"Duncan has."

Billie stopped and touched Mara's arm. "And you've
waited until now to tell me?"

"Iain's coming home today. He may be there already."

"I see."

"I dinna think you do. He asked Duncan no' to tell you."

"And so Duncan told you?"

"Aye. And I had promised Iain nowt."

"What should I do?"

"Your love must be strong."

"I'm beginning to think that's my mantra. Give me a candle and I'll chant it until I'm enlightened."

"I've learned that you joke when you feel something most deeply."

"I should be joking all the time, then."

"Go to him."

The advice was good, but Billie found her heart slam-dancing with her ribs. She was afraid to see Iain again. He didn't even want her to know that he had come back. He had made a decision about them, and he hadn't consulted her.

"I don't know...."

"He loves you."

Billie's worst fear surfaced. Her voice dropped. "If he doesn't, it wouldn't be the first time I've made a mistake."

"You mentioned once that there was another man. Did you love him as much?"

"No." Billie was surprised at herself. The word escaped with such force she couldn't have held it back. "It wasn't the same thing at all."

"And why was it different?"

Because Iain was her heart. Billie didn't believe in soul mates, in predestination, reincarnation or any other nation that wasn't solid, inhabited land. She didn't, couldn't, believe in any of those things.

But she believed that Iain was her heart.

"Because my love *is* strong." She touched Mara's arm. "Strong enough, I hope, to see this through."

Mara fished in her pocket and held up a familiar car key. "I will no' be needing it all day or night."

"I hardly know you, yet you've become such a good friend. The best one I've ever had."

Mara clasped her hand. "Walk with care, Billie. Watch everything and everyone. Take no advice that does no' ring true in your heart. And listen for the things that are no' said as well as those screamed in anger."

Billie was transfixed by the way Mara's eyes seemed to grow paler as she spoke. "Yes. All right."

Mara nodded; then she pulled her green cape around her and started down the hotel walkway. Billie stood and watched. At the stairs that led inside, Mara stepped into a pool of cloud-filtered sunlight. For a moment she didn't look like Mara at all. She was radiant, unearthly somehow, as if she were no longer made of flesh.

Then she turned and waved just before she stepped inside and closed the door behind her.

Billie found Iain in the conservatory. He wasn't pruning today. He was lounging on a stone bench, staring through the glass at the drab winter afternoon. He stood when she approached, but he didn't speak.

She did. "Mara told me you'd come back. Next time you'll have to swear her to secrecy, too."

"Don't make this more difficult than it has to be."

Iain looked composed, with just the correct hint of regret in his eyes. She wondered how many times he had played out this farewell scene, because obviously he had mastered it. But she was different from the other women he'd known. He had not chosen her because she would be easy to leave.

She folded her arms. "How difficult does it have to be?"

"Difficult enough. But I've never lied to you. I've told you, right from the beginning, that I intend to spend my life alone."

"We've had some good times, but now they're over?" She raised a brow. "Or let's see what other clichés come to mind. How about 'you're too warm and wonderful a woman, Billie, to waste yourself on a man like me'? Or 'you'll always have a special place in my heart'?"

"There's no point in ending this with sarcasm."

"There's no point in ending this. You love me. I love you. We can work out our problems."

"Problems?" Something flared behind his stern control. "That doesn't begin to cover it."

"What does cover it?"

"Basic incompatibility. We're from two different worlds, and you don't understand mine. You don't understand my life, and you refuse to understand what I've been telling you all along."

"Maybe I'll understand this time. Go ahead and say it again."

"I don't want a relationship."

"Maybe I'll understand if you're specific, Iain. Be specific this time. Be very specific, and say it like you mean it."

"Why are you torturing us both?"

"Am I torturing you?"

He realized his mistake. She could see it in his eyes. Something clicked shut in them, but not before she had seen it. "I don't want to hurt you," he said.

"Nice retraction. But I'm waiting for you to tell me that you don't want a relationship with *me*. With me specifically. Tell me that you don't love me. And if you can say it so that I believe it, then I'll go."

"I know I told you I loved you on the moor, and I'm sorry. But I confused my feelings of protectiveness and concern for love."

"Did you?"

He took a step toward her. "Why do you insist on this?"

"Because I come from a different world, remember? And in my world we like to dissect every little feeling. And we also like to know exactly where we stand. So, where do I stand?"

"You can't stand beside me."

"You mean you won't let me."

"I mean I don't want you to. You *are* a warm and wonderful woman. I regret that's a cliché, but it's true. And we have had good times together. But now they're over."

"You still haven't told me that you don't love me."

"I'm trying not to hurt you!"

She let her arms fall to her sides. "You're not succeeding."

"I think my feelings are clear, even if you refuse to see them."

Her love was strong, but for a moment it faltered. Despite herself, she wondered if she had been wrong about Iain all along. He was a lonely man, even at times a tormented one. Had he reached out to her in his loneliness? And afterward, had he regretted it?

She had been wrong before.

He seemed to know the exact moment when her defenses cracked. "I don't think I have it in me to love anyone," he said. "I'm sorry that it seemed otherwise."

She realized that she couldn't fight him any longer. She had been battling from the beginning, but she was a victim of forces she didn't understand and of a man who wanted to protect her from them. She could have fought forever if she had been sure of his love. But she was no longer sure of anything.

"All right. I guess that's close enough." She turned and looked through the greenery for the door. Everything was blurred by the tears that seemed to have appeared from nowhere.

"I'll be spending the next months traveling. I won't see you again. But you've nothing to worry about from Martin Carlton-Jones. You'll be safe now. I've seen to it."

Billie remembered that Ruaridh had avoided Christina the same way. He had traveled all of Scotland and beyond to keep from seeking her out. But Ruaridh and Iain were not the same man. Clearly Iain would not be back before Billie's time in Scotland was up.

She saw the door and started toward it, blinking back tears that she would not let Iain see her cry. She summoned her strength and turned in the doorway to say goodbye.

She had caught him unprepared. The yearning in his eyes was so naked, so intense, that it almost bridged the distance between them.

Relief so strong she could taste it coursed through her. "You're a phony!" She stalked back toward him. "My God, you almost made me believe you."

"I don't know what you're talking about."

She knew better than to start the conversation again. She would only get more of the same from him. His tongue would not falter, but his eyes had given him away.

"Oh, don't worry, I'll leave in a moment. But before I do, I want to tell you a story I learned from Flora."

"This hardly seems the time."

"It's the perfect time." Her hands were shaking. She thrust them in the pockets of her jeans.

"I know the entire legend of Ruaridh and Christina, Billie. And it makes no difference."

"This is about wild swans. Do you know their story?"

He lifted a brow. She could almost see him struggle to stay distant.

"Do you know that some people here in the north call wild swans the enchanted sons of kings?"

"I can't see what this has to do with anything."

"Those sad, sad princes are under a spell, Iain. That's why they've been turned into swans. Each day they fly from place to place, anywhere the wind will take them, because seeing new sights, new fields and mountains and trees, is all that's left to them."

He remained silent, but she had expected nothing different. She went on. "Some say that if you watch for the swans on lonely mountain streams or lakes, just as the sun passes over the horizon, you can see them remove their coverings. For that brief moment they struggle to become men again and free themselves from enchantment. But they can't, not until the spell is lifted."

"Why are you telling me this?"

"The wild swan is mentioned in the MacFarlane curse. Now I think I understand why. You're like the swan. You fly from place to place because there's no place you can really call your own, not even this incredible old house. That's why you've never done anything to make it a home. You can't settle, and you can't find joy. I think you want to find a way to cast off the spell that binds you, but you can't, because you don't know how. I can tell you how, and I've tried, but you refuse to listen because you want so badly to protect me."

"I can't do anything about who I am and what may happen to me."

She shook her head. "The real curse isn't the disease that's stalked your family. It's your fear of living. And I'm the very worst threat. Because for the first time in a long time I made you feel alive. I made you want to fight.''

She hadn't expected an answer, and she didn't get one. But he turned away from her. It was answer enough.

"My love is strong, Iain. But yours has to be strong, too, or the curse will never end."

This time she left without looking back. Because nothing she might see on his face now could change what was between them.

# Chapter 15

A lacy veil of snow had fallen in the last hour, and the wreckage of Cumhann Moor was cloaked beneath it. Billie could see the moor from Ceo Castle tower, as well as the silver sheen of the loch and the cloud-tipped mountains. After her encounter with Iain, she had yearned for a last long look at the countryside that had so beguiled her. She had to leave Druidheachd, and Scotland, too. She had mountains of research, enough for a dissertation and possibly, someday, a book. Now she had contacts here who would answer letters and telephone calls, and lists of librarians throughout the country who would respond enthusiastically to questions.

She had no reason to stay, and more than enough to leave.

She wondered what the view would look like in the springtime. She had come at the gloomiest time of year, at a time when only the hardiest professed love for their native land. Yet she had come to love this country like her own. There was something in the jagged peaks, the slate gray mists, the wind-roughened waves of Loch Ceo, that called to her and tugged at cords binding her to her family's past. She had fallen in love with the Highlands when they were most difficult to love.

She specialized in loving that which she could not keep forever.

The sky was fast growing darker, and she knew that she should leave. Her ankle had twinged as she climbed, and she knew she needed time, light and courage to get back down. She lingered for one last look and saw a familiar car slowly cruising the loch road. It slowed and turned onto the track leading to the gate where she had parked.

She wondered what Alasdair Melville was doing at Ceo Castle.

She started down the tower stairs to greet him. Between her ankle and the fading light, the trip down was worse than the one up. She was forced to move so slowly that the walls seemed to close in on her. By the time she got to the bottom she was limping again.

When she emerged from the tower, Alasdair was crossing the depression that had once been a defensive ditch. She hobbled toward him, through the remains of what had been the great hall. "Alasdair." She called and waved. "I'm over here."

He started toward her. She didn't want company. She was too numb to talk to anyone, but she waited for him. From the beginning Alasdair had been unfailingly kind to her.

He covered the distance with long strides. "Billie, what are you doing here?"

She didn't want to tell Alasdair she was leaving Druidheachd. She wasn't sure she could. Not yet. She needed time to summon the strength to deal with more partings. "I just came for a view. I know I'm not supposed to be here, but there's no finer scenery anywhere than from that tower."

"I used to come here often as a lad."

"With Iain and his friends?"

"No. I was never part of their fun. I was younger and no' one of them."

She thought she detected a well-masked note of bitterness. She dredged up comfort from the wreckage of her heart. "Well, I was the youngest of four children, so I know what you mean. No one wanted me tagging along, either. And my brothers are older.''

''You came along far behind the others?''

''Technically they're my half-brothers. Their mother died young, but my mother raised them as if they were her own.''

''Now that's interesting. Then they are no' Mac-Farlanes?''

''No. In fact, their mother's people were from Germany, so they aren't even Scots. Just me.''

''And are there many of your mother's family left in the States?''

''None that I know of. My mother was an only child. Her father was an only child. As far as I know, I may be the last remnant of that sorry portion of the clan.''

''Sorry portion?''

''It's hard to be thrilled with my roots.'' She gestured expansively. Wind swept across the open field where once a castle stalwartly had stood. ''Look around and what do you see? A history of betrayal and battles and men standing by as their own children were slaughtered. And then, of course, there's the curse.''

''Dinna tell me that you hold any stock in that?''

''Then I won't.''

''You believe that it still exists?''

''I don't know what I believe, exactly. But I know that the power of suggestion can be astonishing. I've been influenced by it, too. And if the curse is nothing more than that, it's still vile enough.'' She sighed. ''But this is no way to spend the evening. I'm heading back to my car. Are you going up in the tower?''

''No' tonight. I'll walk with you.''

She didn't want Alasdair's company or anyone's, but she didn't know how to tell him. She walked slowly beside him. Her ankle hurt, the wind chilled her to the bone, and her car seemed very far away.

''I'm surprised that Iain isn't here with you.''

''What was he like as a boy, Alasdair? You said once that he was good at everything, and that you wanted to be like him.''

"Why do you ask?"

She'd asked because now she wondered what Iain might have become without the terrible pressure of his future. The boy was almost always the embryo of the man. "Just curious. And who better to tell me?"

"He was painfully polite to me. He was ordered to be polite by his parents, of course. Lady Mary, in particular. But when he was no' with me, he laughed, I'm sure. I had a wee stutter, and when I would try to talk with him, it always grew worse."

"It's hard to imagine Iain laughing at anyone, even as a boy. Raising an eyebrow, perhaps, but laughing? Uh-uh."

"You've no idea what it's like to be different, no' to be able to speak as quick as your thoughts. I suspect he thought I was slow-witted."

"I seriously doubt it. But if he did, you certainly fooled him."

"What do you mean?"

"Well, look at you. You're a successful doctor, and I don't know about here, but in the States you'd be every mother's dream of a son-in-law."

"How about your dream, Billie?"

She almost stumbled. "Alasdair." She stopped and faced him. "I don't know what to say."

"You've had no idea I was interested in you?"

"None." She touched his arm. "And I'm incredibly flattered. But I think of you as a friend. A good friend. Can't that be enough?"

"Do you think of Iain Ross as more?"

She was startled, but when she looked in his eyes she saw nothing but affection and perhaps a trace of concern for her. She was relieved. "It doesn't matter. Iain doesn't want me."

"Then he's a bit of a fool."

"No, he's not. It's just too complicated to explain." Her hand dropped to her side. "I hope you understand."

"I certainly do."

Billie started toward their cars again, but when Alasdair spoke, she stopped. "Have you had the whole tour of the ruins, Billie?"

"Iain showed them to me."

"I know something about the castle that even Iain doesn't know."

"What's that?"

"A secret room." He pointed. "Over there. I found it as a child. It was my own special hiding place. I went there when I had no one to play with."

"It sounds like you were a resourceful little boy."

"Would you like to see?"

She didn't want to see anything. She wanted to go back to Flora's and make arrangements to leave. But she owed Alasdair something. His feelings for her were deeper than hers for him, and he had been kind to her. He was still being kind, even though she had gently dashed his hopes. "It's getting dark," she hedged.

"It won't take long."

"Okay. But then I really do have to get back. Flora will worry."

"You'll be glad you saw this. It's a true slice of medieval Scotland." He reached for her hand. Since the snow had begun again and his hand seemed more an aid than a romantic gesture, she allowed it. They wound along the ditch, across the great hall again, then turned and ducked under the shelter of the walkway between the towers.

"Exactly where are we going?" She was unhappy that they had backtracked so completely.

"We're almost there."

"I'm afraid my ankle's hurting worse."

"You should have said something before. Well, we'll have a spot to rest out of the snow when we get there, and I'll have a look at it."

She had to content herself with that. She let him pull her along, but she stopped when they reached the second tower. "I don't think this is safe, is it?"

"Oh, we're no' going up. I'd never take you up these stairs."

"Then what?"

"Come and see."

He sounded as excited as a small boy sharing his clubhouse with a friend. As shattered as she felt, she could not refuse.

The massive tower door hung slightly askew. With a surprisingly mighty thrust Alasdair moved it far enough to one side that they could enter. "It was always locked when I was a lad, but my father had a key, and, like all lads, I had ways of getting what I wanted."

There were narrow ventilation slits along one wall, but the room was almost pitch black. "I'm not sure this was such a great idea," Billie said. "I think we'd better come back when it's lighter outside."

"Don't go yet. Wait. I'll need to look at that ankle."

Seconds passed; then a light wavered in the far corner. For a moment Billie was transfixed; then she realized what it was. "A candle. Alasdair, where did it come from?"

"I kept a cache in here as a boy. A tin of them. The room was nearly untouched the last time I came here. The tin was still here, so I brought new candles. For auld lang syne."

It seemed an odd tribute to his childhood, but she was grateful for the light. "So this is your secret room." It was fairly large, but gloomy, as only windowless rooms can be. "I can see you here as a boy. Plotting and planning."

"Plotting?"

"Well, I was always plotting against my brothers. Didn't you plot terrible crimes against Iain and the others?"

"On the contrary. I plotted ways to make them admire me."

She felt a thrill of sympathy for the friendless boy he had been. "Did you miss this place when you moved away? Did you find another secret room somewhere?"

"There was no time to play after we moved from Fearnshader. I was forced to grow up quickly."

"Oh, I'm sorry. Then it wasn't a good move?"

"My father was a hard man. He became harder after Lord Ross fired him."

"Fired? I didn't realize. Iain never said..."

"I doubt he knew. You see, Lord Ross was losing his mind by then. He discovered something about my father that sent him over the edge."

A shiver crept along Billie's spine. She didn't like the room. She felt trapped, enclosed, despite how spacious it was. She forced herself to breathe slowly. There was plenty of air. "What?" She wanted the conversation to end.

"He discovered that my father was a MacFarlane."

For a moment she thought she hadn't heard him right. "A MacFarlane?"

"Aye. On his mother's side. Just like you, Billie. Exactly like you."

"Then you and I . . ."

"Are cousins. Aye. Distant, distant cousins. You come from the family of Christina's oldest brother, and I come from the family of the cousin she was betrothed to marry."

Fear exploded inside her. Mara's words rang in her head. *Watch everything and everyone. And listen for the things that are not said, as well as those screamed in anger.* She started toward the door, but Alasdair reached it before she did. "There's more to see. You can no' go yet."

"I'm very tired, and my ankle hurts like heck. I really do have to go. We'll come back. You can show me later." She was babbling.

"I want to show you now." He took her arm.

She was afraid to scream, afraid she had misread this entire situation and was overreacting. She had come through too much today to trust her instincts. But Mara's words continued to beat a steady rhythm inside her. *Walk with care, Billie.*

"I don't like being in here." She tried to pull away. "You can tell me the rest of the story outside."

"There's no' much more to tell. Lord Ross had to file some legal papers on each of his employees. My father could no' hide the truth. When Lord Ross saw that my father's middle name was MacFarlane, he fired him then and there. He was afraid, you see, that my father would bring the curse down on his head. By then, of course, he was already quite mad, already a victim of the MacFarlane curse." Alasdair laughed. There was nothing pleasant about the sound.

"Alasdair, let me go! I'm beginning to feel frightened."

"I suppose Christina felt frightened, too, when she realized she had no place to run."

She tried once again to jerk her arm from his. When he didn't let go, she lunged at him. But Alasdair was not Jeremy Fletcher. He easily avoided her, twisting her arm so that she was trapped against him.

"My father never found another position. Lord Ross would no' recommend him. And he had been a good keeper, one of the best in Scotland. Every April I went with him to the moors to burn off strips of the land. He knew every bush, every rock, every game bird. The deer would eat from his hand...."

"Your father taught you to burn the land?"

"Aye. And I learned the skill well." His teeth flashed white in the darkness. "I remember it still."

She brought the heel of her boot down sharply on his instep. His grip loosened for a moment, and she broke free. But she had no more reached the door than he had her again.

"You've no' seen my secret room!"

She struggled, but he dragged her slowly back toward the center. She managed one shrill scream, but he clapped his hand over her mouth. "My father began to drink too much after he was sacked. And when he drank, he was a violent man. Lord Ross did that to him, and to me. And every time my father beat me, I told myself that I would come back to Druidheachd someday, and I would make Iain suffer for his father's sins, just as I had suffered for them!"

He was insane. Now it was so clear that Billie couldn't believe he'd hidden it. She wanted to plead with him, but his hand was firmly covering her mouth. She was losing ground. He wasn't a large man, but he was strong and in superb condition. Between her injured ankle and inferior size, she couldn't stop him from dragging her.

She felt him kick at the floor with his foot. Once, then again. She used the third time to try to break free, but he

held fast. "My secret room has an interesting secret itself."
He laughed. The sound was terrifying. "Once this was a
prison cell, Billie, and below us is the dungeon. Historians
would call it a bottle dungeon now, because the top is narrow and the bottom just a wee bit wider. You'll see."

She twisted and turned, trying desperately to escape. But
a hole appeared in the floor where the planks he had kicked
away had covered it. She felt him force her toward it, despite her struggles.

"Iain had *you,* too." He sounded sad. "He had everything, and I was left with nowt."

She couldn't plead, and struggling did no good. She was
helpless. When he removed his hand from her mouth and
shoved her toward the hole in the floor she gave a piercing
scream. But as she fell through the horrifying darkness, she
knew that no one had heard her.

# Chapter 16

Hollyhock whined. Iain watched the dog leap to his over-size feet and start for the window. Once there he rose on his hind legs and rested his front paws against the sill, soulfully gazing into the darkness.

Iain couldn't remember when he had last taken the dog for a walk. He was already a large animal, growing larger, and he needed exercise. Thanks to Billie's intervention he was no longer impossible to restrain on walks. He came when he was called—most of the time—and obligingly fetched sticks that Iain threw for him. Iain hadn't wanted a dog. He had only taken Hollyhock for April's sake. But somewhere along the way—and reluctantly—Iain had grown fond of him.

"What do you see, Hollyhock?" Iain went to the window, too. He was talking to a dog. His life had come to that. His days stretched ahead of him, days when a dog would be his best hope of a conversation, days when he would isolate himself more strenuously to wait.

He wondered if Billie truly understood that his worst fears of slowly going mad had been for the people he loved and not for himself. He wondered if she would ever realize that it wasn't cowardice but courage that had made him set her free.

*For the first time I made you feel alive. I made you want to fight.*

Iain could almost hear her saying the words. They were true. She had done both. He had almost succumbed to the lure of life coursing through his veins, to hope and passion and joy. He had almost forgotten that he was destined to writhe in agony and terror for the remainder of his days, and that if she was at his side, she would share in that horror.

He was a twentieth century man. He didn't believe in the MacFarlane curse.

But he believed in its legacy.

Hollyhock whined again and pawed at the glass.

Through the window Iain could see that the snow had picked up in intensity. As a boy he, Duncan and Andrew had often gone for walks on evenings like this one. Their whole lives had been ahead of them, and they had been impatient for the fun to begin. They had planned and plotted in turn, each boy more grandiose than the last.

Iain knew he could lose the dog in a drift if they waited much longer. "All right. A short walk. And you'd better stay with me, or there'll be no more walks at night."

Hollyhock started for the door.

Outside, the air was frigid. Hollyhock bounded to the nearest drift and dove into it. Iain shoved his gloved hands in his jacket pockets and started down the drive. There had been no forecast of a storm, but weather in the Highlands was difficult to predict. Billie had once joked that the weathermen in Scotland chose predictions from a hat, because on any given day, one was as accurate as another. A little rain, a little snow, a little sun.

Billie.

Hollyhock raced past, stopped and shook the snow off his coat, then took off at a run again.

Iain whistled, but the dog—who could hear the rattle of food tumbling into his bowl from any of Fearnshader's fifty rooms—ignored him.

"Hollyhock!"

The dog was a dark streak against the white snow. A rapidly disappearing dark streak.

Hollyhock was headed the back way toward Ceo Castle, the same path that Iain had used to carry Billie to Fearnshader after she'd nearly drowned. Iain called again and whistled shrilly, but Hollyhock was out of sight.

Iain considered what to do. He could go back home and wait for Hollyhock to return—if he did. Or he could go in search. It took only a moment to decide. He had already suffered too many losses. He turned back home for Hollyhock's leash before he started in the direction the dog had gone.

There was little traffic on the loch road because of the hour and weather. Hollyhock would probably be safe from cars, but Iain didn't trust the dog's sense of direction in the snow. If the night worsened, he might die of exposure.

Iain was halfway to the castle when he heard Hollyhock barking somewhere up ahead. He shouted again and followed with another whistle, but Hollyhock didn't appear. Every few hundred meters he stopped and shouted again. Hollyhock barked once, as if to let Iain know the game was still on, but he didn't return.

Iain was beginning to feel the chill through his coat. The landscape was white, but landmarks were easily detectable. He wrapped his scarf tighter around his neck, the same scarf he had used to help Billie screen the smoke when Cumhann Moor had burned.

Billie.

Where was she now? Had she gotten home before snow glazed the loch road? She was from Florida, renowned for sand and sun. What did she know about snow or ice? She still had trouble remembering which side of the road to drive on.

He understood that he would worry about her for the rest of his life. He would wonder where she was and what she was doing. He would remember their night together, a night he never should have allowed but would dream about always.

Billie.

He was nearing the castle when Hollyhock barked again. Iain thought of old television shows he'd seen as a child. Lassie leading a small boy to people or animals in trouble. Lassie barking, then running ahead to show the way. He would have smiled if a smile had been left inside him somewhere. Perhaps Hollyhock was part collie as well as a hundred other things, but the resemblance ended there.

He rounded a corner, and Ceo Castle loomed in the faded moonlight. Outlined in snow, the ruins were a magnificent reminder of all that was wrong in his life.

"Hollyhock! Bloody hell!"

He was colder than he remembered being in a long time. He didn't want to be anywhere, but least of all here. He would never look at the castle again without thinking of Billie.

He thought he heard the dog bark again, but now the sound echoed off stone, vaulted over walls and slipped through crevices. He couldn't be sure where it came from.

He couldn't even be sure that it was a dog.

Suddenly he was chilled to the marrow of his bones, and he shuddered uncontrollably. He was filled with such a feeling of foreboding that he couldn't move. Fear froze him to the spot.

The view began to dim. The ruins quivered, as if at last all that remained of the castle would finally tumble to the ground. Snow became mists, formless wraiths sliding across the earth with arms outstretched. Somewhere deep inside his mind he heard a woman scream.

"Billie." He whispered her name. It warmed him not a trace. Vague unease was fast being transformed into terror. He swayed on his feet, and his head grew light. The freezing air warmed, but not pleasantly. He was sweating, he could feel beads of it dampen his cheeks and chest. His arm grew numb, as if it had been held in one position too long, and the sweet fragrance of apothecary's rose blended with the odor of horses and panic.

He closed his eyes and heard the thunder of hoofs. He felt the soft pressure of a woman's body against his, felt the frantic stretch of his own horse beneath him. Something whistled through the air, and a woman cried his name.

The ground was iron-hard beneath him, the frozen ground of Cumhann Moor. He had held the woman in his arms as they tumbled to the ground. Pain stabbed through him, through every limb and tissue. As he clung to her a flying hoof shattered his arm. He could feel it hanging limp....

"Hold on to me," he whispered. "No matter what happens, *mo boirionnach boidheach*. Whatever happens, I will hold you forever."

Iain opened his eyes and saw the castle through a haze. "Lord God..."

Ceo Castle stood before him in its entirety. He could see the Ross standard waving from a parapet, see the sturdy stone causeway leading over a wide, deep ditch. Then, as he stood motionless and frantically willed it to disappear, it did. Slowly, by degrees, just as it had throughout the ages. Stone by stone. Until it was nothing more than familiar ruins.

His knees were weak. His head throbbed. "Billie." She was here somewhere. He was sure of it, although he didn't know why. Perhaps he was insane. The last few moments had nearly convinced him that he was beginning the downward spiral he had expected all his life.

*But Billie was here.*

He started across the grounds, calling her name. Hollyhock materialized from behind a wall, but he didn't spare the dog a moment's look. "Billie! Where are you?"

Hollyhock joined him. Iain started toward the tower with the dog at his heels. It seemed the likeliest place to begin. From the very beginning Billie had been fascinated by the view.

The wind picked up, screaming mercilessly and flailing snow in every direction. He entered the tower, but before he could start up the steps, he heard someone calling him from the walkway overhead.

"Iain, is that you?"

"Who's there?"

"It's Alasdair."

"What in the bloody hell are you doing here?"

"I saw Mara's car parked at the gate and guessed Billie had been driving it. I was worried, because of the snow, so I came to find her."

"Is she up there?"

"Aye, and hurt. Come quickly. She fell, I think. She's unconscious. I'll need your help to bring her down."

Iain didn't have time to question how he'd been right about Billie. He hadn't seen Mara's car. He had come a different way. But he had known that Billie was in danger. Forever, he would know, no matter how far away she was from him.

He took the steps at a near run. He could hear Hollyhock whining below as he ascended. He didn't stumble once, but he was winded when he reached the top and lunged out to the walkway.

"Where—"

His head exploded. He had the momentary impression that it had split into two separate parts. He saw two men gazing sorrowfully at each other across a divide as deep and wide as Ceo Castle's ditch. *Two men who were him.*

Madness.

He awoke on his back, his head resting on stone. Pain nearly shattered him, washing through his head like an angry sea everytime his heart beat. He struggled to sit up, but a foot was firmly planted on his chest.

"I thought maybe you wouldn't be coming to at all."

Iain gazed above him and saw the shape of a man silhouetted against the dark sky. But his mind, fogged and twisted, would not divulge an identity.

"I'm glad you're awake, Iain. It would pain me to kill you without your knowing why."

"Kill...me?" The words formed without conscious assistance. Desperately he tried to pull his thoughts together, but like the head that sheltered them, they seemed to have been splintered into pieces.

"Aye. Trained to heal, born to kill."

He placed the voice with effort. "Alasdair?"

"Alasdair MacFarlane Melville. Quite a mouthful for a wee laddie, only I was never allowed to repeat my middle name, no' while I lived in Druidheachd. My father warned me that it might set off your father."

Iain lay very still. "I don't...understand."

"I was born to kill you, Iain. Born to bring you to retribution."

"I...see."

"Do you?" Alasdair leaned forward and rested more of his weight on Iain. The breath left Iain's body, and darkness surged through his brain. "I think no', though I'm certainly no' one to argue with the laird. Who would I be to argue with my betters?"

"I have never pretended to be better...than anyone."

Alasdair laughed and relaxed his foot, and as air rushed back into Iain's lungs, his thoughts began to coalesce. He was on the floor of the tower walkway. He had come to find Billie. "Billie. Where is she?"

"Oh, no' here. But dinna take a notion to feel relief. She's in a place where she will no' be found until she's dead. No' till she's been long dead."

"Dead?"

"Aye. You always learned quickly, Iain."

"Why?"

"For what you and yours have done to me and mine."

"I don't...understand."

"I'll give you a moment to try. Then I shall kill you."

Iain knew he had only one chance. He had to act as he would if he hadn't been injured. He had to act quickly and decisively. He struggled to ready himself, despite the agonizing pain in his head and the weight bearing down on his chest. "I can't hear you." He whispered the words. For a moment his mind drifted to the hours when he, Duncan and Andrew had made up stories and acted them out here. He had always gotten the best parts, because he had always had a flair for the dramatic. "I can't hear what you're...saying."

"Can't you?" Alasdair laughed. "Did the blow affect your ears?"

"Speak...up, please. What are you saying?" Iain put fear in his voice. The effort almost made him pass out.

"I am going to kill you." Alasdair shouted the words. When Iain didn't respond, he bent lower to shout them again.

Iain grabbed the foot bearing down on his chest and jerked it with all his strength. Alasdair wobbled, and his arms flapped for balance. Iain jerked again, and Alasdair crashed to the ground.

"No, you're not!" Iain grabbed him in a crushing bear hug and rolled on top of him. He was larger than Alasdair and probably stronger, but Alasdair had the advantage of a clear head.

He grabbed Iain's shoulders and shoved. Iain grabbed his and thrust them against the stone. But not with enough force. Alasdair rolled to his side and took Iain with him.

Iain's head exploded against the walkway. His grip slackened, and Alasdair used that moment to scramble away. Then with the force of momentum he leapt at Iain. "You're going...to die!" He slammed his fist into Iain's face. He raised his fist again, and at the moment it descended, Iain twisted away. Alasdair's fist connected with stone.

He screamed in protest.

Iain slammed his knee between Alasdair's legs, and the other man screamed again. "Bastard!" Iain grunted. Adrenaline pumped through him now, and the fog in his head was clearing. Billie was in terrible danger, and he stood between her and death.

*He had not saved her before. Once before he had failed to save her.*

He threw himself on Alasdair and straddled him, holding Alasdair's arms against the walkway floor. "Where' Billie? Tell me...or I'll throw you...over the bloody side!"

Alasdair bucked and twisted. It was all Iain could do to keep him on the floor. He was tiring quickly, but Alasdair was not. "Where is she?"

Alasdair quieted gradually. Finally he lay still, but Iain wasn't fooled. "If I show you," Alasdair said, panting heavily, "what...will you do?"

"I'll...give you a head start...out of here. That's it, and that's all."

"You would do that?"

"Don't count on it to save you. I'll hunt you down, you slimy bastard. If one hair...on Billie's head is harmed, I'll hunt you down!"

"You're cursed, Iain. The two of you will die together."

"I'll take my chances. You'd better do the same."

Alasdair gave a strangled laugh. "Do you think so?"

Enraged, Iain probed Alasdair's greatest vulnerability. "I've always been bigger and better than you!"

Alasdair's eyes narrowed in hatred. Iain lifted Alasdair's shoulders and slammed them against the stone. "Are you going to tell me?"

"In the boot."

"What?"

"She's in the boot of my car. I planned to take her coat and leave her...on Bein Domhain, somewhere too far from civilization to walk...before she froze."

Iain slammed his shoulders against the stone one more time. "Then what were you doing up here?"

"I found her here. We struggled before I got her in the car. Then I heard you calling your dog. I thought I'd gotten lucky. I though I could...get you both."

This time Alasdair's head bounced against the stones. "You're insane!" Iain said. "Why should I believe you?"

"Show you," Alasdair mumbled.

Iain didn't trust a word of the story. Yet it could be true. Billie, who had once confessed her hatred of enclosed places, could be locked in the boot of Alasdair's car. "All right." Iain knew what he was risking. His head was still pounding mercilessly, and he was painfully weakened. Alasdair could escape. "Give me your keys."

"You'll have to let go of my arms."

"One arm. Which side?"

"Right."

"If you're lying, you're a dead man."

"Get them."

Iain twisted Alasdair's right arm under his head and held it with his left hand, but his grip was precarious. He was watchful as he reached for Alasdair's pocket and his fingers closed around the keys, but he wasn't quick enough.

Alasdair twisted and dumped him to the floor. He sprang to his feet and started toward the steps. Iain threw himself at the fleeing figure and just grasped his ankles. Alasdair crumpled to his knees. Iain slung himself on top of him, but now Alasdair was fighting for his life. He pounded and throttled Iain, screaming obscenities as he did. They rolled over once, then again.

Iain crashed against the walkway wall. The old battlements were sturdy, but there were substantial spaces where stones were missing. His own sense of direction was useless. He didn't know where they were, or in how much danger. Alasdair gouged at his eyes, and Iain knocked his hand away. They rolled to one side, then the other.

Iain's world was growing darker. Pain had become a constant, debilitating force that was as much a threat as the hands that wrapped around his throat and spasmodically squeezed. His eyesight dimmed; his breath rattled in his chest. He would die here locked in a struggle with the personification of all that had nearly destroyed his life.

He gave one last heave, one mighty thrust, and Alasdair fell backwards. Iain kicked out at him with all his waning strength, once, then again. The third time he kicked nothing but air. He heard a terrible, choking gasp, a startled cry.

And a scream that went on and on until it shattered into silence.


"Billie..." Iain stumbled through the ruins. He had ceased to define where the cold stopped and his injuries began. He had half woven, half crawled to Alasdair's car. As he'd suspected, Billie was not there. But she was somewhere nearby, because Mara's tiny Morris Minor was still parked beside Alasdair's.

"Billie..." He couldn't shout. He could barely choke out her name. He had already checked the narrow strip of forest between the castle and the loch. And he had been completely over the ruins once, stumbling, falling, picking himself up to fall yet again.

He guessed that nearly an hour had passed since he had heard Alasdair's final scream. The young doctor's body lay in a twisted heap at the side of the tower. As horrifying as his death had been, perhaps it was more merciful than what he had planned for Billie.

Iain was sure that if she was dead, he would know somehow. The connection between them had not been severed, but it wasn't strong enough to lead him to her. His cheeks were wet, and not from snow. He had never felt so desperate or so helpless.

As he searched, he had forgotten about Hollyhock. Now he heard the dog barking somewhere near the tower. Iain wondered if Hollyhock had just discovered Alasdair's body. The barking ceased, then began again.

Iain had to go home for help. There was no other way. The constable, Andrew, Duncan... He wanted his old friends with him now. He had never quite been strong enough to push them from his life, despite his fears of what they might suffer for loving him. Now he was grateful. They would help him....

"Billie..."

Hollyhock answered instead. He bounded toward Iain from the direction of the ruined tower. Iain started in the opposite direction, and the dog circled him, before heading back toward the tower, barking as he ran.

Iain turned and stared. He had been through the tower once already, searched every inch of the lone room at the bottom, even felt his way up the hundred or so crumbling steps to see if there was something he might have missed. The tower had been as empty as his heart.

Hollyhock disappeared inside. As a lad Iain had never been allowed to go there. Until recently the foot-thick door had been securely padlocked to discourage intruders. Now Iain recalled that several months ago his grounds keeper had reported finding the ancient lock on the ground, rusted through and useless. Iain had authorized him to replace it, but there had been no sign of a new one today.

He had never been allowed in the tower. Now he tried to remember if there had been a reason other than its ruined state. Something nagged at him but refused to take shape.

He started after the dog.

*We'd like your permission to do some excavation.*

As he staggered toward the tower, the voice leapt out of Iain's memory. His head was clouded, but he placed the words immediately. Last year a young professor from the University of Edinburgh had wanted desperately to dig at Ceo Castle, but Iain hadn't been convinced that the proper safeguards were going to be enforced. He had wanted to be certain that whoever took on the castle as a project was committed to its entire history, layer by layer. And this man had been only interested in the rumor of an infamous bottle dungeon somewhere on the grounds.

*There is nowt in that tower for our family to be proud of. Keep it locked, and keep away those who would exploit our past.*

The second voice was Malcolm Ross's. Iain had been eight. They had stood amidst the ruins, and his father had warned him of his responsibilities. Lord Ross had begun early to train his son, perhaps fearing his inability to do it later.

"Billie." Iain moved faster, willing himself to cover the distance without falling. Hollyhock was barking from inside.

Iain had already been inside once. He had called Billie' name. He had seen nothing.

He stumbled on.

The door was ajar. It hadn't been completely closed th first time he'd entered. Now, as he hadn't then, he realized how strange that was. Nearly as strange as his ground keeper delaying the installation of a new padlock—if indeed he had.

"Billie..." He pushed his way inside. The room was pitc dark, even with the door open wide. "Billie!"

Hollyhock barked from a corner. Iain stood very still. "Quiet!" For once that evening the dog obeyed.

Iain could hear the keening of the wind outside, but nothing else. Nothing else...

Weeping.

For a moment he wondered again if he truly had been reduced to madness. His legs would no longer hold him. He fell to his hands and knees and began to search the floor. "Billie..." Her name rasped from his throat without force. If she was under here somewhere, she probably wouldn't be able to hear him. He discovered that beneath a thick layer of earth at least part of the floor was covered with planks. He clawed at them, testing to find one that was loose. He circled, inch by inch, trying desperately to stay conscious and to find the strength to keep going.

Frustration warred with exhaustion and pain. There was nothing here. Nothing. He banged his fist against the floor.

There was a hollow echo beneath him.

It took precious minutes to clear the earth away. He realized now that it had been disturbed recently. It wasn't packed solid like the rest of the floor. It gave easily under his clawing fingers, but there was so much of it...so much.

Calling Billie's name, he struggled with a plank. He summoned what strength he had left for a single, powerful heave. The plank gave way, then the one beside it.

"Billie!"

Now he clearly heard weeping.

"Billie, it's Iain."

There was silence.

"It's Iain. Billie, it's me. Alasdair's dead. I'm going to get you out."

"Iain...?"

His heart began to pound harder, faster. She was there. Alive. "Are you hurt?"

"Iain..." She began to sob again. Wild, wrenching cries that tore him apart.

"I'm right above you. You've got to help me. I can't do this without you. Be brave a little longer. I'm going to get you out. I can't see anything. How far down are you?"

"Candles . . . There are candles there."

"Where, do you know?"

"On a ledge."

"I'll look. Talk to me while I do."

"Alasdair . . ."

"Alasdair fell from the tower. He can't hurt you again." He stood and felt his way to the wall, moving around the room as he felt for a ledge. When he found it, he searched until he came across something wedged into a crack in the wall. It was a tin of some sort, and when the top snapped open he felt half a dozen narrow candles and a box of matches.

"I've got them. Billie, be brave. I'm going to get you out."

Feeling his way, he crawled back to the center. He buried the bottoms of two of the candles in the mounds of earth he'd piled to one side and lit them both. "Can you see the light?"

"Iain . . ."

He lit another and held it over the opening. He could see the top of her head, but she was too far below him to grab. There were wardrobes at Fearnshader that were wider than the space where she was huddled, and the opening leading into the dungeon was long and treacherously narrow. His skin crawled. She was obviously terrified. His brave and beautiful woman.

His mind raced for a way to rescue her. But he couldn't reach her, and he was too weak to pull her up with a rope—even if he could find one.

"Take deep breaths. You've plenty of air now. Breathe, Billie."

"He said he was going to kill you. . . ."

Tears tightened in his chest and throat. "Well, he didn't." He felt in the tin for the remainder of the candles. Now he knew what he had to do. He buried them at intervals around the opening. He couldn't leave her there while he went for help. She couldn't wait for rescue. If he left her, it would be twenty minutes or more before he could return—if he remained conscious that long. She was so frightened.

"I'm coming down." He stripped off his jacket, afraid that he might get stuck if he wore it. Twentieth century men were larger than their medieval counterparts, and the opening to the dungeon hadn't widened with time.

"No! No, Iain!"

"Move to one side."

He tossed the jacket in, watching carefully how long it took to fall. If he was wrong about the dungeon's depth, they were going to die together.

But he wasn't wrong. The jacket fell beside her in seconds. The dungeon was carved from rock, but through the centuries dirt had sifted in and raised the floor. He lay flat and swung his feet toward the opening. Then with a push he slid down to join her.

She was in his arms before he had fully landed. His hands trembled as he held her. She was sobbing so hard she couldn't speak.

The space seemed to close in around them. There was hardly room to maneuver. "Listen, Billie." He threaded his fingers through her hair and tilted her head back. "You have to listen."

He watched her struggle for control. She nodded, but her eyes were wild.

"There's only one way out now. You have to get on my shoulders and climb out. It's going to be close, but you can do it. Once you're out, drive back to Fearnshader. Take Mara's car, or Alasdair's. His keys are on the boot. Ring Duncan and Andrew. Ring Constable Terrill. Send them to get me."

"Iain..." Her fingers traced his face as if she were still trying to be sure it was really him. Her voice was husky with tears and terror. "I was so scared you were dead."

He held her for a moment. He could feel her heart pounding unevenly against his. "I want you to stand. Just under the opening there. I'll get beneath you, and I want you to straddle my shoulders. As I rise, use your hands to propel yourself into the right position. When I'm on my feet, I'll grab your ankles and lift you to my shoulders. But I'm weak, Billie. We may have only one chance."

She nodded. Her fingers continued to flutter over his face. "He hurt you. The bastard!"

"Not badly enough." His lips touched hers; he whispered against them. "I stayed alive to find you."

"I can't leave you here."

He kissed her quickly. Her lips trembled beneath his. He could feel the terror in every part of her that touched him. "You have very little choice. It's up to you now to save us both."

"I love you, Iain."

Her voice wobbled with emotion. He could hear her struggle to be brave. Whatever resolve he'd been left with crumbled. "You're my heart. My woman."

"Iain..."

He set her away from him, as far as he could. Then he motioned for her to crawl beneath the opening and stand. "One chance. Let's make this work."

She positioned herself and rose to her feet. He crawled beneath her and settled her legs around his neck. Then, with every bit of his waning strength, he pushed himself to stand. He wavered. The effort was more than he'd expected. He saw bright colors and flashes of light, but he strained on. His hands closed around her ankles. "Now!"

She scrambled to his shoulders, weaving dangerously. He moved back and forth to steady her. He could hear her soft cries. One foot settled against his hair, and she pushed against his skull.

He crumpled to the floor in agony. The lights faded, colors spun like a pinwheel he had loved as a child. "Billie..."

Darkness fell. He gave in to it with something close to pleasure.

# Chapter 17

Dr. Angus Sutherland lowered his substantial bulk to the bed that Iain had recently vacated. "I can no' forgive myself, lad. We should have seen it. One of us should have seen."

Iain finished packing the few clothes that had been brought to the hospital from Fearnshader four days before. "We none of us saw it, Angus. Alasdair hid his insanity well. He was warped by a childhood he had no control over and his belief that my family had caused all his misfortune. His pain festered until it erupted."

"Aye, but if I'd just seen it . . ."

"There's nothing you could have done." Iain faced him. "Have you found someone to replace him?"

"Next week I'm interviewing a young woman with a husband and two wee bairns. And no ties to the village. I made certain."

"A good choice. You won't bully a woman so badly."

Angus humphed to cover a smile. "You're certain you're ready to go home, lad? You had a particularly nasty concussion. I will never know how you found the strength to fight off a murdering madman and rescue Billie."

Billie, whom Iain hadn't seen since his own rescue. Each day he had expected her, and each day she had stayed away. She was well. That much he knew. And still in Druidheachd. Beyond that he knew nothing.

"She was a powerful incentive," he said, placing the last shirt in his case.

"You will no' forget to take things slowly? You may still have dizzy spells from time to time. No hearty exercise. No driving your car for at least a week. Plenty of sleep. And a phone call to me if you suddenly have more pain than you're having now?"

"I promise." Iain turned. "Angus..."

"Aye?"

"When I went to the castle, before I knew that Billie was in trouble..." He stopped, unsure how to proceed.

"What? Did something happen?"

"I saw things...I couldn't have seen." Iain watched Angus closely, waiting for his reaction.

"What sort?"

"A scene from the past. And not my own. Another time when Ceo Castle stood whole and proud."

"And what came from that vision?"

"I realized that Billie was in danger, and that I had to save her."

Angus sat forward. "And now you're afraid that you've begun to slip into insanity, as your father did."

Iain gave a short, reluctant nod.

Angus's gaze softened. "Iain, lad. There was a time when I might have thought you had reason to worry, before I had lived in these bens and braes and seen all that I have. But now I know there are many more things that we dinna understand than those we do."

"Then you don't think...?"

"No. I dinna." Angus stood and clapped Iain on the back. "Go home, Iain. I'll expect you back in a day or two for a quick look over. And in three months for the wee talk we've scheduled."

"Thank you."

"Get away with you now." Angus's voice was husky. "And I'm glad you have nowt more than a bump on your skull and some bruises to show for all you've been through."

In the corridor Iain accepted Jeanne Sutherland's good wishes and those of another hospital patient. Duncan and Andrew were waiting in the reception area. They stood as one when he walked through the doorway.

"I think he looks pale and frail," Andrew said. "What do you think, Dunc?"

"At least he's on his feet and not napping at the bottom of a cozy hole in the ground. What some people won't do for a little privacy."

Iain strode to them and enclosed them both in a bear hug. Something clutched at his throat. "Thank you for coming. Now and before."

The two men were silent; the hugs were huge.

Finally Iain stepped away. "I'm ready."

"Are you sure you want to go back to Fearnshader?" Duncan asked. "Mara insists you come to the hotel so she can keep an eye on you."

"And I would no' mind the company at my place," Andrew said.

"No. Thank you both, but I want to go home."

The two men caught him up on village news as Duncan drove them toward Fearnshader. "Carlton-Jones seems to have stopped trying to get folk with loch cottages to sell," Andrew said.

"That's because I believed he was the one who'd started the fire on the moor. I threatened him, and I suppose that, at least temporarily, he's taken me seriously. But he'll be back, Andrew. His kind always are."

"Then the fire was Alasdair's doing?"

"Aye. He helped his father burn off land when he was a wee lad. He knew exactly what to do and how to do it. Apparently the constable found enough supplies at his house to burn half a dozen moors."

"And the brakes on your car?"

"Most likely Alasdair, too. He was there at the wedding that night. And Angus told the constable that Alasdair was as good a mechanic as a doctor."

"Jeremy Fletcher was arrested in Spain yesterday," Duncan said. "Drug trafficking. Seems our boy's been smuggling cocaine for years. He has a long list of offenses and a longer list of enemies. It's unlikely you'll ever have to worry about him again."

"How did you hear that?"

Both men were silent.

Iain's suspicions grew. "I was having him watched. Were you having him watched, too? To protect me?"

"Iain was always sure he was more important to us than he really was. Don't you remember?" Duncan asked Andrew.

"Aye, I remember a time..."


Billie confirmed her flight to Florida for the following Monday. "Now, you're sure Steuart doesn't mind driving me to Glasgow to catch the train?" she asked a loitering Flora after she hung up the telephone.

"I told ye before, lass. He's business there."

"Then I guess I'm all set."

"No' quite."

Billie knew what was coming. "I don't want to hear anything about Iain, Flora."

"He's out of hospital. Just this morning."

"I know." Billie bit her lip. She hadn't intended to let that slip.

"And how do ye?"

"I called Jeanne Sutherland. I couldn't leave without knowing he was all right."

"You owe him yer thanks face-to-face."

"I'll write him."

"A letter's poor thanks for saving yer life."

"Trust me, Flora, he doesn't want to see me."

"Trust ye?" Flora made a noise that united myriad cultures. "You dinna trust yerself. Should I trust a woman s torn between what she wants and what she fears that she can no' even say a simple thank ye?''

Torn between what she wanted and what she feared. The words had a familiar ring. Billie had said something similar to Iain.

Flora shook her head. "Ye will no' forgive yourself if ye dinna see him one last time."

Billie had been tempted to go to the hospital many times. But every time she had remembered that last scene in Iain's conservatory. She didn't think she could bear another. Iain loved her; she was sure of that now. But his fears for the future were stronger.

Flora touched her shoulder. "Go to him."

"I don't have a car. I'll call him."

Flora reached in her pocket. "Steuart's keys."

Billie's eyes widened. "Does he know?"

"Aye. And he's resigned." When Billie didn't reach for them, Flora took her hand and placed them inside, locking her fingers around them. "But Steuart's no' patient, lass. Ye'll have to go soon, or ye'll miss yer chance. The car's parked on the road." She left the room.

Billie stared down at her hand. For days she had been asking herself what could hurt worse than losing Iain forever. For days she had almost convinced herself that another terrible confrontation was the answer.

Her hours in the dungeon had affected her courage. She had been sure that she would die there, buried in a hole beneath the earth. She had shivered and whimpered and cried out for Iain. She had almost allowed Alasdair to destroy her. But Alasdair was dead, and unless she went to see Iain one last time, she would always know that because of him, she had given in to cowardice at the most important time in her life.

She made her decision. She slid on her jacket with trembling fingers; the car key trembled as she stuck it in the ignition. But by the time she had slowly followed the loch road and pulled into Fearnshader's drive, she had gained a fragile composure. She would see this through. Whatever the outcome. Because not to was to give a dead man control of her life.

She parked and started up the walk. The door opened before she could knock, and Gertie stood there.

Billie held up her hands. "I don't have an ounce of fight left in me."

"Come in, Miss." Gertie pulled her inside. She didn't let go of Billie's arms after she'd kicked the door closed. "Let me look at you."

"I thought you were gone for good."

"An old woman's foolishness. Are you well? Have you recovered?"

"Mostly." She didn't add that since the rescue she slept with her door open, and sometimes her window, despite the freezing temperature. She avoided cellars and dark closets and even warm hugs that went on too long. But she had faith that would change as she readjusted. She would recover.

"Gertie, I want to see Iain, and I don't want to fight you."

Gertie dropped her hand. "Fight me? And why would that be?"

"I know what you think of my family."

"It was never you, nor your family, either. I've been told there were fine MacFarlanes here, as well as some who were no' so fine. It was your safety and Master Iain's that worried me." Gertie paused. "It more than worried me," she admitted. "I should no' have carried on as I did. But Master Iain is like a son to me. And I watched his father take sick...."

Billie was touched. "It must have been terrible."

"Master Iain's in the sitting room. I threatened to lock him there if he does no' stay put. He's wandered the halls back and forth, since he came home. And he needs rest."

"I won't stay long."

"Stay as long as you like." Gertie gave her an assessing look. Then she nodded. "Stay every bit as long." She turned and started down the hall. At the door to the sitting room

Gertie stopped. "I'll let you show yourself in," she whispered. "And I will no' be disturbing you."

"Thank you."

"Take good care of him."

"You're asking the impossible."

"I dinna think so."

Billie waited at the door until Gertie was gone. Then she knocked and opened it.

The room was lit only by the evening sunset and the flickering flames in the fireplace. Iain was sitting in front of it. He looked up, and for a moment there was naked emotion in his eyes. "Billie."

"Hello, Iain."

He started to his feet, but she waved him down. "I'm under orders to be sure you don't overdo."

"How are you?"

"As well as can be expected, I guess. A lot better than I'd be if you hadn't found me."

He sank back to his chair. "You look wonderful."

"What about you?" She crossed the room and leaned against the fireplace. They were still miles apart. "Does your head hurt, or has that subsided?"

He shrugged. "For days I was sure my head had split into two pieces. Now at least I believe what I see in the mirror."

"I keep trying to forgive Alasdair. Someday maybe I'll manage."

"If I know you at all, it will be soon."

"And you?"

"He's dead because of me. The least I can do is forgive him."

She shivered, and he stood. "Are you cold?"

"No. I'm fine." Warily she watched him move closer. "Iain, I came to say thank you. I didn't want to leave without saying it. I didn't want you to think that I wasn't grateful. If it weren't for you..."

"If it weren't for me, you wouldn't have been there in the first place." He stopped just in front of her.

"Maybe not. But Alasdair would have come after me somewhere else, and you, too. It was just a matter of time."

"When I think of what you went through in that hell-hole."

"I can't think about it." She looked beyond him, because she couldn't look at him. Her eyes focused on Hollyhock, stretched out in a comfortable armchair, like a king. The dog was so replete and satisfied with himself that he hadn't even wagged his tail when she'd entered the room. "You need to train that dog, Iain. I won't be here anymore to do it."

"For the rest of his life Hollyhock gets whatever he desires. I'm his willing slave. He's the one who found you."

"Hollyhock?"

At last the dog deigned to wag. Then he slipped off the chair and wandered from the room, as if he were looking for an undisturbed place to sleep—or another slice of roast beef.

"His barking led me to you," Iain said. "I think he heard you when I couldn't."

Billie met Iain's eyes. "Then I have you both to thank. I'll send him a genuine American buffalo bone."

"I was coming to see you tomorrow. I'd already arranged the ride. I've been warned not to drive until all the dizziness is gone."

"Dizziness? Should you be standing?"

"I'm perfectly fine."

"Why were you coming tomorrow?"

"To do this." He lightly touched her hair. She started to move away, but he cupped her head to keep her there. He lowered his face to hers. She closed her eyes because she didn't want to see doubt in his. "Open your eyes," he whispered.

She did. All she saw in his eyes was desire. The feeling of his lips against hers was as old as love and as new as commitment. He wooed her to open to him, slowly, gently.

Instead, she moved away. "We already know we're good at that. Did you need more proof?"

"I need you."

Her heart was pounding uncontrollably. "I can't go on this way, Iain. I almost died, and you did, too. But that doesn't change anything. You still don't want me in your life.

for more than a night or two. I need to leave now, before you tear my heart to pieces.''

"Stay with me."

"Did you hear anything I said?"

"I've taken the blood test."

For a moment she didn't understand. Then she realized what he meant. "The genetic test?"

He took both her hands. "Aye."

She couldn't speak. She was a tapestry of emotions and thoughts, all woven into a form she couldn't see clearly. Then the pattern, the entirety of it, leapt out at her.

And she knew that they could never be together.

She pulled her hands from his. "I see."

"Do you?"

"Yes. You've used the results to make your decision about us. Heads, you're free to love me. Tails, you'll face the rest of your life alone."

"Is that so bad?"

"Yes! I'm glad your news is good, happier than you can imagine. But, Iain, you've never learned what you really needed to know about me. I loved you, and whatever the future held, I would have faced it with you. I didn't need a note from your doctor. Maybe the news is good this time, but what about next? There are a thousand diseases that could strike you down. And what about me? Do I have to come to you complete with a guarantee?"

"Billie..."

He said her name so tenderly that for a moment she almost wavered. But she steeled herself to go on. "I never asked for proof that our future together would be perfect. I loved you without it. But you've never loved me enough to believe that."

He took her hands again and raised them to his lips. His eyes gleamed. He kissed one palm, then another. "I *don't* have the results, Billie. I've come to you without them. I won't know for three months what the blood test will conclude, but I know what my own heart tells me. If you'll have me, I'll give you the very best life I can. If we have five years or fifty, I'll live every day with a prayer of thanksgiving on my lips."

She searched his eyes. "You really don't know?"

"I don't. It's a complex test, and there's still a chance that we'll know very little when it's completed. Still a good chance we'll never be able to have children." He held her hands to his heart. "Will you take me this way? With no guarantees at all? Just me as I am?"

There must have been questions in her eyes, because he smiled sadly. "I refuse to lose you again. I'll keep you here any way I have to. Alasdair, in all his madness, taught me how much I love you."

She launched herself into his arms, and he held her tightly against him. "I'll take you any way, Iain. Every way!"

"It may not be easy."

"I never asked for easy."

"Then I'm yours. No guarantees, no conditions."

She lifted her face to his. There was nothing in his eyes that she couldn't read. He was open to her in a way he had never been before. No part of him was held back. "Sold," she whispered.

He took her lips in a kiss that was deceptive in its tenderness. He drained her of every drop of doubt, every fear that had haunted the perimeter of her mind. When at last he pulled away, she knew that in the most important ways he would never pull away from her again.

Now there was no need for a gentle wooing. He locked the door, and their clothing drifted like flower petals to the floor. Dressed in firelight, they moved together as if they had made love a thousand times.

"I thought of this when I was in the dungeon," she said. "I was afraid you would never hold me again."

"I stayed alive so I could hold you."

She traced his bruises with her tongue, baptizing each of them with warm, soft kisses. He held her carefully, as if he could feel her need for air and space.

They avoided the sofa and sank to the rug in front of the fire. Time was a new luxury, and they stretched each moment to its breaking point. Each texture, each taste an sound was worthy of exploration. Desire built quickly, but they allowed it, aware that they had freedom to let the storm break when they chose.

Billie cherished Iain's hands at her breast; she cherished the way that her own hands set him aflame. She couldn't seem to stop trying to satisfy herself that he was there and whole, and so was she. She knew it would take time to truly believe that they were safe and together.

But he had given her time.

They joined together at last when desire had soared so high that they could no longer pull back, even for seconds. He drew her over him after he had protected himself and gave her the freedom of movement that he sensed she still needed. As she felt them slowly become one, she knew that they would never be truly apart again.

"Iain…" She knew whose name she called, what man she loved.

"My woman. My beautiful woman."

She opened her eyes and looked into his as they found the supreme pleasure together.

"Iain Ross's woman," she whispered at last, when she lay half across him, boneless and fulfilled.

"Never forget it."

She kissed his shoulder, slid damp, exuberant kisses up his neck, covered his jaw with them and, finally, found his lips. "Billie Harper's man," she whispered against them.

"Forever and a day."

# *Epilogue*

Spring came to the Highlands, and with it longer days, fields of daffodils and baby lambs frolicking in sunlight.

On the first day of spring there was another wedding at the ancient chapel on Fearnshader's grounds. All of Druid heachd was there, as well as a mob of Floridians who oohed and aahed over Billie's new home. She wore her grandmother's satin wedding dress and pearls of Mara's, and although no one had asked him to, Hollyhock wandered in at the first wail of bagpipes to help Billie's father escort her down the aisle.

She was surprised to discover how quickly her family accepted her new life. She convinced her father not to inventory all Fearnshader's antique-smothered rooms, and she convinced her youngest brother not to chase after the village daughters unless he was willing to stay in Scotland forevermore.

Her mother served a more useful purpose.

"You're sure you know what you're doing?" Sandy Harper asked two days after the ceremony, as she eyed Andrew's sturdy boat.

"Yes." Billie kissed her mother's cheek. Sandra was the vision of what Billie would look like in twenty-five years, and Iain claimed he anticipated it with satisfaction.

"It seems like a sacrilege. That stone's been in the tower for centuries."

"Well, the time's come for that to change."

"I think I hear them coming."

Billie turned. It had taken Andrew, Iain and Duncan the better part of three days to remove the inscribed stone from the tower wall. And now it took all of them to carry it to Andrew's boat.

But instead of setting it at the stern, where its matching half waited, the men set the stone on the ground beside Sandra.

"We've discovered something we didn't suspect," Iain said.

"There's another inscription on the other side, the side that couldn't be seen."

Billie thrust her hands in the pockets of her jeans. She was suddenly cold all over. "I don't want to know."

"Nonsense," Sandra said. "I didn't raise you to hide your head in the sand, Billie."

"There's very little sand to hide in here, Mom."

"Can you read it?" Iain asked his new mother-in-law. "We've cleaned it off as best we can."

Sandra knelt and peered closely at the inscription. "Someone give me a pen and some paper."

Both were fetched. Sandra scribbled, crossed out her own letters and scribbled some more. Then she stood. "This is something you and Iain will want to share when you're alone, Billie. I'll translate it for you."

Billie watched the men hoist the stone into the boat as her mother used a fresh sheet of paper for the translation.

"Mom . . ."

"Go. Do what you have to."

Billie took the paper and shoved it in her pocket. "I love you. We'll be back before long."

"Don't hurry. I'll be here for the rest of the week."

Billie walked out on the dock where the boat was moored
It was a large boat, fitted out to take tourists to look for
glimpse of the resident creature—the creature that Andrew
called his darling. The two halves of the stone were perched
on the rear of the stern.

"Now, you're certain you know how to operate her?"
Andrew asked Iain.

"I'm certain."

"I could come and help."

"No, this is something Billie and I have to do ourselves."

"When you reach your destination, warn my darling. I'
no' have her clobbered from above."

Hollyhock barked from the dock, but Poppy, Andrew'
dog and Hollyhock's brother, engaged his attention, and i
a moment the two were running in circles.

"Time to cast off," Iain said.

Billie watched Iain guide the boat into deep waters. H
handled the boat with ease, this new husband of hers, ju:
as he did nearly everything. The spray was icy cold, but sh
reveled in the feel of it against her face. At high speed the
reached the deepest waters in fifteen minutes.

Iain cut the engine. It was silent this far from shore, an
the loch was as smooth as glass.

"It's time," Iain said.

The scholar in Billie warred with the woman. "Are v
sure this is the right thing to do? We're destroying a piece
history... two pieces."

"It's right."

They walked to the back of the boat, hand in hand. '
feel like we should say some words," she said.

"I have some to say."

She was surprised at the seriousness of his tone, and su
denly afraid again. She thrust her hands in her pockets ar
felt the paper with her mother's translation. "Well, I gue
I've been given some words, too." She took it out. "Wh
should go first?"

"Read what your mother gave you."

"I don't know if I want to...."

"Read it, Billie. Let's be done with this."

She unfolded it and ignored the temptation to read it silently first.

"But if their love is as true, as pure as the love of Christina and Ruaridh, may this curse be lifted for all time, and my family and his live in peace and in harmony." She stared at the paper.

Iain spoke. "It's the final portion of the curse. The part that we thought had been lost forever. Don't you see? It's talking about what can happen if children of the two families fall in love again. It's the part that Christina's father added when he realized how terribly he had doomed his own descendants. It's the way they can free themselves of the curse. Love true and pure. Whoever chiseled the curse into the stone added this later, after the stone was split, in the same way the ending was added to the curse."

"Do you think the curse is over for all time, then?"

He brushed her cheek with his wedding ring, the only ring he wore now. "Two days ago you took me for better or worse."

Her fear blossomed, and suddenly she knew what he was going to say. "Iain, did you get the test results already?"

"Aye. They came back sooner than expected. Dr. Sutherland called this morning."

"Tell me."

"You got the better, not the worse, Billie. I'm one of the lucky ones. The test was absolutely conclusive. I don't have the gene. I won't die as my father did."

She threw herself into his arms and began to cry. He stroked her hair. "It's over. There are no more Rosses alive to pass down the disease. For my family, at least, it's over. When you and I have children, they'll be safe from it."

"Children." She lifted her face to his. "Little lords and ladies?"

"Not if your parents have anything to say about raising them."

She laughed through her tears. He kissed her, and for a moment they clung together. Then Iain turned her toward the distant view of Ceo Castle. They stood locked in each other's arms until wind began to ruffle the calm waters.

"It's time," Iain said.

"Aye."

He smiled at her accent. "Will you help?"

"I will, but you have to warn Andrew's darling first."

They knelt on the seat behind the stones and he called a warning. Then together, using all their combined strength, they pushed the first stone into the water. In a moment the second joined the first deep in the loch.

Billie didn't know what to say. The moment was charged with the same awe she'd experienced as she repeated her wedding vows in the chapel where Duncan and Mara had been married.

In the reverent silence she heard the beating of wings from the sky just above them. She shaded her eyes and pointed "Iain, look."

A trio of wild swans flew overhead, returning to the Highlands for the warmer season.

"May they be freed from enchantment and find what they're looking for," Iain said. "May they become what they were always destined to be."

"I wish them well." Billie gazed up at her husband. "May they someday be as happy as we are."

He kissed her again as the loch gently rocked the boat beneath them. And it was far later than either of them had intended before they finally reached the shore.

*     *     *     *     *

# INTIMATE MOMENTS® Silhouette®

# COMING NEXT MONTH

Men and women hungering for passion to soothe
their lonely souls.

The intriguing Intimate Moments miniseries by

# Beverly Bird

concludes in July 1995 with

**A MAN WITHOUT A WIFE (Intimate Moments #652)**
Seven years ago, Ellen Lonetree had made a decision
that haunted her days and nights. Now she had the
chance to be reunited with the child she'd lost—if
she could resist the attraction she felt for the little
boy's adoptive father...and keep both of them
from discovering her secret.

And if you missed the beginning of this compelling
series, pick up the first and second books:

**A MAN WITHOUT LOVE (Intimate Moments #630)**
Catherine Landano was running scared—and straight
into the arms of enigmatic Navajo Jericho Bedonie.
Would he be her savior...or her destruction?

**A MAN WITHOUT A HAVEN (Intimate Moments #641)**
The word *forever* was not in Mac Tshongely's
vocabulary. Nevertheless, he found himself drawn
to headstrong Shadow Bedonie and the promise of
tomorrow that this sultry woman offered. Could home
really be where the heart is?

▼*Silhouette*® ...where passion lives.      BBWW-3

# He's Too Hot To Handle...but she can take a little heat.

SILHOUETTE
Summer
Sizzlers

This summer don't be left in the cold, join Silhouette for the hottest Summer Sizzlers collection. The perfect summer read, on the beach or while vacationing, Summer Sizzlers features sexy heroes who are "Too Hot To Handle." This collection of three new stories is written by bestselling authors Mary Lynn Baxter, Ann Major and Laura Parker.

Available this July wherever Silhouette books are sold.

SS95

## SPELLBOUND
### ROMANCE

**HIS ACCIDENTAL ANGEL**
**SANDRA PAUL**

No sooner had Bree Shepherd entered heaven
than she was sent back down, this time as an
angel, to reform cynical lawyer Devlin Hunt.
Difficult and charming, Devlin was a man to test
an angel's patience—and somehow still be
able to steal her heart.

**SPELLBOUND: BECAUSE LOVE
CAN CONQUER ANYTHING**

**AVAILABLE THIS MONTH ONLY FROM**

*Silhouette* ROMANCE™

SPELL10

# INTIMATE MOMENTS®
## ™ Silhouette®

## Blood *is* thicker than water...

*A Family Circle*

a new Silhouette Intimate Moments miniseries by

## DALLAS SCHULZE

They have a bond so strong, *nothing* can
tear them apart!

Read the second book in this heartwarming series,
coming in June 1995:
**ANOTHER MAN'S WIFE**, Intimate Moments #643

Gage Walker's best friend's widow and child
desperately needed his help. And Gage was not the
kind of man to turn his back on responsibility. Trouble
was, his "friendship" with Kelsey was stirring up all
kinds of emotions that Gage had long ago buried
and *definitely* didn't want to feel—such as passion,
commitment and pure, raw *need*. And those feelings
could only lead to one thing....

Look for future books in this delightful series.

**V** *Silhouette*® ...where passion lives.

DSFC-1

ANNOUNCING THE

# PRIZE SURPRISE SWEEPSTAKES!

This month's prize:

# L-A-R-G-E—SCREEN PANASONIC TV!

This month, as a special surprise, we're giving away a fabulous FREE TV!

Imagine how delighted you and your family will be to own this brand-new 31" Panasonic** television! It comes with all the latest high-tech features, like a SuperFlat picture tube for a clear, crisp picture...unified remote control...closed-caption decoder...clock and sleep timer, and much more!

The facing page contains two Entry Coupons (as does every book you received this shipment). Complete and return *all* the entry coupons; **the more times you enter, the better your chances of winning the TV!**

Then keep your fingers crossed, because you'll find out by July 15, 1995 if you're the winner!

Remember: The more times you enter, the better your chances of winning!*

*NO PURCHASE OR OBLIGATION TO CONTINUE BEING A SUBSCRIBER NECESSARY TO ENTER. SEE THE REVERSE SIDE OF ANY ENTRY COUPON FOR ALTERNATE MEANS OF ENTRY.

**THE PROPRIETORS OF THE TRADEMARK ARE NOT ASSOCIATED WITH THIS PROMOTION.

PTV KAL

## PRIZE SURPRISE
### SWEEPSTAKES
## OFFICIAL ENTRY COUPON

This entry must be received by: JUNE 30, 1995
This month's winner will be notified by: JULY 15, 1995

**YES,** I want to win the Panasonic 31" TV! Please enter me in the drawing and let me know if I've won!

Name_____

Address _____ Apt. _____

City _____ State/Prov. _____ Zip/Postal Code

Account #_____

Return entry with invoice in reply envelope.

© 1995 HARLEQUIN ENTERPRISES LTD.                    CTV KAL

---

## PRIZE SURPRISE
### SWEEPSTAKES
## OFFICIAL ENTRY COUPON

This entry must be received by: JUNE 30, 1995
This month's winner will be notified by: JULY 15, 1995

**YES,** I want to win the Panasonic 31" TV! Please enter me in the drawing and let me know if I've won!

Name_____

Address _____ Apt. _____

City _____ State/Prov. _____ Zip/Postal Code

Account #_____

Return entry with invoice in reply envelope.

© 1995 HARLEQUIN ENTERPRISES LTD.                    CTV KAL

## OFFICIAL RULES
# PRIZE SURPRISE SWEEPSTAKES 3448
### NO PURCHASE OR OBLIGATION NECESSARY

Three Harlequin Reader Service 1995 shipments will contain respectively, coupons for entry into three different prize drawings, one for a Panasonic 31" wide-screen TV, another for a 5-piece Wedgwood china service for eight and the third for a Sharp ViewCam camcorder. To enter any drawing using an Entry Coupon, simply complete and mail according to directions.

There is no obligation to continue using the Reader Service to enter and be eligible for any prize drawing. You may also enter any drawing by hand printing the words "Prize Surprise," your name and address on a 3"x5" card and the name of the prize you wish that entry to be considered for (i.e., Panasonic wide-screen TV, Wedgwood china or Sharp ViewCam). Send your 3"x5" entries via first-class mail (limit: one per envelope) to: Prize Surprise Sweepstakes 3448, c/o the prize you wish that entry to be considered for, P.O. Box 1315, Buffalo, NY 14269-1315, USA or P.O. Box 610, Fort Erie, Ontario L2A 5X3, Canada.

To be eligible for the Panasonic wide-screen TV, entries must be received by 6/30/95; for the Wedgwood china, 8/30/95; and for the Sharp ViewCam, 10/30/95.

Winners will be determined in random drawings conducted under the supervision of D.L. Blair, Inc., an independent judging organization whose decisions are final, from among all eligible entries received for that drawing. Approximate prize values are as follows: Panasonic wide-screen TV ($1,800); Wedgwood china ($840) and Sharp ViewCam ($2,000). Sweepstakes open to residents of the U.S. (except Puerto Rico) and Canada, 18 years of age or older. Employees and immediate family members of Harlequin Enterprises, Ltd., D.L. Blair, Inc., their affiliates, subsidiaries and all other agencies, entities and persons connected with the use, marketing or conduct of this sweepstakes are not eligible. Odds of winning a prize are dependent upon the number of eligible entries received for that drawing. Prize drawing and winner notification for each drawing will occur no later than 15 days after deadline for entry eligibility for that drawing. Limit: one prize to an individual, family or organization. All applicable laws and regulations apply. Sweepstakes offer void wherever prohibited by law. Any litigation in the province of Quebec respecting the conduct and awarding of the prizes in this sweepstakes must be submitted to the Regies des loteries et Courses du Quebec. In order to win a prize, residents of Canada will be required to correctly answer a time-limited arithmetical skill-testing question. Value of prizes are in U.S. currency.

Winners will be obligated to sign and return an Affidavit of Eligibility within 30 days of notification. In the event of noncompliance within this time period, prize may not be awarded. If any prize or prize notification is returned as undeliverable, that prize will not be awarded. By acceptance of a prize, winner consents to use of his/her name, photograph or other likeness for purposes of advertising, trade and promotion on behalf of Harlequin Enterprises, Ltd., without further compensation, unless prohibited by law.

For the names of prizewinners (available after 12/31/95), send a self-addressed, stamped envelope to: Prize Surprise Sweepstakes 3448 Winners, P.O. Box 4200, Blair, NE 68009.

RPZ KAL